BOOT CAMP SERIES

BY ROBERT MUCHAMORE

The Rock War series:
Rock War
Boot Camp
Gone Wild

and coming soon . . .

Crash Landing

The CHERUB series:
Start reading with *The Recruit*

The Henderson's Boys series:
Start reading with *The Escape*

ROBERT MUCHAMORE

GONE
WILD

Hodder
Children's
Books

HODDER CHILDREN'S BOOKS

First published in Great Britain in 2016 by Hodder and Stoughton

1 3 5 7 9 10 8 6 4 2

Text copyright © Robert Muchamore, 2016

The moral right of the author has been asserted.

A CIP catalogue record for this book is available from the British Library.

ISBN 978 1 444 91459 7

Typeset in Goudy by Avon DataSet Ltd, Bidford-on-Avon, Warwickshire

Printed and bound in Great Britain by Clays Ltd, St Ives plc

The paper and board used in this book are made from wood
from responsible sources.

Hodder Children's Books
An imprint of Hachette Children's Group
Part of Hodder and Stoughton
Carmelite House
50 Victoria Embankment
London EC4Y 0DZ

An Hachette UK Company
www.hachette.co.uk

www.hachettechildrens.co.uk

1. Peanut Buttocks

Noah U da bestest! I vote twenty times 4 Frosty Vader afta every Rock War episodd. You in tha BEST band EVA. The others r all Willy heads LOLS and I hope Summer nevva comes bak!
YouTube post by FrostyFan609

'It's a little ghostly round here these days,' Noah observed.

The fourteen-year-old rolled over black and white checkerboard tiles. Oak doors on one side of the balcony. The other had carved wooden rods, overhanging the grand ballroom at the heart of Rock War Manor. There was a GoPro camera mounted on the side of Noah's wheelchair, recording footage for the sixty-three thousand followers of his vlog. His T-shirt had been sent in by a fan and read *Token Disabled Kid* in giant red letters.

'All these bedrooms had contestants back in the summer hols,' Noah told the camera, as he slowed down, nudged a door and turned the little camera to look into a room.

There were bare IKEA mattresses. A squashed shampoo bottle and tatty neon pool shoes had been abandoned beneath a tubular metal bed frame.

'Teresa and Jess from Dead Cat Bounce slept in here,' Noah said, as his mind flashed with an image of Jess by the pool with lilac-painted toenails. 'Voted off *Rock War* in week two. And I guess this whole house will be empty in five weeks' time. Until season two . . . *Rock War* is pulling in the viewers, so season two is a safe bet.'

Noah took a right through a pair of swing doors, catching dust wafting from the manor's decrepit warm-air heating system. Something came off his tyre tread on to his hand. Oily, light brown. He sniffed his palm.

'One of the joys of being in a wheelchair,' Noah told the camera, as he foraged for a tissue with his clean hand. 'Peanut butter is far from the worst thing you can roll through.'

After wiping off, a swing left took Noah into one of three rooms that had been converted into classrooms. Traditional, graffitied wooden desks had been purchased by *Rock War*'s set-design team from some long-defunct boarding school, but the teacher's workspace, storage cabinets and display board were clinically modern.

'Ah-ha,' the bearded Mr Fogel said, as he rose from the back of the empty classroom, behind a pile of exercise books. 'The hotly anticipated essay, I presume.'

Fogel wore drainpipe Levi's, thin tie and tan Dr Martens, like he'd done every day for the past thirty years. Noah slid three lined sheets out of a pouch clipped to the arm of his chair.

'Eight hundred words on *Political Change in pre-1917 Russia,*' he said joylessly.

Fogel snatched the essay, then slammed it in his desk drawer like it had cooties. 'I suppose you're free to go and play with your little friends then,' he said.

Noah seethed as he saw that Fogel's pile of marking was topped by a half-finished crossword. Back home in Northern Ireland, Noah was a top student. But Venus TV – the company behind *Rock War* – had an eye on profit and kept the education budget to a minimum. Fogel and the other four teachers were fairly useless, and Noah realised that lessons at the manor were mostly about meeting laws on compulsory schooling, rather than teaching stuff that would actually be useful when he got back to his real school.

Getting to the ground floor meant backtracking past the ballroom to ride the only stair lift, then he wheeled outside and down the ramp at the manor's main door. The main gate lay four hundred metres down a gravel path. But since there had been no recent scandals, journalists smoking outside the press tent were outnumbered by burly guards, dressed in rain-pelted bomber jackets.

Light drizzle crisped the November air, which Noah preferred to the fuzzy heat inside the manor. His hands were covered in gravel by the time he'd wheeled around to a former stable block that had been converted into rehearsal rooms for each of the twelve bands who'd been through the *Rock War* summer boot camp, plus two larger studios for music lessons.

'Sadie?' Noah asked, searching for his band mate and bestie as he rolled into his band, Frosty Vader's, room.

But the light was out. The four members of Brontobyte were trying to play The Who's 'My Generation' next door, and since Noah didn't want to interrupt them, he chased down the chatter he could hear coming out of studio one.

It was crowded inside. Brothers Jay and Adam from Jet sprawled on beanbags, their permanently-hooded drummer Babatunde sat behind a kit, while the four members of Half Term Haircut sprawled out across the room. Up back, Dylan from Pandas of Doom sat in a cigarette haze, while Michelle from Industrial Scale Slaughter sat with her back resting against his piano stool.

'Anyone seen Sadie?' Noah asked. 'Or my other band mates?'

'Is that GoPro running?' a lad from Half Term Haircut, who held a half-drunk beer, asked anxiously. 'My 'rents will blow up if they see us boozing.'

Noah's eyes stung from smoke as he looked around, seeing a dozen empty beer bottles on the floor as Dylan frantically stubbed out a hand-rolled cigarette and Michelle shouted, 'Noah's a narc!'

'Camera's off,' Noah blurted, not actually sure whether it was or wasn't. 'I'm cool!'

Then there was a whole lot of drunk giggling.

'Is that a spliff you're smoking?' Noah asked.

'This is a no smoking area,' Dylan grinned. 'Any smoke you see is caused by a short circuit in my Hammond organ.'

'Sure,' Noah said, smiling awkwardly.

There was more guilty laughter as Noah raised his hands and started turning his chair around to exit. 'I'm sorry I interrupted,' he said stiffly. 'If you see Sadie—'

'Stick around,' Jay interrupted. 'We know you're not a narc, Noah. Michelle's just being psycho, as normal.'

Babatunde reached into a cooler hidden under a beanbag chair and pulled a green bottle. 'Stay and have a beer with us.'

The muscular drummer's words slurred like he'd drunk a couple already. Noah was only looking for Sadie out of habit, so he shut the door and rolled up to grab the just-opened beer.

'Cheers, everyone,' Noah said, not loving the taste as he sucked foam creeping from the bottle's neck.

Noah wheeled over towards the three members of Jet. He got on OK with them, while he'd always found Half Term Haircut a touch snobby.

'You finish that essay?' Jay's older brother, Adam, asked.

'Forced me to,' Noah said weakly. 'Mr Fogel's an ass.'

'I heard he got sacked from two schools,' Babatunde said. 'Can't control a class, then gets all macho and comes down on kids he thinks won't fight back.'

'Fogel properly sucks,' Noah agreed, as he did a little beer belch. 'All the catching up I'll have to do when I get back to school . . .'

'Not going back to school,' Adam said, smirking. 'This time next year, I'll be playing stadiums and licking beer off swimwear models.'

'Drink to that,' Babatunde said, raising his beer.

The guys from Half Term Haircut raised their drinks too.

'You think *you'll* win?' their lead singer, Owen, shouted.

'We sure as hell can't *all* win,' Noah said. Which made everyone go quiet.

'All hail Lord Buzzkill,' Michelle said, as she gave Noah evil eyes.

'Noah's not wrong though,' Jay said, sensing his friend's discomfort.

'Did that whole bag of plums get eaten?' Michelle asked drunkenly. 'They were the *best* plums.'

'Actually, Noah, you have a good ear,' Dylan noted.

'Plums, plums, plums!' Michelle shouted, as she stood up and stomped around. But she was drunk and tilted into the wall, almost knocking the Hammond organ off its stand.

'We've been working on our original compositions for Saturday's show,' Dylan explained. 'Jay came up with this riff for a song he's working on. But Half Term Haircut kinda tweaked it and they both claim their version is best.'

Noah liked that his opinion mattered. 'I'm all ears.'

Jay grabbed an acoustic guitar and started playing the intro to a song. It had a good beat and Jay spoke as he played. 'So here's where Theo cuts in with the lyric. *Cut me slowly cos you're cruel. Knife to my heart, something, something, something.*'

'Where *is* Theo?' Noah asked, as he realised Jet were a man down.

'Magazine interview in London,' Jay explained. 'He's not big on rehearsals.'

As Jay stopped playing, the guitarist from Half Term Haircut cut in with a similar riff, only faster. And Owen sang the lyric. 'Life gone in a puff. Yesterday I had love. Today I'm just a shaaaaa-dow . . .'

When the guitar stopped, Noah held every eye in the room. He took a slow mouthful of beer while deciding what to say.

'Half Term Haircut have the better lyric, obviously,' he began.

Jay sounded irritated. 'I'm not asking about the lyric.'

Noah twisted in his chair. He honestly preferred the faster version played by Half Term Haircut. But Half Term Haircut were the clean-cut, good-looking sort who'd always say the right thing to your face, while bitching behind your back. Whereas Jet were rough around the edges, but genuinely nice guys.

'I guess I prefer Jay's original,' Noah lied. 'But they're *both* good. Now I guess the question is, who gets to use the riff?'

'Well it's mine, obviously,' Jay said. 'Theirs is just an adaptation.'

Dylan shook his head. 'Jay, you can't float something like that in a songwriting session and then claim dibs. We're bouncing ideas. Half Term Haircut's version is different. It's not like they stole a finished song.'

Jay wasn't pleased, but dismissed this with his hand. 'I've got *heaps* of other ideas I can use.'

Adam put a hand in front of his brother's mouth. 'Keep 'em to yourself this time, dumbass.'

'Noah's right, both variants work,' Dylan said. 'Once you've polished them up, I'd be happy to work on the arrangements and record them with you.'

The four Haircuts and three members of Jet all nodded. Noah gave Dylan a confused look. 'Why are you helping these guys with their songs? What about your *own* band?'

Dylan shrugged. 'Eve and Max are writing the Pandas' song. She's barely speaking to me since we broke up and her brother never liked me to start with. Got sick of fighting every inch, so now I just rock up and play what I'm told.'

Jay laughed. 'But you're *full* of ideas, Dylan! I'd much rather you recorded our songs than the alleged professionals up at the manor.'

'Appreciated, bro,' Dylan said. 'I'd sooner be producing in a studio with a comfy chair and a nice fat joint than out on stage getting all sweaty.'

'Good job too,' Babatunde said, grinning. 'You ain't got the looks to be a pop star.'

Dylan scoffed, 'Says the boy in the permanent hoodie and ten-dollar shades.'

Babatunde gave Dylan a friendly finger, as Adam stood up, scratching his belly.

'Screw all of yous,' Adam said, as he rose from his beanbag and headed for the exit. 'Arse is numb, bladder's full, and my belly says dinner-time.'

Jay stood up too, holding his back like he was old. 'I'd better shift too. Publicity wants me to get my hair trimmed before tonight's premiere.'

2. Reality Bites

TV Hits magazine, November 18th issue

MONTHLY HIGHLIGHT
Rock War: Battle Zone – *Saturdays, 8 p.m.,*
Channel Six

While the revival of Karen Trim's Hit Machine *has struggled to rekindle the audiences that once made it Channel Six's biggest show, teen upstart* Rock War *has risen phoenix-like to become the most watched reality show on British telly.*

The warts-and-all approach puts the show in stark contrast to glitzier reality rivals, while strong online presence and contestant vlogs have made it a smash hit amongst tweens and teens.

The contestants' outrageous behaviour led to the withdrawal of show sponsor Rage Cola and almost to the show's financial collapse. But Rock War *now has new*

*backers and a huge fan base, reflected in the fact that the
Rock War format has already sold to seven overseas
territories, including Spain, France and Japan.*

*The next few weeks of Battle Zone will be crunch time
for the teenage contestants. By the time you read this
article, Rock War's original twelve bands will be whittled
down to six. Upcoming shows will see three more bands
getting the boot, leaving a final trio to battle it out in the
season's finale, which has now been moved from its original
mid-December slot to be shown live on Christmas Eve.*

*Bookmakers now rate heartthrob rockers Half Term
Haircut and Theo Richardson's outrageously behaved
Jet as joint favourites to win the competition. But
hard-core rockers Industrial Scale Slaughter remain in the
competition, minus their talented lead singer, Summer
Smith.*

*Summer remains in hospital, recovering from a broken
arm and serious internal injuries sustained in a motorbike
collision that aired live on the BBC News channel.*

*While Rock War's producers remain tight-lipped,
rumours persist that Summer could return for the final
rounds. Always assuming that her band doesn't get voted
off first.*

London's Leicester Square was roped off. Forty-metre banners
hung down from the giant Empire cinema, showing a flash
Audi careering up a ramp, plugging the European premiere of
Chequered Flag IV – Ultimate Heist. Supercars had been parked

in the square's centre, and there were flashes and squeals as DeAngelo Hunt stepped out of the cinema, waving a hand decked with huge gold rings.

Cast in hit US sitcom *Minefield* as a chubby eleven-year-old, DeAngelo had packed on muscle after the show ended, reinventing himself as the action hero in the billion-dollar-grossing *Chequered Flag* movies and spin-off video games. Still only twenty-four, a Hollywood producer couldn't even think of having him in their movie without cutting a cheque for twenty-five million.

DeAngelo worked the crowd the way he'd been doing his whole life. High fives, autographs and near hysteria when he pulled his trademark move: removing a gold ring and throwing it into the crowd.

'You're beautiful,' he told them. 'You my people!'

But he was barely halfway down the red carpet when a bigger cheer upstaged him. A girl started rattling her autograph pad and yelled, 'Theo,' right in DeAngelo's ear.

'Whoa!' DeAngelo said, cupping his ear. 'You got lungs, girl!'

'Theo,' she repeated, rattling the notebook.

DeAngelo looked back towards the cinema, seeing four teenagers getting engulfed in screams and shielding their eyes from camera flashes. He stepped back into the centre of the red carpet and caught the ear of a leggy publicist.

'Who's all that?'

'They're from *Rock War*.'

'Am I supposed to know what that is?'

The publicist smiled. 'It's a reality show that's been a huge hit with your key teen demographic.'

'So, I should go say hi?' DeAngelo asked.

'They'll run that picture for sure,' the publicist said brightly. 'The tall good-looking one is Theo. Adam's the blond one, Jay's the skinny one and the black dude is Babatunde.'

'The white boys all alike,' DeAngelo noted.

'They're brothers.'

Jay was blinded by the flashes and shielded his eyes, even though media training taught him never to do that, unless he wanted to see a hundred pictures of himself looking gormless. Theo and Adam had dived off to kiss girls and sign autographs, so Jay found himself alone on the red carpet as a dozen gold rings reached out to shake.

'They tell me your show is hot stuff,' DeAngelo said.

Jay had seen *Chequered Flag III* at the Wood Green Cineworld with his mate Salman. He'd spent summer mornings watching Channel Four reruns of *Minefield* with his cousin Erin. *Now I'm on a red carpet with a movie star, a thousand screaming girls and two hundred people taking my photograph. DeAngelo has a really strong handshake and those rings dig right in.*

'Hey,' Jay said, hiding the pain in his hand as a TV journalist stuck a microphone in his face. 'How d'you like DeAngelo's new movie?'

'Great,' Jay said, as if he'd say anything else with DeAngelo's bulk looming. 'Maybe the best *Chequered Flag* yet. Roll on number five!'

'That's what I like to hear,' DeAngelo beamed, as he gave

Jay an almighty slap on the back. 'We're so proud of this movie, know what I'm sayin'? Lotta movie franchises go stale, but *Chequered Flag* is still at the top of its game.'

While Jay was the creative heart of his band, Theo was the bad-boy lead singer who was getting his name chanted by the crowd. The media wanted Theo and DeAngelo in the same shot.

'Good to meet you, dude,' Theo said, high-fiving DeAngelo and making Jay envy his brother's cocky confidence.

'I've never seen this *Rock War* show,' DeAngelo told the camera, as a hundred flashes popped. 'Judging by this crowd, I'd better catch a few episodes before I head back stateside.'

Theo looked good in wingtips and a tailored suit, but his skinhead and neck tattoo still gave off menace.

'So, Theo, was this your first movie premiere?' the journalist asked.

'Old hand,' Theo said. 'Went to one a few weeks back.'

'How was the new *Chequered Flag*?' the TV journalist asked, as DeAngelo smiled expectantly.

'Dick fungus,' Theo said. 'Cheesiest thing I've seen in a long time. Girl in that orange bikini was the only thing worth watching.'

Anger ripped across DeAngelo's face.

'Got no respect,' DeAngelo snarled, wagging a finger. 'People got a right to their opinion, but you just a rude little boy.'

Theo flipped DeAngelo off, then craned his neck and licked the TV camera lens.

Every camera flashed as someone in the crowd shouted, 'Mess him up, Theo.'

The journalist faked horror for the camera, but was actually delighted to have something other than bland statements about how great the movie was. Theo would have happily tussled on the red carpet, but DeAngelo was a pro and cracked a smile as he eyed another TV reporter.

'Where you been lately, sugar?' DeAngelo purred, giving the reporter a kiss. 'That dress is beautiful.'

Adam shook his head at Jay as he followed Theo towards their waiting limo. 'I won't be holding my breath for another premiere invitation.'

3. Ward Round

Summer spent all day waiting for her consultant. The doctor arrived after eight p.m. Her scrubs were printed with Lego mini figures, reminding Summer that she was still in a kids' ward and still, legally, a child.

'Feeling good?' the consultant asked, faking cheer through glazed eyes.

Summer set a half-read copy of Malala Yousafzai's autobiography on her hospital bed. 'Bored,' she sighed. The consultant had left the door open and a kid on a Micro Scooter rattled down the hallway outside.

'Sorry I kept you waiting so long,' the consultant said. 'I try and deal with the little ones before they get too tired. The good news is that the most recent scan shows your bones healing nicely, though you'll still need the cast on your wrist for another couple of weeks. The lab results are back, and the latest swab from the infection you picked up after the operation on your leg is all clear.'

Summer smiled anxiously. 'What about the fluid?'

The consultant smiled back as she sat on the edge of Summer's bed. 'That's the *really* good news. When you hit your head on that kerb, you bruised your brain, making it bleed and swell. That's what caused the headaches and blackouts, and made me reluctant to let you leave hospital. But it's been a while now, hasn't it?'

Summer nodded. 'Two weeks since I had a blackout. I had a bad headache a week ago, maybe. But even that wasn't as bad as they used to be.'

The consultant peeled two coloured printouts from a stack of Summer's notes. 'What you're telling me is consistent with your latest MRI scan. Your brain floats inside your skull. This first MRI picture was taken at the beginning of October when you were suffering daily blackouts. You see the big gap between your skull and the edge of your brain?'

Summer nodded.

'At that time, excess fluid was literally squashing your whole brain, and the surgeon had to drill through your skull to release some of it. Now, the spacing between skull and brain looks normal, which fits in with the fact that you're not getting blackouts and serious headaches.'

Summer leaned forward. 'You said I could go home if the MRI looked good.'

The consultant smiled. 'You're well on the path to a full recovery. I'll still want to see you in two weeks, and for three-monthly check-ups after that. No contact sports, especially soccer or anything else where you head the ball or get hit.

And obviously, if you start getting headaches or blackouts again I need to know immediately. But I've already told the social care team that they can start making arrangements to send you home.'

'Awesome,' Summer said.

She smiled as the consultant backed out, but the thought of social workers had killed the good vibes. Summer had always lived with, and looked after, her nan, who suffered with severe asthma. Her nan was currently staying in a nursing home, and Summer had already been visited by a social worker, who'd suggested that she needed to live with a foster family, and would *possibly* be allowed to return to living with her nan after an assessment when she was fully recovered.

But Summer had spent her whole life battling teachers, social workers, sniffy school secretaries, NHS helplines and doctors' receptionists who all thought they knew best. She stared at the Malala book in her lap, and decided that she wasn't giving up without a fight.

*

The post-premiere party was in full flow at Thrust nightclub. DJ Zane Bobcat at the turntables, Premier League players ignoring the free bar to buy jeroboams of champagne, B-list celebrities on the dance floor and a chromed Audi R8 dangling like a giant disco ball.

Theo was drunk and dripping sweat from a dance floor encounter with a beautiful Laura, who said she worked for an F1 team. He urinated next to the Welsh rugby captain in the club's uber-swanky bathroom and got irritated by a bathroom attendant offering aftershave and hot towels when he just wanted to stand by the mirror and catch his breath.

He was heading back into the melee, hoping to pick Laura's stunning yellow dress out of the crowd and hopefully get her back to his hotel room. But a skinny guy stood in the doorway of a little office. Greased back hair, Ray-Bans and stupidly pointy shoes.

'Mr Thomas, can I have two minutes?'

'I'm looking for someone,' Theo said, catching a glimpse of the crammed dance floor and realising he'd struggle.

'Just step into the room. I'll make you an offer you can't refuse.'

Theo gave his I-might-just-hit-you-if-you're-bullshitting frown and raised two fingers. 'Two minutes. It better be good.'

He followed the guy and was alarmed to realise that his office was actually the disabled toilet. An open briefcase lay on the toilet lid, with two rows of watches sparkling amidst red velour.

'Like what you see?' the guy asked, as he closed the door. 'Take your pick, any watch you like. You heard of Louis Vacchero?'

'Vaguely,' Theo said, thinking of a billboard. 'The underwear, modelled by that French footballer.'

'You got it, pal,' skinny guy beamed. 'The Louis Vacchero underwear range is one of the most successful of our fashion ranges with annual sales over one hundred million dollars. Now Mr Vacchero is branching out into fabulous watches. The designs are inspired by Louis's work, and manufactured by one of Switzerland's oldest watchmakers. They've just hit London jewellers, retailing for between three and seven thousand pounds.'

The guy picked a chunky black and silver watch out of the case. 'How about this beauty? This one is titanium, with eight diamonds in the face. Retail six and a half thousand. I think it would look great, and if you're happy to wear it around town, maybe roll your sleeves up a little, it's yours.'

'Six grand, just to be seen wearing your watch?' Theo said, disbelievingly.

'This is luxury business, Theo,' the guy explained. 'The watch probably costs a hundred pounds to make. If one guy sees it on your wrist and likes it, we'll make our money back fiftyfold.'

Theo slid the watch over his hand, but his wrist was too chunky for the clasp to lock.

'Don't worry about that, just a few seconds to adjust,' the guy said, as he grabbed the watch and fiddled with the strap.

Theo stepped anxiously towards the door. 'My girl's gonna think I've ditched her.'

'Wait,' the guy said, as he grabbed a bag of white powder from inside his suit. 'You give your girl a sniff of this and you'll have to fight her off.'

'Cocaine?' Theo said, eyeing the bag suspiciously.

'Best quality,' the guy said. 'In one minute I'll make good with this strap, give you the baggie as a little present. Do we have a deal-a-roo?'

Theo worked out and did boxing, so drugs weren't his

thing. But he'd grown up sneaking fivers out of his mum's purse and shaking down kids for change. He guessed he could sell the cocaine for five hundred, wear the watch a couple of times and hopefully sell that for even more.

'Just get moving with that strap,' Theo said.

'All right, beautiful,' the guy said, as he put down a little set of pliers and handed back the watch. 'Here, try again.'

It was slightly tight, but Theo said it was fine because he wanted to get back out on the floor. They'd pumped up the dry ice and the drop was 'Freaks' by Timmy Trumpet. Laura had found her way towards the exit of the gents and was a vision, with her yellow dress bathed in swirls of dry ice.

'Where you been all my life, beautiful?' Theo said cheesily, as he kissed her neck and grabbed her ass. 'It's so cool that you came to find me.'

4. Midnight Run

Summer's hospital room was stuffed. She'd been sent make-up, clothes, more cards than she could count, and the younger kids loved visiting her room because she always had chocolates to give away. But she had to pack light.

Summer grabbed the wheeled suitcase that her band mates Lucy and Michelle's dad had used to bring clothes and toiletries when she'd first regained consciousness. She packed jeans, trainers, underwear, phone charger, the Malala book, an envelope containing items of jewellery, and a couple of handmade cards from fans that had made her all emotional when she'd first opened them.

A November chill erupted as she opened the window at the back of her room, just about squeezed the case through the gap and watched it crash into shrubs, two storeys below. It was noisier than she'd expected and she hoped nobody had heard as she slid socked feet into furry slippers and put a winter coat over her pyjamas.

She was anxious, but to avoid suspicion she moved at hospital speed: the speed you go when you've got nothing to do but shuffle down to the vending machines before another night stuck in your room. A kid was screaming hysterically in one room, held down by Daddy as a nurse tried to get a blood sample.

Summer knew the PIN for the door at the end of the hallway, then took another door into a little outdoor play deck. She'd hoped it would be empty, but two mums sat on a metal bench, smoking.

'How'd Elliot's op go?' Summer asked.

'Not bad,' the chunkier of the two mums answered. 'Puked up his dinner, but the nurse gave him a sedative and he's finally gone to sleep.'

'Where you off to at this time of night?' the other mum asked.

'No Doritos in the vending machine,' Summer explained, as she pointed backwards with a thumb. 'Gonna check the machine by the cancer ward. It's always stocked cos none of the poor sods can eat.'

'You're looking a lot better, pet,' the chunky one said, as smoke billowed out of her nostrils.

'Back on that *Rock War* before you know it,' the other one added.

'I highly doubt that,' Summer said, trying to sound cheerful as she pushed another door at the far side of the play area. But she was almost tearful, thinking about kind nurses and a couple of cute patients who deserved a proper goodbye.

Just shy of the cancer ward, Summer took a left into the deserted corridor where the oncologists had their offices, then down four flights and out of a door. After anxious seconds, she worked out that it had been bolted for the night and she went on tiptoes to take it off.

She hoped there wasn't a silent alarm as the outdoor air hit again. She doubled back, only this time she was outside of the building. She had to shake branches to get her case down the last metre, then she opened it up, removed a few items and started to change.

She pulled jeans and hoodie over her pyjamas, swapped slippers for Nikes, then put her coat back on. She pulled her phone from her pocket, and dialled the number she'd seen on taxis driving through the car park.

'Not at the hospital reception,' she told the controller, as she crossed the car park with her case wheels rattling. 'Across the street, by the bus stop outside the Esso station.'

She was relieved when the taxi arrived, but alarmed at how fast the meter burned her money. She had fifty-five pounds, and the meter was on forty-eight by the time it pulled up at the base of a familiar Dudley tower block.

It was a dodgy area and Summer walked fast, keeping her face low, hoping not to be recognised by the lads hanging out by the entrance to the underground car parks. She hadn't walked further than the cancer ward in three months and wasn't used to cold. Her right leg, which now had several metal pins and a twenty-centimetre operation scar, felt like it had completely seized up.

The lift rattled, the light flickered and she tried to ignore a wall decorated with vomit. But at least the damned thing was working for once.

Her heart raced as she neared home. The flat had been unoccupied for almost four months and she feared broken glass and ransacking. But nothing seemed dramatically wrong from the outside. Just pizza leaflets sticking out of the letterbox and a new multicoloured masterpiece from graffiti artist Bezzo8 on the brickwork next to the kitchen window.

The door needed an almighty shove as mail got trapped beneath, and she wheeled her case inside, over the mound. Amidst the flyers were quite a few get well cards, handwritten notes from a journalist who would *love to get in touch for an interview* and some ketchup-smeared chips from some joker who'd decided to post the remains of his takeaway.

The familiar smell cheered her up, though a vague whiff of drains had built up. The rooms felt strangely small and Summer was reminded of how little they had. Her nan's chair, and her oxygen stand. The old TV and VHS player. Unmatched plates and the tatty Woolworths mugs they'd had her whole life.

Summer had tidied everywhere before going off to *Rock War* boot camp, so the place didn't look too bad. The electric was on and, after a few splutters of limescale, water ran from the kitchen tap.

In the morning she'd open the windows to air the place out, tip disinfectant down the loo and sinks, give everywhere a good dusting and then call up her nan and tell her that she could come home.

Summer had enough experience dealing with social services to know that they were overworked and understaffed. By taking the initiative and leaving hospital early, Summer hoped she'd have the flat in good order and her nan back living with her before social services knew what was happening.

Once that had happened, and they came and saw that she could cope, they'd find it much harder to justify putting her nan back in a home and placing Summer with a foster family.

After switching the timer so that the heating would come on at seven, Summer huddled under sheets of a wonderfully familiar bed. Her smartphone had been gifted by a Chinese mobile maker, and it seemed ludicrously futuristic as she reached under her desk to unplug a tatty bedside lamp and replace it with her phone charger.

She liked her own duvet and pillows. Liked the smallness of her bed and the way her big toe touched the wardrobe door when she stretched out. But even though it was cosy, she couldn't sleep. Her leg ached and the cast on her wrist made it a job to get comfortable.

She lay awake, worrying about how the taxi from the hospital had gobbled almost all of her money. She barely had enough left to buy food from the local shop.

5. Bad DJ

By one a.m., premiere guests were trickling out of Thrust nightclub. Jay managed to grab a vacated VIP booth, complete with half-drunk cocktails and stickiness on the circular leather bench. He felt out of place. There were no girls his age and he wouldn't have been brave enough to speak to one if there were.

But Jay wasn't alone for long. Babatunde had found a woman old enough to know better and started making out. Then Theo rocked up with Laura and sat on the other side of the bench with his tongue exploring her mouth and hands all over.

Enveloped by lust and jealous of his band mates' sexual prowess, Jay briefly entertained a fantasy of being with Summer, before having more practical thoughts of escaping under the table and heading back to his hotel room in nearby Covent Garden.

For the past hour, DeAngelo had done a guest DJ slot at the

turntables, which had gone flat and greatly contributed to the number of people who'd left. As Zane Bobcat got back behind the decks to wild cheers and a resurgent dance floor, DeAngelo came off stage, bitter about the muted reception to his set. Jay was close enough to catch him snarling at some flunky, blaming his failings on the club's sound system.

Jay sensed trouble as DeAngelo eyed Theo, who was too entangled with Laura to notice. Jay kept a wary eye out, as DeAngelo found a couple of powerfully built doormen and dropped money in their pockets.

'Theo,' Jay warned, batting his brother's shoulder as DeAngelo led the doormen towards their table.

'You diss my movie?' DeAngelo growled, cracking his knuckles, though the music was too loud for anyone to hear. 'You boys under age, and it's way past your bedtime.'

Theo straightened up with a face smeared with lipstick. 'Big man, DeAngelo,' he sneered. 'So bold with a two-man backup?'

DeAngelo looked at Laura. 'This chump *wants* to be a star. How about smearing some of that lipstick on someone that *already* made it?'

DeAngelo was a big star. Despite the dark, noise, and flashing lights, clubbers had spotted the tension and were gathering to watch.

Theo slugged his beer. 'Maybe she wants a real man's body,' he taunted. 'I hear those plastic pecs don't look so good close up.'

'She'll find out it's all real, soon enough,' DeAngelo grunted. 'So how 'bout it, babe? Things dying off here, but I got the finest suite at the Savoy and my party's gonna roll deep into the AM.'

Laura narrowed her eyes at DeAngelo and spoke perfect, posh-girl English. 'My family owns two Formula One teams and an airline, so your status doesn't impress me, Mr Hollywood. And I am absolutely not your *babe*.'

To make her point, Laura grabbed a half-drunk cocktail left by one of the table's previous occupants and flung melted ice and soggy mint leaves in DeAngelo's face. Smartphones recorded DeAngelo stumbling back in shock, then rearing up and looking at the doormen.

'Get these *children* outta my party.'

Ten million people had been watching *Rock War*, but the two doormen worked Saturday nights and had no idea that Theo was a champion boxer. As one big lump made a grab, Theo shot forwards, spun out of reach and threw an almighty punch.

It was a one-shot deal. As DeAngelo's nose and upper lip exploded into a bloody mess, the two huge doormen jumped on Theo and barged him to the ground. Once he was down, Theo took kicks and punches, and would have copped worse but for the smartphones recording every angle.

Two more doormen jogged on to the scene as the first pair yanked Theo to his feet and started dragging him towards an exit.

'Get them out of my party,' DeAngelo slurred, as he felt two wobbly front teeth with the tip of a bleeding tongue.

Laura had vanished and Adam hadn't been seen for hours,

but Jay, Babatunde and the soccer mom he'd pulled put up no resistance as they headed towards a side exit. The press hadn't been allowed inside the club, but there were a dozen photographers waiting for the stars to leave and they charged down the side of the club as Theo got flung into an alleyway.

Theo was chuffed at landing a good shot on DeAngelo, but pissed at the bouncers who'd stomped him while he was down. He acted half unconscious while they dragged him out, but the instant the pair let go, Theo stumbled towards a freestanding metal post, which connected velvet rope around the club's outdoor smoking area.

He grabbed the post, then swung, going for the back of the doorman's head, but stumbling and catching his upper back. As one doorman sprawled, the photographers flashed and Theo jabbed the post backwards, hitting the second doorman in the guts with the pointy end before breaking into a drunken sprint.

The second pair of doormen didn't react well, and furious expressions were enough to send Jay and Babatunde running, pursued by photographers and Babatunde's woman, who'd stopped briefly to ditch needlepoint heels.

Unfortunately for Theo, Thrust was in the heart of London's clubland. CCTV operators inside had called the cops at the first sign of trouble. As Theo rounded a corner at the rear of the club, he eyed a taxi with its hire light on and decided to climb in. Before he got there a cop car rolled up with lights flashing and the cabbie took fright and hit the gas as Theo lunged for the door.

Theo spun, but faced a dead-end. His choices were to try barging through the cops, or head back down the alley where the four angry doormen would be waiting for round two.

As Theo decided to try bundling past the cops, Jay and Babatunde emerged from the alleyway with the posse of photographers a few steps behind. Jay thought Theo was about to knock him flying and flinched as he closed in.

'Hold on to this,' Theo whispered, before turning back and running full pelt towards the cops.

Jay looked down, expecting a knife. But it was a clear bag filled with white powder. He froze for an instant, before pocketing it in a state of complete horror.

'Stop running, stop running!' a cop shouted, spreading himself wide to block Theo's charge.

Theo was younger and faster than the cop, but he wasn't faster than the Taser bolt wielded by his colleague. Jay winced as the metal barb hit his big brother and gave fifty thousand volts to his upper thigh. Caught mid-stride, Theo's leg spasmed from the blast and he ploughed forwards, hitting pavement hard.

'Pigs,' Theo shouted, as the cops closed in, handcuffs at the ready and pepper spray poised just in case.

Jay knew he'd be in deep shit if the police searched him and found the bag of coke. And the bag had both his and Theo's fingerprints on, so ditching wasn't an option.

While the photographers fired off pictures and shot video of Theo's zapping and arrest, Jay grabbed Babatunde's arm.

'I'm outta here.'

'What about your brother?'

'What can we do?' Jay gasped, tasting sick in his mouth as he set off back along the alleyway. 'I'm always cleaning up his shit.'

Babatunde found his woman and put an arm across her back. The doormen had retreated inside the club. Jay shuddered as he saw one of them in the open doorway, moaning while his neck was attended to by a first-aider.

The boys were worried there might be a stray photographer or a reaction from someone inside the club, but all the attention was on Theo's arrest and Jay felt like he'd won a war when he broke into the area in front of Thrust and began the short walk towards their hotel with nobody in tow.

6. Baldie Head

The kids' ward had been constantly noisy. Food trolleys, patient trolleys, brats yelling and running around. Summer thought she'd appreciate quiet, but the empty flat just made her more anxious. What was she going to do about money? What if social services knocked on the door? How would her nan react to what she'd done?

Summer tried to beat her thoughts down by keeping busy. She got out of bed at seven, checked the boiler pressure, opened windows to air the place out, ran the taps, put bleach down all the plugholes. There was no milk, but she found a couple of Weetabix in the cupboard and ate them dry, with a sprinkle of raisins and weak black tea.

After a shower, she stood side on to the mirror, lifted some hair and studied the stubbly square above her right ear, which had been shaved bald before her skull got drilled. There was no getting around its freakiness and it made Summer feel ugly as she put on black leggings and a Zara T-shirt that was a hand-me-down from her band mate Lucy.

It was still too early to call Nan, but Summer had a brainwave as she dried her hair. She scooted into the living room, opened the little cupboard next to her nan's chair, and took out an orange Jacob's Crackers tin.

There were a few coins rattling inside, a leaky tube of eye drops, postage stamps and a set of telephone banking details. Summer always called the bank in a state of angst, hoping benefits had cleared so that she could pay a bill, or draw food money. But today the synthesised voice brought good news.

'*Your balance is. Four hundred, thirty-two pounds, sixteen pence. Your available balance is. Four hundred, thirty-two pounds, sixteen pence.*'

'Thank you, god!' Summer gasped, staring up at a yellowed plastic light fitting and hugging her phone. The main bills like council tax and TV licence were automatically paid by direct debit, but benefits money had built up because they hadn't been buying food and household stuff while Summer was in hospital and her nan was in a care home.

Summer found her nan's cash card. She knew the PIN because her nan was rarely well enough to draw cash herself. The world felt like a better place as Summer strode down to the estate's little Spar supermarket, took forty pounds from the in-store cashpoint and filled a basket with groceries.

She was waiting to pay when her eyes caught the tabloids shelved beside the counter: ROCK WAR RAMPAGE – *DeANGELO LOSES TEETH IN NIGHT CLUB RUCK*, *THEO THUMPS* CHEQUERED FLAG *SUPERSTAR*. The third paper had THEO TASERED, above two pics. The left-hand picture showed Theo being dragged into a cop car, the second showed DeAngelo being helped out of Thrust, holding hands over his face and blood streaked down his shirt.

'Can I jump by?' the guy in a day-glo vest standing behind asked, as Summer gawped. 'It's only a coffee.'

'Go ahead,' Summer said absently, as she opened the full spread on pages two and three. It said that Theo was in police custody. DeAngelo was having stitches and emergency dental at the fancy hospital where the Queen had had her hip done. But Summer's eyes were drawn to a picture of the arrest, with Jay in the background. He looked smart in a tailored jacket, but his expression was almost tearful as he tugged anxiously at Babatunde's arm.

'We're not a library,' the assistant growled, pointing at a handwritten *no reading* sign.

'Sorry,' Summer said.

The paper cost eighty pence, so Summer put it back and decided to read up on her phone when she got indoors.

'I just realised who you are!' the checkout guy said, as he blipped a bottle of milk. 'Bloody hell! When'd you get out of hospital?'

'I . . .' Summer mumbled.

The guy reached over the counter to grab the paper Summer had been looking at, then found the big Sharpie he used to price up fruit and veg.

'Would you sign this for us? My kid sister *loves* you. You're the biggest thing to come out of Dudley since Lenny Henry.'

Summer sighed, shoved bananas deeper into her plastic bag and turned around to see a shopper snapping her with their iPhone.

'So when are you back on the show?' the assistant asked. 'Is your singing voice OK?'

'Can I have a selfie?' the iPhone woman asked. 'Lasses at the hairdressers' will cack their drawers!'

Summer turned her stubbly patch away from the camera and faked a smile, then felt violated as she walked through the automatic door and up the concrete path to her tower block. Her leg was hurting by the time she reached the lift and she kept thinking about Jay's fearful expression in the newspaper photo.

Summer had been given her first smartphone just before her accident, so she lacked the skills of teens who'd handled touchscreens their whole lives. As the lift clattered up, she hit the Facebook Messenger icon, touched the last message from Jay and slowly typed out:

Saw you in the paper. You OK?

Usual Theo nonsense SIGH!!!, Jay replied, as Summer exited on to the ninth-floor balcony.

Two guys made her jump. Instinct said rapists or muggers, but they looked too posh and one snapped her with a Canon EOS, while the other held a tiny video camera in her face. There was also a woman, down the balcony by her front door.

'Summer, is it true you left hospital without permission?'

Summer walked with a hand in front of her face and kept silent.

'Are you here alone, Summer? Is anyone looking after you?' The woman journalist spoke as Summer closed on her front door. 'Are you going to sing with Industrial Scale Slaughter on Saturday's show? The *Rock War* organisers seemed to think you're still in hospital. Michelle and Lucy's dad is refusing to comment and your grandmother *must* be worried.'

'No comment,' Summer said. 'This shopping is heavy, get outta my way.'

'There's no response from the nursing home,' the guy videoing added. 'Have you contacted your grandmother since you left hospital?'

Summer put her shopping bag down and fumbled to find her key. 'Leave my bloody nan alone,' she said irritably. 'She's been through enough already.'

'But you must have known she'd worry if you ran away from hospital?'

Summer felt like screaming as she stepped inside. She'd yet to pick up the flyers and skidded on *Jalfrezi Hut FREE delivery*, sending a pain shooting up her bad leg, and saving herself by grabbing a coat hook with her plastered wrist. The near-fall hurt in several places and she fumed as she launched a backwards kick, slamming the door in the journalists' faces.

'Leave me alone, assholes,' Summer yelled, mainly to herself.

She clutched her leg as she hopped around, picking up groceries that had spilled out of the bag. Someone at the hospital must have told the press that she'd done a runner, and if there was media coverage there was no way she could get her nan back home before social services found out.

A tear welled as Summer carried the groceries into the kitchen. Then a lens tapped on the window and a flashgun popped.

7. Throbbing Meat

Theo had a bandaged thigh, arm in a sling, bruised ribs and a touch of hangover as the custody officer took his handcuffs off. He looked around at battered white paint, table and chairs bolted to the floor and Sergeant McQueen, sat behind the desk with a hipster beard and a cuppa.

'Theo, Theo, my old friend,' McQueen sneered. 'Take a pew.'

'I always preferred Interrogation Room C,' Theo said, cockily. 'It's slightly bigger, with the corner aspect and those lovely beige light fittings.'

'What a wag you are,' McQueen purred, as he slid a Louis Vacchero watch across the tabletop. 'Last I heard, you were on a suspended six-month sentence for nicking cars. Now, your dust-up with a movie star could play out any number of ways, but I'd *really* like to know how you came by this little beauty.'

'Is this an official interrogation?' Theo asked, his ribs aching as he tried to sit comfortably. 'Because I didn't hear a caution and I don't see the tape recorder running.'

'More of a friendly chat,' McQueen said. 'You might have celebrity status, but I know that Theo Richardson is the same nasty, thieving little runt I've been collaring since he was twelve years old. And someone, somewhere, is missing this very expensive watch. And that's going to cop you a theft charge, and a second vacation in young offenders'.'

'It's my watch,' Theo said, as McQueen eased back and placed confident hands behind his head.

McQueen laughed. 'Then I'm sure you have a receipt.'

'It was a gift.'

'If this is yours, I assume it fits.'

'It's tight,' Theo admitted. 'Needs adjusting. That's why it was in my jacket, not on my wrist.'

'Who *gave* you the watch?'

'Some guy, in the disabled toilet at Thrust.'

McQueen burst out laughing. 'Some guy in a toilet randomly decides to give you a five-grand diamond watch. Do I *really* look that dumb?'

'This isn't even legal,' Theo said. 'You're just trying to scare me.'

'This is for real, Theo,' McQueen carped. 'I had your big brother in this very room. He liked mouthing off too, until he went down for four years.'

This jarred Theo, but he kept up the act. 'I wasn't scared of you when you busted me at twelve. You think I'm worried now?'

'Got a future at stake now, Theodore.'

'My name's Theo. It's not short for anything.'

'Hmm,' McQueen said, as he sipped from his paper cup. 'But you've got something to lose now, Theo. Magistrate sends you down, you'll miss your TV show and your shot at fame. But *maybe* I can help. *If* you co-operate. Tell us where you stole the watch and admit you tried to assault the police officer, we can put in a good word. Get you off with a formal caution.'

'Let me guess,' Theo said, mocking the sergeant's tone. 'This is a private deal, just between me and my bestest pal, Sergeant McQueen. But if I get my lawyer involved, this deal is off the table.'

McQueen shot forwards and yelled. 'You think you're so bastard clever, don't you?'

'Never claimed to be a genius,' Theo said. 'But I'm brighter than the smackheads and pregnant shoplifters who fall for your sweet talk.'

There was a knock at the door.

'Yup,' McQueen shouted.

The door opened, admitting a tiny, fierce-looking woman. She had a grey pinstripe suit and a shrill Scottish accent.

'Officer McQueen, is this an illegal interview with an underage suspect?' she demanded.

'I . . .'

'I'm Megan Seebag, senior criminal solicitor at Buick Partners.'

McQueen had never met Seebag, but he knew that Buick was one of London's most prestigious criminal law firms. Their £750-an-hour starting rate meant they were more likely to represent Bentley drivers who splattered a few cyclists, or women who'd shot their millionaire husbands, than the likes of Theo Richardson.

'Buick Partners?' McQueen stuttered, narrowing his eyes. 'Who engaged you?'

'I believe my costs are being paid by Venus Television, on behalf of Mr Richardson. My intention is to photograph the apparently extensive injuries sustained during and since Theo's arrest. I will then file complaint. I also have four separate pieces of video evidence, showing my client being assaulted with a stun weapon. This violates Metropolitan Police conduct codes, stating that such weapons should only be used if there is a direct and immediate danger to an officer or another person, and that these weapons should never be used on anyone under the age of eighteen. Furthermore, I shall now be launching a complaint about my underage client being interviewed without the presence of an adult.'

McQueen looked riled, but thought he had a way to fight back. 'What about our movie star, DeAngelo? He'll have a big-shot lawyer all of his own.'

The tiny Seebag scraped a blood-red nail on the interview table. 'Sergeant, do you really think a macho Hollywood star will be prepared to make multiple trips to London, to give evidence in a criminal assault case, which will involve him admitting that he got sucker-punched by a boy who recently turned seventeen?

'I've already discussed this matter with the management of Thrust nightclub and with Mr Hunt's publicity and legal team.

Parties will release a joint statement, saying that a minor scrap took place inside the club, that the incident is much regretted by all concerned but that no further action will be taken.'

'What about this?' McQueen said, twirling the watch.

'Has anyone complained that they're missing a watch?' Seebag asked.

'Not yet,' McQueen admitted.

Theo pointed a thumb backwards and grinned. 'She's good, isn't she, Sergeant?'

'Shut up, Theo,' Seebag said, inhaling deeply. 'Unless I missed a few classes at law school, there's no law against having a watch in your jacket pocket. So, I would suggest you return my client's property upon his release, which I expect to take place *very* shortly.'

'You can smarm your way out of theft and assaulting DeAngelo,' McQueen said. 'But my fellow officers . . .'

'My office has produced this no-fault agreement,' Seebag said, as she pulled a stapled document from a plastic file. 'If my client is released within the next hour, the two officers involved in Theo's arrest will be allowed to sign a statement agreeing that no assault took place and that my client did not resist arrest. In return, my client will agree to withdraw any complaint regarding his brutal treatment and your illegal use of electric stun guns and pepper spray in the arrest of a minor. I will also *generously* overlook this illegal interview, and the complaint I was planning to file against *you*, Officer McQueen.'

Theo wore a big smile as McQueen turned bright red and took the document.

'I'll need to speak to the station commander,' McQueen said reluctantly. 'This kind of agreement is *way* above my pay grade.'

Seebag passed over a blue Post-it, written with two telephone numbers. 'Give these to your commander. The first is the personal number for Deputy Commissioner Grant, she plays golf with the senior partner in my department at Buick. The second number is for Matt Cromwell. He's senior solicitor currently on duty in Met Police legal. I've already had a brief conversation, and he's agreed to get these documents checked through and signed off within the hour.'

'Amazing what money can buy in this country,' McQueen said contemptuously, shaking his head as he stood up. 'I'll show this paperwork to the boss and leave you here to confer with your delightful young client.'

Theo gasped with relief as McQueen stepped out of the room. 'I don't know who you are but I love you,' he blurted, reaching out to shake Seebag's hand.

The petite solicitor was unmoved. 'You got *very* lucky, Mr Richardson. You, the cops, DeAngelo, the bouncers who assaulted you and Thrust nightclub all come out of this badly if matters proceed. But don't count on the cards falling your way every time you decide to thump someone.'

'I know,' Theo nodded, laying on his good-boy voice. 'I appreciate your help and hard work. This has been a real wake-up call. I'm gonna watch my temper and stay out of trouble from here on in.'

Seebag burst out laughing. 'I'd suggest lessons if you're

planning on going into acting. This is my business card, I suspect you'll need it sooner rather than later. Buick Partners' minimum charge is two thousand – three thousand if you call after ten p.m.'

'Cheers,' Theo said.

'I'm eyeing full partnership in my law firm and a Ferrari California,' Seebag said, as she flicked up a cheeky eyebrow. 'The likes of you might earn me both.'

8. Still A Thing

It was Friday, seven a.m. Jay was using a selfie stick for his vlog as he crawled across his metal-framed bed towards the window.

'That's my room-mate, Babatunde, snoring,' Jay whispered to the camera. 'All the rumours are true: he even sleeps with the hoodie on. Frankly, I'm starting to think it's glued. So, I'm just going to open a crack in the curtain.'

Jay wiped condensation off the glass, before turning his camera out over the lawns in front of Rock War Manor, crisped with early morning frost.

'That's the press tent, down by the main gate,' Jay explained. 'But I've *never* seen so many people out there. The publicists have even put a big table outside with coffee and bacon rolls, because the tent is full and there's still a queue of cars at the gate. Also, you see the line of TV vans? There's CBS, NBC, ABC. So I guess the Yanks got interested when my brother decided to punch out a film star's central incisors.

'It's all gone crazy. *Rock War* was in all the papers yesterday and Theo getting zapped was the second story on BBC news. There's four different recordings on YouTube, with zillions of hits, and some joker even listed one of DeAngelo's teeth on eBay.

'Then there's Summer doing a runner. #willSummersing was trending on Twitter last night. Social media has gone crazy. I picked up eight thousand new followers for my vlog. But I've only got like, thirty thousand and I think Theo and Summer are both close to a million. Which is kind of a joke, because Theo broke two cameras. He's only vlogged twice and one was a video of the mole in his armpit.

'They're saying tomorrow night's show could get our biggest viewing figures yet. But I guess I'm more worried about our performance. Theo's been up in London most of the week and I don't even know if he's learned the lyrics of the song I co-wrote with Babatunde.'

Jay switched off his camera and crept out, so as not to wake Babatunde. He wore filthy red slipper socks for the manor's cold floors, checked pyjama bottoms and a Ramones T-shirt which had the neck all stretched out from a poolside incident where Adam and Theo had yanked it and tipped ice down his back.

He rode the curved aluminium slide down to the ground floor. The sofas and games that usually covered the ballroom had been stacked in the little basketball court at the far end. Crew members were setting up an elevated stage, with *Rock War* backdrop and a long desk. Unpaid interns had set out lines of chairs, but were now stacking them up again, because they could only fit all the journalists and TV cameras in by making everyone stand.

Jay spoke to a set guy named Roger as he cut across the floor towards the canteen. 'What time's the press conference?'

Roger glanced at his wrist. 'Supposed to be five past eight, so that Sky and Channel Six can show it live on their breakfast shows, right after the news headlines. But there's so many journalists out there I don't know if we'll be ready. I've got *sixty* requests to have microphones on stage.'

'At least we're not being ignored,' Jay said, deciding against further questions because Roger looked frazzled.

The journalists were being held outside, but TV cameramen were being allowed in to set up. Jay had to dive out of the way as a group of Koreans wheeled in an ultra-high-resolution camera, four times the size of anything used to film *Rock War*.

'Morning, Jay,' Karolina Kundt said brightly. 'You down for breakfast?'

'Sure,' Jay said, slightly perturbed by the warmth coming from the matter-of-fact German boss of Venus TV. The crew called her Angela Merkel, but never to her face.

'I need contestants out of the ballroom during the press conference,' Karolina said. 'Go outside and around by the pool on your way back.'

Jay looked down at his slipper socks. 'It's frosty out, I'd better get some trainers.'

But Karolina snapped her fingers and a skinny intern came running.

'Jay needs shoes.'

'What size?' the intern asked.

'From his room, genius,' Karolina said.

'Blue Converse under my bed,' Jay added. 'I'll be in the dining room.'

Karolina looked at Jay, clearly chuffed about the big press conference and the wave of publicity. 'Go get breakfast and stay out of sight.' Then she yelled at a publicist. 'Get someone upstairs. I don't want any more contestants down here.'

Jay didn't move, and Karolina narrowed her eyes. 'You're still here,' she noted.

The leggy German made Jay nervous. 'I need a favour,' he said, going all goose-pimply.

'You see how busy I am?' Karolina said.

'We still haven't rehearsed this week's songs,' Jay explained. 'Theo was up in London doing interviews half of Tuesday and all day Wednesday. Then this whole DeAngelo thing blew up.'

'Theo is box office,' Karolina said, pointing to the giant camera. 'That's NHK. Punch a movie star, and even the Japanese want a piece of you.'

Jay was irritated and found a burst of confidence. 'Theo's your biggest star. If you don't want him voted off, we *need* rehearsal time.'

Karolina glowered, Jay shuddered. But she was smart enough to see Jay was right and patted his shoulder reassuringly. 'You'll rehearse at ten, and again this afternoon. Even if I have to handcuff Theo to the microphone stand.'

Jay smiled at the thought. 'But we've got lessons this morning.'

'My cheque book pays the education staff,' Karolina said, tailing off as the intern came back, holding a pair of size-ten Nike basketball boots. 'Look at the size of Jay,' she yelled, making the intern squirm. 'I can see they're Babatunde's from here. Go fetch the Converse, like we told you.'

The intern bolted off, but Karolina kept yelling.

'I got fifty résumés just yesterday, Kieran. Buck up your ideas or I'll have your replacement down on the afternoon train.'

Jay half smiled, scratching his armpit and yawning as he padded into the dining room. He raised a hand and said, 'Morning,' to a bunch of weary-looking crew, then stepped up to the service counter, looking for the chef who made omelettes to order.

'Eggs are full of cholesterol,' Summer said cheerily.

Jay hadn't spotted her, because the publicists wanted her out of sight of any stray journalists. She was nestled behind the fruit and cereal table. Made up for the cameras, red mini-dress, arm in a cast and striped stockings that made her legs look amazing.

'Wow!' Jay said, cracking a huge smile. Then he remembered his baggy top, bacterial-hazard slipper socks, uncombed hair and the hand buried in his armpit. 'Just rolled out of bed,' he said apologetically. 'I'm kinda grungy.'

'I'd never have known,' Summer smirked.

'I missed you,' Jay said, as Summer stood and gave him a kiss.

It was only a peck, but he caught her taste and smell, even if the make-up took the edge off. It was like being dipped in a giant chocolate fountain.

'Missed you too,' Summer said.

Jay and Summer had paired up just before her accident. They'd messaged every day, but he'd only visited her three times in hospital, and always when there were other people around. Neither was sure if they'd pick up where they'd left off, or just go back to being mates. But Summer's hand was on the table and she didn't pull back when Jay sat opposite and bravely placed his hand on top.

'Life's weird,' Jay said, grinning. 'Why are you all dolled up? I thought the press conference was for Theo.'

'The publicity department like to keep the press on their toes,' Summer said anxiously.

'Nervous?' Jay asked.

'Very,' Summer gasped. 'When was I ever not?'

'So you ran away, or was that all media crap?'

'I thought I could buy time,' Summer sighed. 'Get my nan back in the flat before anyone found out and make it harder for social services to put me into foster care. But the press got tipped off by someone inside the hospital.'

'Bummer,' Jay said, as Kieran the intern arrived and wordlessly threw down his Converse.

'Such a star you have a valet now?' Summer giggled.

'Can't you tell by my super-sleek appearance?'

Summer smiled as she swept her hand through her hair. 'So,' she sighed. 'I had twenty journalists camped on my doorstep by lunchtime. I had no choice but to call up *Rock War* publicity and beg them to come rescue me.'

'So you're back at the manor. What about your nan?'

'God knows,' Summer said. 'I mean, Mr Wei – that's Michelle and Lucy's dad – already agreed to pay to keep Nan in a private care home until ISS got voted out of *Rock War*. But the social will stick their noses in when this is over.'

'But your nan likes the care home, doesn't she?'

Summer nodded. 'She likes the fancy private place she's in now. But that's not the kind of home she'll be put in once Mr Wei stops writing cheques. And I *want* to be with my nan, you know? She's the only one who really cares about me.'

'I care about you,' Jay said, giving Summer's hand a little squeeze.

'I know you do. But you're thirteen.'

'Fourteen,' Jay corrected. 'You know that. You even sent me a recycled *get well* card on my birthday.'

'It wasn't like I could stroll out to Clinton Cards,' Summer said, smirking. 'But . . . Like . . . I obviously care about *you*, Jay. But it's different to the way your mum has cared for you your whole life.'

'Family,' Jay said, nodding. 'Blood thicker than water, and all that jazz.'

'I've looked after Nan my whole life,' Summer said. 'And all *Rock War* has done is made stuff worse.'

'It'll work out,' Jay said, thoughts turning to food as a chef emerged behind the serving counter. 'You want anything?'

'I can't even look at food right now,' Summer said. 'The thought of all those dickheads pointing cameras and churning up my private life.'

9. Pride Before Fall

'No more questions for Summer,' Karolina said, as the rowdy press mob demanded more. 'Theo, can you come on stage please.'

'So will Summer be in tomorrow night's show?' someone shouted.

'Summer arrived here early this morning and no decisions have been made,' Karolina said. 'You'll just have to watch the show tomorrow night, the same as everyone else.'

Summer drank a mouthful of water, before rising out of her seat. Theo was already stepping on to the stage. He was at his most menacing, in filthy ripped jeans, unlaced army boots and a *Camden Boys* boxing vest with washed-out bloodstains down the front. Cameras flashed as he gave Summer a hug and whispered, 'Good to have you back, you did great.'

Before sitting down, Theo struck a bodybuilder's pose, then gave the photographers the shot they wanted by flipping everyone off.

'You all here to write more shit about me?' Theo yelled, as Karolina urged him to sit down. 'Anyone who does better stay beyond the reach of my right fist.'

Theo finally sat down as Karolina picked out a journalist from Channel Six. 'First question to you, Judith.'

'Theo,' the ponytailed woman began. '*Rock War* is a family show. What kind of example do you think you're setting for your young fans?'

Theo shook his head with contempt before answering. 'The clue's in the title. *ROCK War*. If you wanna watch chefs or ballroom dancers, sling your hook. This show's about rock music and not that middle-of-the-road stuff. And if you don't like me, vote for someone else, or better still get your ass off the couch and go out on a Saturday night.'

Karolina pointed at the entertainment correspondent from BBC News.

'Earlier this year you got major publicity for rowing with Karen Trim, who runs your biggest rival show. Now you've assaulted a film star. Isn't it all a bit one-dimensional? Wouldn't you rather be known for your band's music, or the quality of your singing?'

Theo laughed. 'Have you heard me sing, mate? I'm not that great.'

The journalists roared, and Karolina wore a huge smile. 'Rhea Connor, from RTE.'

'Do you have a message, or perhaps even an apology, for DeAngelo Hunt? And do you consider yourself lucky not to have faced police charges?'

'First, let me say that you have the sexiest Irish accent ever,' Theo grinned. 'I went to young offenders' when I was fourteen and I wasn't scared. If they sent me back now, I'd be running the place. As for DeAngelo, all I can say is, if he's such a big man, why does he need two bouncers backing him up to confront a seventeen-year-old, and still end up losing two teeth? If he wants to get in the ring and fight me fair and square, I'll do it. Anytime, anywhere!'

'What about allegations that your attitude towards DeAngelo is racist?' someone asked.

'Stick that up your arse,' Theo said. 'My training partners in boxing since I was thirteen? Both black. I've had black mates and black girlfriends all my life. I'm in a band with a black drummer. This got nothing to do with DeAngelo's skin tone, and everything to do with him being a steroid-jerking weakling who made a terrible movie and doesn't like it when I tell him so.'

'Bob Carlos, from OnlineCow,' Karolina said, as she pointed to a raised hand.

'How do you and the other members of Jet feel about the Instagram post DeAngelo put up twenty minutes ago?'

For the first time, Theo looked less confident. The press were also confused, with a couple of people in the know laughing, but a lot of journalists scrambling to find DeAngelo's post on their smartphones.

'Would you like to see the post?' Bob Carlos asked.

Theo nodded and Bob pushed his way to the stage, before handing over a little tablet computer. The screen showed an

Instagram pic of DeAngelo, with stitches in his top lip and two missing teeth, and the caption *Racist Thug 2, DeAngelo's teeth 0. I'll donate $500,000 to the International Red Cross if Theo Richardson's band Jet get voted off* Rock War *this weekend!*

This was followed by a second post, with a picture of a kiddie in a hospital bed, with a tube coming out of her nose. *Vote for Industrial Scale Slaughter, Brontobyte, Pandas of Doom, Half Term Haircut or Frosty Vader. $500,000 to Red Cross if Theo Richardson's Jet get voted off* Rock War *this weekend!*

Theo was a slow reader and there were a few cheap laughs from the assembled press as Karolina leaned across the stage and mouthed, 'Stay calm, don't let DeAngelo rile you.'

'How do you feel about that?' Bob Carlos asked.

'He's rattled,' someone added.

Theo's awkward silence was broken by a journalist shouting. 'Karen Trim just Tweeted that she'd double the Red Cross donation to a million dollars if Jet get voted off.'

'DeAngelo fighting with his money,' Theo said finally, as he shot out of his seat. 'Here's what I think of your money, big man.'

Theo tried snapping the tablet in his hands, but it was tougher than he expected, so he had to smash it against the front of the desk, knocking several microphones to the floor. Then he hurled the shattered display back in Bob Carlos's face.

'That's what I say to DeAngelo,' Theo roared, as he stormed off stage.

A publicist tried to calm Theo down as Karolina took over

the press conference, but he knocked her flying.

'Mrs Kundt,' someone asked. 'Will you be secretly relieved when Theo and Jet are voted off the show tomorrow night?'

When, not *if*.

Theo didn't hear the answer. Interns and crew looked around as he blitzed through the dining room and out of the back door. As he marched on away from the manor he felt pure rage. Imagining his fists pounding out more of DeAngelo's teeth.

But deep down, Theo knew it was his own fault. Theo's mates had laughed when he thumped his teacher and got expelled, but it meant he'd ended up with the reading level of a nine-year-old. He sneered at the cops when he got busted, but Sergeant McQueen had scraped a nerve when he mentioned his big brother doing a four stretch. And Theo bragged about his hard-man dad. But Vinnie 'Chainsaw' Richardson would be in his sixties when he finally got out of lock-up.

Theo thought about his band mates. Jay, Adam and Babatunde were smart. If *Rock War* ended they'd go to uni. If music didn't work out, they'd have jobs, wives and whatever. Theo was a thug who could barely sing. To begin with, Theo hadn't been sure he wanted to hang out with dorky music kids and make a fool of himself on TV, but now *Rock War* felt like his best hope of amounting to something.

I'll end up in prison. My whole life in a tiny cell breathing another guy's farts.

Public footpaths crossed the land around the manor, so

there was always a chance of a sneaky photographer, but Theo didn't care as he stumbled forward into knee-high grass, slumped against a tree stump and rubbed his palm through a tear streaking down his face.

10. Missing Members

Three quarters of Industrial Scale Slaughter did Friday morning lessons, ate baguettes in the dining room and started the trip out to their rehearsal room. Coco, the slender, crazy-afroed guitar player, Lucy Wei on drums, and her volatile younger sister Michelle, who had been covering vocals in Summer's absence.

'So, what's our plan?' Michelle asked, as she led the trio into their rehearsal room. 'Sit around and await Her Majesty, Summer Smith?'

'Would it kill someone to tell us what's going on?' Coco moaned. 'Would it kill Summer to reply to me?'

'Summer's not the best with tech,' Lucy pointed out.

Lucy was Industrial Scale Slaughter's calmest head. She shrugged as she hunted for her drumsticks and unscrewed the cap on a bottle of water. 'All we can do is practise the songs we've got for tomorrow night.'

Michelle switched on the guitar amps, creating a little

background hum. 'Why?' she blurted. 'It's a massive waste of time if Summer comes back.'

'We're shipping out for London first thing in the morning,' Coco said, slinging her guitar around her neck. 'Even if Summer walks through that door right now, we're gonna struggle to get two decent songs together by this evening.'

'We wrote "Neon Zipper" for Michelle's vocal style,' Lucy said. 'No way that's gonna work with Summer. But I guess we could just use her for "Dream On" . . .'

'There goes Anthony!' Coco said, pointing at wisps of white hair bobbing past the rehearsal room's slot window. 'If anyone knows what's going on . . .'

Michelle and Lucy were already out of the door. Anthony was *Rock War*'s dandyish music co-ordinator. He worked with the bands on their arrangements, making sure that the right equipment was on stage during the show, sorting lighting and backing tracks and, most importantly, timing everything so that the two-hour shows hit their commercial breaks and finished on schedule.

Dressed in red cords, and with a slim frame and upright posture, Anthony looked flustered as the three teens charged him down.

'Is anyone gonna have the decency to tell us what's going on?' Michelle demanded, all pouty and hands on hips.

'Nobody is exactly sure,' Anthony said.

'But Summer's our band mate,' Lucy said. 'Don't you think it's *kind of* important that we know if our vocalist is going to perform with us? This isn't an episode of *Glee*. We can't break spontaneously into song and dance.'

'I'm *fully* aware of your musical limitations,' Anthony said acidly. 'I believe there's an insurance issue.'

'What's that mean?' Coco asked.

'Venus TV has to have insurance, in case we fry one of you with electricity, or a stage light drops on someone's head. But since Summer ran off before being properly discharged from hospital, the insurers are insisting on a medical certificate to prove she's fit to appear in tomorrow's live show. Karolina has been trying to find a doctor. If Summer doesn't get cleared before the insurer's office closes this evening, she'll only be able to appear in a pre-recorded interview.'

'So what do we do?' Lucy asked.

Anthony started looking for a show schedule on his phone. 'Rehearse the songs you were expecting to perform,' he said. Then, when he found what he was looking for, 'We're also running long in section four of the show. So you need to cut eighteen seconds from "Neon Zipper". Losing the repeat of the second chorus should do it.'

'So is Summer going to be around later, or what?' Lucy asked.

'I've told you *all* I know,' Anthony said, as he drummed on his watch face. 'Now I'm running late for the production meeting, and Karolina will dump on me from a great height.'

'He's such a dick,' Michelle said, before Anthony was fully out of earshot.

'But this is golden if you *actually* think things through,' Lucy said, as she turned back to the rehearsal room.

'How'd you figure that?' Coco asked.

'This week Summer comes back, does a soft-focus interview, all tearful and whatnot,' Lucy explained. 'Even if we play like crap, we'll never get voted off, because everyone wants to see us play with Summer again in the semi-final. Then the semi comes along in two weeks and it's our big reunion with Summer. Everyone loves her, so we nuke our way into the final.'

Coco saw the logic, but still snorted as they stepped back inside. 'If there's one thing *Rock War* has taught me, it's to never predict *anything*,' she said. 'Remember when Crafty Canard lost to Frosty Vader in the vote-off? Everyone had them as one of the favourites.'

'It was the cripple factor,' Michelle said. 'Little old ladies voting for Noah the wheelchair kid.'

'I like Frosty,' Coco said. 'Their stuff can be *so* weird.'

'And don't say cripple,' Lucy rebuked. 'Especially the way you kick off when you get called a midget.'

'Michelle the Midget,' Coco added.

'Sticks and stones . . .' Michelle said airily, as she strummed her guitar. 'Let's do "Neon Zipper", minus the second chorus.'

'OK,' Lucy said, finally locating her sticks in the back pocket of her jeans as she sat at the drum stool. 'Summer Smith's support bitches are ready to rock!'

'Things could certainly be worse,' Coco said. 'At least we're not Jet.'

Michelle shook her head and smiled. 'Theo cracks me up, but those guys are *so* screwed.'

*

Jet were three rehearsal rooms down. Jay sat on his guitar stool, scrolling his phone, with Adam and Babatunde looming.

'They crucifying us on Twitter?' Adam asked.

Jay shrugged. 'It's quite mixed. Like, there's a guy Tweeting me, saying that he feels bad for us, but that a million bucks will make a real difference for poor people and that he'll vote us off if he gets the chance. There's a lot of people who are like, *big mouth wanker Theo, finally getting what he deserves.* But there's also a backlash against DeAngelo. People saying he's acting like a pussy, and throwing his money around. There are even more people who hate Karen Trim.'

'Her whole TV persona is *mean bitch*,' Babatunde pointed out. 'If anything, her chiming in with an extra half million will work in our favour.'

'But none of this matters if we play a blinder and don't drop into the public vote-off,' Adam said, optimistically.

'How's that gonna happen?' Jay said.

'Six bands left,' Adam said. 'This week the three highest scores from the judges go through automatically. Bottom three go into a vote-off and the audience gets to save two of three in the phone vote.'

'I know how the show works, dumbass,' Jay gasped. 'You think I've been under a rock for the last two months? But in case you haven't noticed, it's two in the afternoon. The live show is tomorrow, our lead singer is AWOL and we've yet to do a full band rehearsal of this week's tracks.'

'If we dip into the phone vote, we'll tank,' Babatunde said.

'No matter how bad the other bands are, people will want the starving babies to get their million buckaroos.'

'What if one of us sings?' Adam asked. 'It's not like Theo's voice is that amazing.'

'It's his stage presence,' Babatunde said. 'Theo *owns* the crowd.'

'The *Guardian* called him a Punk Elvis Presley,' Jay noted.

Six eyes shot up as the door flew open. Theo stumbled in, with grass stuck to a sweaty boxing vest and red-ringed eyes. Jay guessed he was drunk and flinched at the thought of guitars going through windows, but Theo's posture was all slouched.

''Sup guys,' Theo said meekly, running a hand through his hair.

Theo never did meek, so it seemed crazy wrong to his brothers.

'Have you been crying?' Adam asked.

Jay shrank back towards the wall. Adam was the one guy who could ask Theo that without getting a smack, but it was still risky.

'Been walking around in the fields,' Theo said, dabbing one eye. 'I guess it's hay fever or some shit.'

November wasn't hay fever season, but nobody pushed it. Theo broke silence with a slight sob.

'I guess I screwed this up for all of yous,' Theo said. 'Like everything else in my life . . .'

Jay watched a streaking tear, then cleared his throat. 'It's not over, bro,' he said. 'We just need to rehearse.

We've written a *decent* song.'

'There's time to get it right,' Babatunde added. 'We'll hole up here till midnight if needs be.'

Theo moved closer to his microphone, clutching the stand like he needed it to stay on his feet. 'I always act like I don't give a shit. But when I heard DeAngelo was campaigning to get us kicked off . . . Made me realise how much I want to win.'

Theo turned to Jay. 'I'm sorry about the cocaine. I know nobody believes a word I say, but for the record, I'm not into drugs. It got given to me inside Thrust and I was gonna sell it.'

Jay smiled. 'So you're a drug dealer, not a drug taker . . .'

There was a flash of Theo's normal menace. 'Watch it, shrimp.' Then he shook his head and cooled back down. 'Smart lawyer wouldn't have got me off if I'd been holding drugs. Jay saved my ass.'

'Not for the first time,' Adam added.

Theo plucked Jay off his stool and gave him a hug. Jay was touched, but getting clamped by the boxer bod was a depressing reminder of how puny he was compared to his half-brothers.

'Got your back, little brother,' Theo said, as he finally let Jay breathe.

Babatunde slammed his kit. 'So, we rehearsing these songs, or what?'

'Best set ever,' Adam grinned.

'Ready here,' Jay said. 'You need the words, Theo?'

'Memorised,' Theo said, tapping his skull. 'So, I guess I'm not completely useless.'

Babatunde rapped his sticks together, 'One, two, three, four . . .'

And then things got noisy.

11. Back In Black

London Live Radio, with Rosh Patel

'Tonight's weather: a cool, clear December night, thirty per cent chance of rain and temperatures close to freezing, so wrap up warm if you're heading out. I'm Rosh Patel and you're listening to *The Talk Hour* on London Live Radio, eight zero eight FM.

'Now, a few miles north of this studio, Alexandra Palace is hosting tonight's live episode of *Rock War*. It all kicks off in a little bit over two hours. It's the show everyone is talking about, and after so much time in the news this week, people are even saying the Channel Six show could beat soap opera stalwarts and top this week's TV viewing charts.

'And get *this*. A few weeks back, Venus TV, the company that makes *Rock War*, *gave away* three thousand tickets for tonight's show. Now, those tickets are changing hands for up to four hundred pounds each. We want to hear what you think about this. Is *Rock War* the best thing to happen in

British TV in years? Or does it show our obsession with reality TV plumbing new depths?

'Lines are open and our first caller is Doreen, who I understand lives in Muswell Hill, right on the doorstep of tonight's show. Is that right, Doreen?'

An old lady crackled, 'Hello?'

'You're live on air, Doreen. What's it like up there?'

'Chaotic,' the caller said. 'We've come to expect a little disruption when there's a concert at the Palace. But this seems to have attracted all kinds of young people. Milling around, with banners and flags. They were queuing out the door of Nichol's off-licence. Buying vodka and all sorts . . .'

'So it's a big crowd, not just inside the venue?'

'As if there's nowhere better to stand around on a chilly Saturday night! And some of the girls are wearing practically nothing. They *must* be frozen.'

'Interesting,' Rosh said. 'What about the show itself, Doreen? Are you a *Rock War* fan?'

'I think it's horrible,' Doreen said. 'My granddaughters are in a beautiful choir that sang at the Royal Festival Hall. Those are the sort of young people who deserve to be on television, not a bunch of hooligans banging and crashing.'

'Thank you, Doreen,' Rosh said, as he cut the call. 'We've also had a text from Matt, a cabbie from Peckham. Matt says he just dropped four young *Rock War* fans off at Alexandra Palace. They didn't have tickets and just planned to hang out. Matt says, *The streets behind Ally Pally are crammed with people, and as I turned back towards town, my taxi was surrounded by youngsters thumping on the roof, chanting the names of their favourite contestants. The show doesn't even start for two hours and I'd strongly advise drivers to avoid the area.*

'Thanks for sharing that with us, Matt. What do you listeners think? Call, text or Tweet. We'll be back talking to Zoe from Hammersmith after this short break.'

*

The LED clocks alongside the stage said 19:29. The countdown beneath hit 28 seconds and the crowd of three thousand roared as screens either side of stage lit up with *Rock War*'s opening titles. The set for Battle Zone deliberately lacked the glitz of the talent show's rivals. A matt black stage, with Marshall speakers piled either side, a large neon *Rock War* logo, and the judges off to the side behind a graffitied wooden bar the show's designers had reclaimed from a famed Chicago punk club.

When the cameras cut from the titles, TV viewers saw the Palace stage, with the venue's huge pipe organ behind. There was just enough light to get a sense of the swaying crowd. Normally, host Lorrie would take to the stage, hype the show and do some banter with the judges. Then you'd get the first band, followed by the first commercial break.

In TV land, three seconds of nothing is eternity. The live audience seemed lost. Viewers at home assumed something had gone wrong. Then came a recorded guitar riff. The sound engineers kept it low so you still weren't sure if things were OK, but the audience started to get excited as they recognised the opening riff of AC/DC's classic, 'Back in Black'.

Viewers at home heard a clanking sound effect. A single, high-intensity pin spot shone from the back of the Palace, hitting the girl who'd just strutted on stage.

Summer Smith had never looked this way before. Black boots, black stockings, stiff rubber mini-dress, with a push-up bra giving her major cleavage. Her make-up was in monochrome, and her hair and even the cast on her hand were black. Rather than disguise the stubbly patch, the hair around had been gelled punkishly and the patch left blonde, like some movie robot with an access panel in the side of her skull.

Summer blinked out a tear as she hit her mark in front of the microphone. There was a huge roar from the crowd as she started to sing.

While Summer nailed the song, viewers at home got to see cut-ins from a nursing home, with a bunch of old-timers swaying in front of a telly. They all wore AC/DC baseball caps, with Summer's nan clapping away, centre screen. When the song ended, the roar inside the Palace kept going.

Lorrie, a former student who'd gone from unpaid intern to *Rock War*'s main presenter, stopped beside Summer and gave her a quick hug, before turning towards the audience.

'Do we know how to kick off a show, or do we know how to kick off a show?' Lorrie shouted, as the crowd went bananas. 'Summer, that was *amazing*.'

'I just learned the words last night,' Summer said, dipping her head shyly. 'I think I got a couple of bits wrong.'

'Summer, you haven't seen it here,' Lorrie said, as a screen descended at the back of the stage. 'But the audience at home has been seeing your nan watching your performance. Have you got anything to say to her?'

Summer put her hands over her face and looked totally shocked, as her nan's smile loomed on screen.

'Oh my god, this is such a surprise,' she blurted, exactly like she'd done in rehearsal three hours earlier. 'Nan, I love you *so* much.'

'Love you too, sweetie,' Summer's nan said, as the crowd cooed and the screen disappeared. 'Not so sure about the new look though.'

'So that was quite a comeback,' Lorrie said. 'I'm liking the whole black thing.'

'I'm not,' Summer grinned. 'Rubber's *definitely* not a breathable fabric and I'm hoping this hair dye washes out.'

'Back in blonde,' Lorrie joked, as the audience laughed. 'So you're looking a lot like your old self. What comes next?'

Summer shrugged. 'What with rehearsing this song, and four hours for this crazy hair and make-up job, I've barely had time to catch up with Coco, Lucy and Michelle. But I want to be back rehearsing with my band for the semi-finals. So after everything I've been through, you'd *better* not vote them off the show tonight!'

Summer wagged a finger to a cheering audience as she walked off stage. For the first time the full stage lit up, and the three judges smiled from behind their bar.

'Folks,' Lorrie continued. 'We need to get moving, because tonight's show is packed tighter than DeAngelo

Hunt's wallet. You're going to hear all of our six remaining bands. They'll play one hit, and one original composition. But sadly, only five of them can make it to the semi-final. Now before our first band kicks off, I want a big round of apple sauce for our three judges. Guitar legend, Earl Haart. Mr Sexy Trousers himself, DJ and grunge legend, Jack Pepper.'

Jack was the most popular judge and got a huge roar.

'Last but not least, the incomparable, Beth Winder.'

Nobody had planned it, but over the last weeks of Boot Camp and four previous rounds of Battle Zone, Beth had become *Rock War*'s mean judge. Its answer to *Hit Machine*'s Karen Trim. As boos for Beth subsided, the camera moved around so that the audience at home could see four good-looking band members, led by singer Owen, in skinny jeans and a tweed jacket.

'It's time for a Half Term Haircut!' Lorrie shouted.

12. Top Puff

Besides the concert hall, Alexandra Palace had thousands of square metres of exhibition space. This made life more comfortable than at some previous Battle Zone venues, where contestants spent their Saturday nights crammed into tiny dressing rooms beneath the stage, or dashing between the venue and a marquee in the car park.

Jay found himself sprawled at an indoor picnic table, outside one of the shuttered fast food joints dotted around the cavernous exhibition hall. The crew had set up several TVs on tabletops, though for some reason Jay ended up alone, while a livelier group jostled over an identical screen a few tables across.

The live broadcast ran on a ten-second delay, so that producers could bleep swearing or cut away if something went wrong. This created a weird lag between the TV and the muffled sounds coming from the adjacent concert hall.

Since this was the first knock-out round in London, Half

Term Haircut chose The Clash's 'London Calling' as their cover song. HTH were a Coldplay-style indie band. Jay wasn't convinced that punk was their territory, but the audience were so hyped after seeing Summer they'd have cheered anything.

Jay's interest perked up when HTH segued straight into 'Puff'. It was based on the riff Jay had shared during their Wednesday jamming session. And though he'd acted cool, he still felt ripped-off by them using their own version.

'Puff' had a chorus with a slow 3/2 beat, and by the third time it came around the audience were stamping their feet.

'You can write a tune,' Dylan said, as he sat down opposite Jay, holding a cardboard food tray and a sausage on a stick.

'Where'd you get that?' Jay asked, as the smell made him hungry.

'Catering table,' Dylan said, pointing. 'They just put a bunch of stuff out. Potato crunchies and whatnot.'

They heard stamping from the hall, then watched on screen ten seconds later. The camera panned over an audience having the night of their lives.

'This is clever,' Jay said thoughtfully. 'Keep the original song simple. Something the audience can get their hooks into first time they hear it.'

'Accessibility,' Dylan agreed, nodding as he pushed the box of chips, and mini spring rolls, into the middle of the picnic table. 'Dig in.'

'Ta,' Jay said, diving for chips.

'Owen kinda reminds me of Buddy Holly,' Dylan noted,

as they watched Half Term Haircut doing a piece of choreography where they bowed to each other, and then to the audience.

'That was peculiar,' Jay said, as the screen cut to the judges. 'When are the Pandas playing?'

'We're fourth,' Dylan said. 'But I'm not optimistic. The song Max wrote is about as far from a foot-stamper as you'll get.'

Jay cracked up laughing. 'Good old Max!'

'Guy is so up himself,' Dylan said, shaking his head. 'And to top it off, Eve's got an horrific cold. They're giving her steam and shit, but she can barely sing.'

Jay tried to cheer his friend up as he grabbed another spring roll. 'Maybe the adrenaline will help. She's only got to hold it together for six minutes.'

'Here's hoping,' Dylan said, leaning in closer. 'There's actually something else I wanted to ask you.'

'Ten out of ten,' Jay gasped, pointing at the little TV as Earl gave Half Term Haircut their first mark. 'I didn't think "London Calling" was anything special.'

'Not much wrong with it,' Dylan said, then changed the subject. 'I heard Theo passed some cocaine to you, before he got busted.'

Jay shot upright. 'Where'd you hear that?'

'A certain hoodied drummer.'

'Who should have kept his mouth shut,' Jay sighed. 'What about it?'

'You still got it?'

'I really wanted to toss it, but I thought Theo might want it back. And he's not the kind of guy you want to piss off.'

'Can I buy it off you?' Dylan asked.

On screen, Jack Pepper gave Half Term Haircut 10/10.

'Wow, two tens,' Jay blurted. Then in a whisper to Dylan, 'Why would you want the cocaine?'

'Never tried it,' Dylan said. 'Don't tell me you weren't tempted to have a snort.'

'Cocaine!' Jay spluttered. 'Not in the slightest. That stuff wrecks people.'

Jay was shocked. He knew Dylan smoked roll-ups, and that one of the runners sold him weed. But cocaine was a whole different level.

'My dad's been snorting coke for years,' Dylan said casually. 'He's still alive and kicking.'

'I'm not taking responsibility for it,' Jay said, as a huge cheer erupted from the concert hall.

'Thirty points!' Sadie from Frosty Vader shouted at the next table, and a few seconds later the TV caught up, with Beth Winder holding up a number ten and Lorrie almost losing it over Half Term Haircut being the first band to score full marks in a Battle Zone round.

'They weren't *that* good,' Jay said irritably.

'So?' Dylan asked. 'The coke?'

'Once I'm sure Theo's forgotten, I'm flushing it,' Jay said firmly.

'Hundred and fifty quid,' Dylan said, as he flashed a roll of fifty-pound notes.

'I'm not a drug dealer,' Jay said. 'And you're crazy wanting to try that shit.'

'Don't be such a narc,' Dylan said. 'Tell you what. There's two-fifty here. Take *all* of it. I've seen where you live, Jay. Take the money.'

Jay was offended by the *seen where you live* line, but two hundred and fifty quid was two hundred and fifty quid. A new tablet. A big chunk of the Year Ten skiing trip which his mum would never stretch for, or a gift that would blow Summer's mind. It didn't feel right, but he needed the money and it wasn't like he was selling the only cocaine on the planet. Dylan's family was minted, and if he was curious about drugs he'd find another supplier.

'It's back at the manor,' Jay said, as he reluctantly palmed the fifties. 'But swear you'll be careful with that shit.'

Dylan tapped Jay's shoulder. 'Don't sweat it, Jay, you're making too big a deal out of this.'

'If you get voted off, I'll sneak it into your luggage before the runners pack your stuff.'

Forty metres away, Owen led Half Term Haircut into the exhibition space. There were some pats on the back from the crew, but the contestants were more muted. A perfect score reduced everyone else's chance of reaching the semi-final.

'Nailed it!' Owen shouted.

As Half Term Haircut joined Jay at the table, one of the make-up girls called Dylan away.

'You saved us, pal,' Owen admitted, as he slapped Jay on the back. 'We had *nothing* before that jam session. Did you hear them stamping their feet?'

'Glad to help,' Jay said, grinding teeth as he faked as much sincerity as he could.

*

Brontobyte played second, scoring a respectable eighteen points. Frosty Vader played third and they were gathered around Lorrie on stage, sweating and smiling.

'Twenty-five points,' Lorrie said brightly. 'Really good score. Do you think that's enough to carry you through?'

Sadie, Otis and Cal's expressions said yes, but Noah spoke diplomatically. 'That's the highest we've scored in *Rock War* so far, but the standard gets higher every week, so I'm still keeping fingers crossed.'

'OK, good luck, guys,' Lorrie said, as Frosty walked off. 'Now, I've never written a song myself, but I'm told it's not easy.'

As the live audience and TV viewers got to watch a pre-recorded package of contestants song-writing in various spots around the manor, Dylan walked on to the unlit stage with his band mates. He didn't get super-nervous like Summer, but hated the idea of everyone watching and liked being able to hide up back, behind a vintage Yamaha synth and with his Chicago Cubs cap over his eyes.

Leo was the Pandas of Doom's overweight bass player. The *Rock War* team had performed a minor miracle, making Leo cool, with shoulder pads stitched into his shirt to counter round shoulders and blond streaks in his hair.

Drummer and lead singer Eve had been Dylan's girlfriend

for a while, though he now realised it had been about sexual curiosity with the only girl he knew, rather than a proper relationship.

Slim and chronically shy, Eve looked tortured as she sat by her kit, shivering from her cold as the assistant stage director stood anxiously alongside, poised with iced water and a menthol throat spray.

The Pandas' final component was Eve's twin, Max. Arrogant and stuffy, Max had voted against Dylan joining the Pandas in the first place and things didn't improve when Dylan dumped his twin and left her feeling like crap.

There were three monitors on the stage floor between Dylan and Leo, angled so both lads could see. One showed the schedule clock, currently green and indicating that the show was running fourteen seconds ahead. The second repeated what the audience were watching on the giant stage-side screens. The third had a clock counting down the seconds until the director cut back to the stage, and a live scroll of the show's running order which currently read:

0205 VT 005 Song Writing
0206 Lorrie intro (FAST)
0207 Pandas LIVE set
0208 End part 4
AD BREAK 5

Eve's cough erupted, as Dylan's attention was caught by a clip from the Wednesday jam session, where he'd worked up songs with Jet and Half Term Haircut. Owen and Jay sat on cushions, laughing as they worked on something. Babatunde was behind, goofing for the camera with a drumstick up one nostril, and Dylan was up the back of the room, looking chilled.

It jarred Dylan that he felt more relaxed with Jet and HTH than amongst his own band mates. Leo was decent, but never said much, and Eve had barely spoken to him since the break-up. If Dylan wanted any say in the band, he had to battle Max's ego. But he was too laid-back to fight every decision.

'Good to see the bands putting in so much hard work,' Lorrie said, as the package ended and stage lights came up. 'And now it's the Pandas. Kicking off with ELO's "Mr Blue Sky".'

Eve was a solid drummer and Dylan had done a good job arranging the opening synthesiser parts. Some of the crowd recognised the song and got excited, but it fell flat when the vocal kicked in. Eve usually sang with her brother, but as her cold had worsened, Max had decided to take the reins for her first track.

Eve's high voice and shy body language were quirky and sexy. The Pandas' style was low-fi, but tonight, Max had decided he was a rock god. He'd kept things simple in rehearsal, but the audience went to his head and he posed centre stage, like some hammy Shakespearean actor, with his feet far apart and his shirt buttons open to a hairless and not very muscular chest. Max's vocal was fine, but his skinny frame and macho delusions gave off the vibe of a drunk schoolboy at a karaoke night.

The audience had been pumped since Summer's opening number, but as Dylan played the song's wind-down on his keyboard the Palace went eerily quiet. Like the whole audience had caught a bad smell and taken three steps backwards.

As Dylan exchanged *what-the-hell* glances with Leo, Eve stood at her kit and reached for her microphone. She was burning up, as the director cut to a close shot of her face.

'My sister will now sing a song I wrote,' Max said stiffly, apparently undented by the audience reaction. 'It's called "Peace in Africa".'

Dylan cringed every time he heard Max's song title, but he obediently flipped some settings on the synth and played the opening, which had a kind of camp *Lion King* atmosphere. Eve was wobbling at the microphone and her voice was flat as she started to sing.

'There's a lonely boy, under a mosquito net, in the heart of Africa . . .'

Dylan pulled his hat down even further.

13. The Old Scoreboard

@RockWarFan007 For all da hype about Summer and Theo, #HalfTermHaircut get 1st or 2nd every week. Favourites surely?

4 REPLIES

@FlamingoedUp #HalfTermHaircut are boring as. It's the fans who vote for the winner in the final, so still between Jet and Industrial Scale Slaughter IMO.

@AllysCarpetCleaning #FrostyVader FTW

@LizzzieSmith Nobody will beat #ISS now Summer is back. She da nuclear bomb!!!!

@AlleyBalls #HalfTermHaircut not boring! They're actual musicians instead of attention seeking dick holes.

The audience stayed quiet as Earl Haart leaned over the bar, scratched his big moustache and made a sigh.

'I'm seeing bands getting better and better. Forming their identities, building their skills. But that performance by the Pandas of Doom missed the mark. It gives me no pleasure, but I can only give three out of ten.'

Low marks often brought jeers from the audience, but not this time. The Pandas had stunk the place out. The director cut to Jack Pepper, generating a few screams from girls in the audience.

'I know Eve's suffering with a cold,' Jack began. 'But Max, if you wanna be a leading man, you gotta work with what god gave you. And your original song was trying to do too much. Frankly, it was a little pretentious.'

Dylan enjoyed the fury on Max's face.

'I'll give you one more than Earl, because your song didn't really work, but I admire people with the ambition to try something different.'

Jack held up a number four, as the camera panned across to Beth Winder. Beth didn't hold back and the audience hummed, expecting zingers.

'I've had three babies,' Beth began, as she stuck fingers in her ears. 'First one had me in labour for thirty-two hours, but it was less painful than listening to that Africa song.'

The audience laughed, as Eve started coughing and Max turned red.

'I hate to break it to you, Max, but you're not Jimmy Page. You're not Axl Rose. You're more like one of the Minions. One point for the Pandas, and that's only because I don't have a zero!'

Lorrie was supposed to get reactions from the band, but Max was already storming off stage.

'Eight points for the Pandas,' Lorrie said, trowelling on her sad voice. 'That leaves them fourth with two bands to play, and means they'll definitely be in tonight's three-way vote-off.

'Brontobyte are currently third with eighteen points, Frosty Vader second with twenty-five, and Half Term Haircut leading the pack with that incredible, perfect, thirty out of thirty.'

'Peasants,' Max roared, as he ripped off his lapel mic and threw it at a stage hand. 'You try anything clever or interesting and they rip you to shreds. All they want is dumb lyrics and foot stamping.'

Dylan smirked as he followed Max down the hallway connecting the stage to the exhibition space.

'We signed up for a TV talent show,' Dylan noted. 'Did you expect the heights of sophistication?'

'Oh, *now* you have a contribution,' Max snarled. 'After I watched clips of you writing and rehearsing with half the other bands in the competition.'

'You *never* listen to me,' Dylan yelled. 'You're an arrogant prick. And guess what, you're *so* up yourself, you can't even see that you wrote a ridiculously pretentious song and made a complete ass of yourself in front of ten million viewers.'

Max tried to give Dylan a shove, but Leo wedged his bulk between them. 'Don't kick off,' he begged, as he pointed to the door into the exhibition space less than five metres away. 'Everyone's gonna be waiting for us through there.'

'Whatever,' Dylan said, stepping back.

'If we get voted off, you're out of the band,' Max snapped. 'You'll never play with the Pandas again.'

Now Leo was annoyed. 'It's not *your* band, Max.'

'So you're on Dylan's side?' Max sneered. 'As per usual.'

'You can't kick me out because I quit,' Dylan said. 'Once we're out of *Rock War*, you can stick this band up your arse.'

Max didn't seem to mind that, but then Leo chimed in. 'I'm out too.'

Now Max looked stunned. 'What if we win?'

'The winners are supposed to record an album,' Eve croaked. 'In the Caribbean.'

Dylan smiled. 'The way we just played, we'll be lucky if we don't get the boot tonight.'

Leo nodded. 'We'd better hope Jet drop into the vote-off. Only the DeAngelo fans can save our asses now.'

*

Rock War's producers knew how to max the drama. Summer's out-of-competition solo song had set things off with a bang, and Jet had been saved until last.

Jay sat in a barber's chair, getting his face dabbed with foundation.

'How's the nerves, love?' El, one of the make-up artists, asked.

'I'll live,' Jay said.

'Lips together, like this.'

Jay made a kissy face and the artist smeared on a tiny blob of lipstick.

'Shall I fix your hair like I did last week?'

'Sure,' Jay said, smiling. 'Looked rather awesome in the playback.'

At the same time, a huge roar erupted from the hall next door.

'Sounds like the girls have done well,' El said, as she cast an anxious glance at the monitor above her mirror.

'We OK for time?' Jay asked, closing his eyes for hairspray.

El nodded. 'We always get behind with Industrial Scale Slaughter. Girls take longer to do, but the producers never account for that.'

Jay opened his eyes and saw his hair all spiked up along the middle. He'd get laughed at if he went to school like that, but it looked the business on stage.

'All done,' El said, as she took a protective bib off Jay's clothes.

Adam, Theo and Babatunde stood in the exhibition space outside the make-up tent, watching a monitor with a couple of make-up ladies.

'How are the girls doing?' Jay asked, ducking as Adam tried to flatten his hair. 'Bog off!'

El shouted from inside the tent. 'If I have to do Jay's hair again, I'll come out there and poke you in the eye.'

'Leave Jay,' Theo told Adam. 'He looks slightly less like a scrawny ponce than usual.'

Theo had shown chinks in his armour the previous afternoon, but his swagger was back. At least for public consumption.

'Six points?' one of the other make-up artists said. 'I thought the girls were better than that.'

'So what happened?' Jay asked.

'Beth just gave them a six. Earl and Jack both gave sevens.'

'Twenty,' Jay said.

'We can beat that if we play like we did in rehearsal,' Babatunde said. 'Frosty and HTH are safe. Brontobyte and Pandas of Doom are in the drop zone. So it's between us and the girls for the last safe spot.'

'I'd love it if Brontobyte got kicked off,' Theo said. 'Tristan is such a loser.'

One of the make-up ladies laughed. 'We got the sense you didn't like Tristan after you bog washed him.'

A runner was jogging towards the make-up tent, gesturing frantically. 'Why are you still here?' she yelped, pointing at the running order on an overhead screen. 'You're on in ninety seconds!'

The make-up artists wished the boys luck as they dashed off. Coco led Michelle and Lucy down the stage corridor and there were high fives and rapid hugs as the two bands passed by.

'Twenty-one or bust,' Jay said, psyching himself up as he reached the edge of the stage. 'Good luck, guys.'

'Who needs luck?' Theo shouted, getting a roar as he stepped up to the edge of stage, before being shoved back into their unlit corner by a furious stage hand.

Jay's hands trembled as he strapped his guitar, and he always felt like peeing before a set. But there was a laptop ad on the monitor and a countdown saying nineteen seconds until Lorrie's introduction. His phone buzzed in his pocket, and since there wasn't time to switch to silent he threw it at a stage hand.

'Catch!'

'Welcome back!' Lorrie told the cheering audience. The lights came up as the stage hand carrying Jay's phone dived out of shot. 'Five bands down and one to go. I give you, Jay, Adam, Babatunde and Theo. It's Jet!'

The audience laughed as the stage-side screens cut to a close-up of Theo's T-shirt. It had the logo for the sitcom *Minefield*, and a picture of a chubby eleven-year-old DeAngelo Hunt eating a sandwich.

'My favourite show,' Theo growled, before spitting on the floor between his boots.

The reaction was mixed. For every Jet fan, the crowd had another who preferred more clean-cut bands like Frosty and HTH. Jay took a deep breath, Babatunde counted in and Adam hit the opening riff of Green Day's 'American Idiot'.

14. Not Even Close

Theo had realised how much he wanted to win and it showed in his performance. For the first time, he'd rehearsed hard and put some thought into what he'd do on stage. Jay and Babatunde had co-written a thumping, super-heavy track called 'Strip'. Big on the chorus, and though different enough for the musically illiterate not to notice, based on the same riff and basic song structure as Half Term Haircut's 'Puff'.

Because it was more hard-core, 'Strip' didn't get the crowd going in the way Half Term Haircut had done, but Jay still felt confident as the set wound down. Theo looked across with a cheeky smile, then stepped to the edge, where a fangirl had been eyeing him the whole time he'd been on stage. She wore an oversized tee, with JET written on the front in marker pen and THEO drawn inside a heart on the back.

Jay saw the stage manager's angst as Theo reached down. His muscled arm effortlessly pulled the girl on stage and she squealed as Theo gave her a sweaty hug.

'What's your name?' he asked.

'Beatriz,' she said, with a heavy French accent.

'I wanna hear the biggest cheer of the night for Beatriz!' Theo roared.

The crowd went bananas as Theo gave her his mic.

'I wanna say hello to my best pal, Jardine. And my sister Emilie, and my mum. And everyone at Ecole Française in Marylebone. Woo!'

Theo backed off, as the director cut off Beatriz's microphone and two stage hands gently encouraged her off stage.

Jay was smiling. Not everyone liked the bad-boy act and dragging up a fangirl had done wonders for a group with a lot of haters.

Lorrie looked anxious as the monitor in front of stage flashed in red, indicating that the show was running twenty-four seconds behind, thanks to Theo's antics.

'Looks like Theo's got one fan, at least!' Lorrie joked, as she rested an elbow on the bar. 'So, judges. The crowd seemed to like Jet's performance. How did it go down with you?'

'Two great songs,' Earl said. 'Easily Theo's best performance of the series, even if he just gave our director a heart attack. Jet has always been a tight unit musically, and when Theo gets the crowd going . . .'

Instead of finishing his sentence, Earl held up a number ten. The crowd had been split when Jet walked on, but their roar showed that Theo had won them over.

Jack had picked up the director's cue to hurry, and spoke in a hammy French accent. 'Jet 'ave one fan in Beatriz, and they 'ave another in me. Dix points!'

Twenty points meant that even if Beth only gave them one, they'd still be ahead of Industrial Scale Slaughter. Jay had just figured this out when he got hit from behind. Babatunde had scrambled away from his kit and wrapped his arms around Jay's neck, hugging and yanking him off his stool in one movement.

'We bloody did it!' Babatunde shouted.

'Bigger than Jesus!' Theo shouted, as he hugged Adam.

The audience at home didn't see this, because Lorrie was approaching the final judge. 'We've had our first perfect score tonight. Beth Winder, do we have another?'

'You know I like to make people happy,' Beth said. 'They were good. But for me, Half Term Haircut *just* edged them out.'

The audience groaned as Beth held up a nine. Lorrie hopped across the stage towards Jet, whose celebrations had ended up with Adam, Theo and Babatunde hugging on the floor, leaving Jay as the only man standing.

'You seem pretty happy with that,' Lorrie noted.

Jay wiped sweat off his brow. 'Such a buzz!' he shouted. 'Especially after the week we've had.'

Theo tried to stand up in the background, but Adam and Babatunde were holding on to his legs, laughing like loons.

'I don't think we're gonna get much sense out of your band mates right now. But are you disappointed not to share the perfect score with Half Term Haircut?'

'Not too fussed,' Jay said. 'Making the semis is what counts.

But I would like to say one thing. There are still poor people suffering in the world. So, who reckons DeAngelo Hunt and Karen Trim should still donate that million dollars to the Red Cross?'

It was usually Theo who spoke on stage. There was a huge roar at Jay's suggestion, then another as Theo flung his vest into the audience.

'Get on Twitter,' Jay shouted. 'Tell those richos to donate their money.'

The stage director had got so desperate about the time situation that he was standing just out of view, grimacing and making throat-cutting gestures to Lorrie.

'So you've heard them all,' Lorrie said. 'Jet are safe, along with Half Term Haircut and Frosty Vader. Now it's down to you, the audience at home.

'Brontobyte, Industrial Scale Slaughter and the Pandas of Doom are all in the drop zone, and the band with the smallest number of votes will *not* make it to the semi-final. To cast your phone votes, listen to the instructions coming up on screen now. We'll be back after the ten-thirty news headlines with the results and you can see live interviews and post-show reactions, starting in just a couple of minutes over on 6point2 and at Rockwar.com. It's been a great show. So get those votes in and we'll see you all later for The Reckoning!'

*

Dylan wanted to split after the Pandas' disastrous performance. He cut across the exhibition hall and squatted against the rear wheel of an equipment truck, parked indoors, just inside the hall's huge cantilevered doors. The way Dylan figured it, too many people would want to see Industrial Scale Slaughter perform with Summer for them to get voted off the show, which left the drop between the Pandas and Brontobyte.

Dylan wondered if he even wanted to stay in the competition and realised there were two different answers. In the long term, the idea of winning and having to put up with Max and the whole embarrassing scene with Eve while recording an album was horrible. But short term, Dylan was in no rush to leave Rock War Manor, with its none-too-serious attitude towards education and mates like Noah, Jay and Summer, who were cool and obsessed with music. Unlike his Scottish boarding school, where rugby and A-stars were all that mattered.

There were no performances or judges in the results show, so the crew were busy, dismantling the performance area, rolling out the bar, and replacing it with three circular white platforms, where the trio of bands on the brink of elimination had to stand in spotlights awaiting their fate.

There was a crash as equipment got thrown into the truck Dylan was leaning against. One of the roadies spotted Dylan's legs and squatted down beneath the open door flaps.

'Can't be here, kid,' the guy said.

Dylan tutted. 'I'm hardly in your way.'

'Forklift coming through in a bit,' the guy said firmly. 'Health and safety. You need to get back to the contestant area.'

Dylan stood reluctantly as the crew hurried off to pick up

the next load. He took a few steps, as if he was doing what he was told, but once the guys were out of sight he doubled back, tapping his pocket to make sure he had cigarettes and lighter, before heading out of a fire door, propped open with a sandbag.

It was the exhibitors' loading dock, with a few lamps, a view over the back doors of the catering stands, and treadmills inside a posh gym a couple of hundred metres away. Alexandra Palace was at the top of a hill, and a blast of wind hit as Dylan backed up to the wall and grabbed a cigarette.

'Thought it was you skulking about,' a woman with a Birmingham accent said, as she stepped out. 'They're looking to interview you for the website.'

Bev was a chain-smoking, chunky-thighed hipster. She managed *Rock War*'s autocue and on-screen graphics departments and while she wasn't conventionally beautiful, Dylan thought her rasping voice and surly attitude were hot.

'Smoke?' Dylan asked, as he offered Bev his packet.

'You heard what I said?' Bev said, as she picked a cigarette. 'Should I feel bad bumming smokes from a schoolboy?'

'Screw their interview,' Dylan said, as he lit up. 'They'll find me when they find me. I'm having a smoke.'

'Amen to nicotine,' Bev said, leaning in so Dylan could light her up. 'You feeling OK? You know, after . . .'

'Fine, I guess,' Dylan said, shrugging. 'I'm figuring we'll get the boot after Max's prancy act.'

Bev puffed and shivered as a gust of wind hit. 'You might get some sympathy because of Eve's cold.'

'Maybe,' Dylan said. 'Have you heard anything about the votes?'

Rumours always flourished in the two-hour voting window between *Rock War*'s main and results shows. For the first two weeks of Battle Zone, an intern with access to the voting system had leaked to anyone who'd listen. But word got back to Karolina, the intern had been fired and the number of people with access to the voting system had been restricted.

'Whoever wins, I'm back on the dole come Christmas Eve,' Bev said, as she pulled out her phone. 'And since you saved me with a smoke . . .'

Dylan was astonished as Bev unlocked her phone and opened an app called *QStat Terminal*. The screen showed a console with a live tally of votes, updating every few seconds.

'Only Karolina is supposed to have access before the lines close,' Bev explained, as rain pelted the screen. 'But I set up the voting system, back when Zig Allen was in charge. Then I updated the system when the new management took over.'

The screen showed that six hundred and eighty thousand phone votes had been cast in the eighteen minutes since lines had opened. A pie chart at the bottom of the screen showed Summer's fan club putting Industrial Scale Slaughter on a whopping seventy-four per cent. Brontobyte had twenty-two, and the Pandas of Doom were way adrift on four.

'Back to boarding school I go,' Dylan said, retaining enough pride in his band to feel wounded by how far they trailed Brontobyte.

'You keep that zipped,' Bev warned, as she pocketed her

phone. 'You caught me in a moment of weakness.'

'I'd never drop you in it,' Dylan said. 'And I appreciate you letting me know. Better to find out from a friend than on stage in front of millions of people.'

'Who knows, eh?' Bev said, as she flicked the remains of her ciggie into a puddle. 'Maybe there'll be a miracle.'

15. Death Blow

Twenty-nine points!

Jay was high on life as he left Alexandra Palace, stepping out of the main entrance behind Theo. His mum, dad, stepdad and three of his youngest siblings waited by the door of a sixteen-seat executive coach.

There were three TV crews on the scene and a dozen cameras flashed, as six-year-old brother Hank leaped into Jay's arms and licked his cheek.

'Eww,' Jay moaned. 'Gross.'

'There's seats on the bus that go back like beds!' Hank blurted, kicking his legs excitedly. 'Come on, I'll show you.'

Babatunde rushed across to hug his parents. Theo said something rude and got cuffed by his mum, as Jay's enormous stepdad, Big Len, reached out and shook Jay's hand.

'Bloody proud of you, boy,' Len said. 'Golden balls gets all the attention, but I know you're the one keeping this band ticking.'

As Len let go, Jay's real dad slapped him on the back. Then a camera got shoved in his face.

'You're live on UK24 News,' a correspondent told Jay. 'We've just had the audience figures, and tonight's *Rock War* was the most watched show of 2016, with fifteen point three million viewers.'

'Nice,' Jay grinned, unable to think of much to say. 'Everyone works so hard, you know? The crew and all the people you never see. Up before we start and still working hours after I'm in bed.'

'So, three bands in the drop zone, which one is for the chop?'

'They're all good,' Jay said, as Hank wriggled in his arms. 'Obviously my cousin Erin and some of my oldest friends form Brontobyte. But they're all great bands.'

'And Summer? You and her were getting pretty close back before her accident.'

'Oh,' Jay said, feeling his face redden. 'We're still good friends . . . I don't know what's going on.'

'And where are you off to now?'

Hank wanted to get down, so Len reached into shot to grab his son. 'I think we're just going to a restaurant. Have a relaxing meal with our families, and watch the results show.'

'Thank you, Jay. And congratulations again on tonight's performance.'

'Cheers!' Jay said, giving a thumbs-up before heading towards the little coach.

The driver wore an old-fashioned chauffeur cap and the

interior was super-posh, with huge leather recliners, each with a table alongside. When Jet and their entourage were aboard, security guards opened up a line of traffic cones. Alexandra Palace was at the top of a steep hill and surrounded by parkland. As the coach rolled out, fans ran in from all directions and started thumping on the sides.

Most ticket holders were still in the Palace, awaiting the results show, so these were the fans who'd spent the evening getting cold and wet, huddled in the moonlit park, watching the show on glitchy phones and iPads.

'Jay,' someone screamed, and when he looked out there were two girls lifting up their shirts.

'Boobs!' Hank squealed, then squirmed as his dad teased him with a hand over his eyes.

Another girl had *Adam call me*, along with her mobile number written on a piece of cardboard.

'I'm writing that down,' Adam yelled cheerfully.

Finally the driver saw a break in the crowd and sped up. The two mums had found a spot together up back, and Babatunde's mum was slowly shaking her head.

'All this attention won't be good for them,' she noted.

Jay, Theo and Adam's mum nodded in agreement. 'At least you've only got *one* to deal with when this all ends in tears.'

*

Dylan had rationalised. Win or lose, he'd have been back at boarding school after Christmas. He'd never got on with Max, so the Pandas breaking up was no biggie. And he'd miss the friends he'd made at the manor, but they'd Snapchat,

WhatsApp and there was already talk of a meet in the Easter holidays. He'd even tapped out a note on his phone:

Ambitions for 2017:

1. Stay in touch with *Rock War* people.
2. Start a new band with dudes I actually like.
3. Get expelled from boarding school.
4. Get laid at least once.
5. Get stoned at least once a week.

The audience was restless after a two-hour wait, trapped in the Palace with grungy toilets and overpriced food. A third had decided to leave rather than wait and the remainder had been herded up close to stage, so that the gaps didn't look obvious.

The stage now comprised three white circles and a podium for Lorrie. Summer, Coco, Lucy and Michelle stood in one, arms around each other's backs, but secretly confident. Brontobyte had a more nervous air. Tristan and Erin held hands. Salman dripped sweat, while *Rock War*'s youngest contestant, Alfie, sat at the edge swinging his legs off stage.

The Pandas of Doom had the leftmost circle. Eve should have been in bed. She kept shivering and the production team had broken precedent and given her a stool to sit on.

The big screens were showing a commercial, which ended as the countdown clock hit zero. Everything went dark, apart from a single spot on Lorrie.

'Welcome back to the *Rock War* Reckoning!' Lorrie said. 'If you haven't voted already it's not too late. Lines close in four minutes, giving you one *final* chance to vote. The numbers will be up on screen while we show you a little recap of what happened earlier this evening.'

Dylan spoke to Eve as the recap package started running on the screens and for the viewers at home. 'You OK?'

Eve shrugged and made a little tut sound. Max laid a protective hand on his sister's shoulder and said, 'I'm looking after her, thank you.'

Dylan looked around for something heavy. He imagined grabbing it the moment the others found out they'd got the boot, belting Max over the back of the head and telling him what a massive wanker he thought he was.

Violence wasn't Dylan's style, but the fantasy played nicely in his head while the folks at home watched the recap.

'And now!' Lorrie said, as the stage lights started to pulse and the audience turned quiet. 'All lines are closed. But you may still be charged, so please stop texting! I just need confirmation from our system that all results have been counted.'

The stage-side screens flashed with *ALL VOTES COUNTED* as the lights over the three white circles went out. A drum roll started echoing around the Palace. 'The first band to make it through to the semi-final is . . .'

Lorrie did a big pause, until the lights came on above the four girls.

'Industrial Scale Slaughter!'

Summer and her band mates did what they were expected to. Hugged and squealed, told Lorrie how grateful they were to all the people who'd voted for them. But nobody was really surprised.

'Now it's between Brontobyte and the Pandas of Doom,' Lorrie said excitably. 'And you can find out, right after these ads.'

*

All the bands were staying near King's Cross and Babatunde's parents had booked a table for Jet and their families at an old-skool curry house nearby. Jay was tucking into a sensational lamb curry, while a TV hung over flock wallpaper showed *Rock War* coming back from commercials. Industrial Scale Slaughter had departed, leaving just the Pandas and Brontobyte in their nerve-racked circles.

'Much as I hate Tristan and Brontobyte,' Jay said, 'the Pandas are getting the axe tonight. Max made an absolute tit of himself.'

Adam stood up and shouted across the table. 'These things *never* work out how you expect. I bet you any money it's Brontobyte.'

'I hate Tristan Jopling *so* much,' Theo growled. 'And his hellcat mother.'

Babatunde's family were quite posh, and his parents weren't comfortable with the rowdy vibe.

'How much you wanna bet, Adam?' Jay yelled, peeling out two fifty-pound notes and waving them.

Jay's mum, Heather, reached across the table and yanked him back to his seat. 'Keep it down,' she warned. 'Everyone's looking. And where'd you get all that money from?'

'Ahh,' Jay spluttered, avoiding the answer by pretending his mouth was full.

'Knew you'd chicken out,' Adam smirked.

Jay gave his brother the finger. Hank copied him.

'Pack it in, all of you,' Heather growled.

Up on screen, Lorrie was ready to make the announcement. 'The band that we'll be seeing in next week's semi-final is . . .'

The lights shone in Dylan's face as he awaited his fate.

'The Pandas of Doom.'

'Yessss!' Adam shouted. 'Jay you loser! I told you. It *never* goes the way you expect.'

'Look at Tristan's face,' Theo jeered. 'Boo-hoo, mommy's boy, you got tha boot!'

'Erin's your cousin,' Len reminded them. 'She looks really upset.'

Jay watched the screen as Leo, Eve and Max jumped up and down. But for some reason, Dylan was in the background looking *really* confused.

16. The Survivor

Dylan shunned his band mates and chose to travel in a taxi with a couple of the interns, arriving at the hotel around midnight. A lot of the other contestants had family visiting, and there were lively groups socialising in the lobby and hotel bar. He sneaked through unnoticed, then bumped into Erin from Brontobyte, coming out of the elevator with a wheelie bag. They'd never been close, but he gave her a hug and told her he was sorry.

'We had a good run,' Erin said, shrugging.

'Not sticking around for breakfast?'

'My mum's waiting,' Erin said. 'We only live ten minutes' drive from here and I feel like being with my family.'

'Good luck with . . .' Dylan said, then paused for thought. 'Wherever life drags you, I guess.'

Dylan envied Erin and all the others downstairs with their families as he rode the lift to seven. His mum was a successful San Francisco-based sculptor, while his dad was a retired rock god who spent his days pottering around the grounds of his remote Scottish estate, tinkering with classic cars and occasionally penning a movie soundtrack.

They'd divorced when Dylan was eleven and sent him off to boarding school a few months later. There had been no parental fuss over him entering *Rock War*, but nor had they shown any enthusiasm. No appearances at concerts, no care packages at the manor. Not even a text message to wish him luck.

Dylan had to slot his room key in the top of the switch to make the lights come on. The room was a tiny single, with a whiff of furniture polish and net curtains grey with dust. The window wouldn't open and he wound up squatted on the narrow bed, kicking off his All Stars.

Sleep would have been great, but loneliness and curiosity made it hard to settle. He thought about the app screen Bev had showed him and wondered how the Pandas had survived.

There might have been some miracle turnaround in the voting. Maybe the telephone number for his band was faulty and there'd been some kind of delay in recording their votes. Or was the app a trick? Bev was a graphics professional, so maybe she'd faked an app on her phone in anticipation of tricking the first contestant dumb enough to ask her how the votes were going. Or maybe there'd been a mix-up with the Pandas' and Brontobyte's scores and now nobody was prepared to admit it.

But Bev wasn't the kind of person who'd put major effort into teasing teenagers. And the other answers didn't completely ring true. Dylan didn't know Bev's mobile number, but most of the *Rock War* crew were staying in the same hotel, so he picked up the handset beside his bed and asked to be connected to Bev Grant's room.

'I'm sorry, Mr Wilton, we don't have a guest of that name.'

'What about Beverly, or something like that?'

'Nobody with that surname, I'm afraid, sir.'

The logical thing was to go to sleep and catch up with Bev in the morning. Dylan stripped, brushed, flipped the lights and got under the covers, but his brain kept churning and he grabbed his phone off the bedside table.

After thinking for several seconds, he typed *Rock War voting* into the Google bar. The first link took him to the official *Rock War* site and a page that said voting was now closed and giving the date of the semi-finals in two weeks' time. There was a link to some terms and conditions at the bottom, and Dylan clicked through to a page of tiny print, which he had no intention of reading. He was about to go back when he noticed the name *QStat* in the data protection statement: *All data collected from* Rock War *voting is held by QStat Technology on behalf of Venus Television and Channel Six Limited, under the terms of the 2004 Data Protection Act . . .*

This jogged Dylan into remembering that the app on Bev's phone had been called *QStat Terminal*. Perhaps he'd misunderstood what he'd seen. After all, it had been dark and wet, and Bev had flashed the screen for all of three seconds.

Dylan realised *QStat Terminal* would be too specialised to be an App Store download, but maybe he could find the company's website and download the app from there, or even just get some clue from a screenshot on their website.

Dylan typed *QStat Technology* into the search bar and was surprised to see a news article about *Rock War* at the top of the results:

Karen Trim Admits Defeat After QStat Deal.

The first part of the article summarised a story Dylan knew well: *Rock War* had been conceived by Zig Allen and his company Venus TV. Channel Six had agreed to screen the show, but most of the cost had been picked up by its sponsors, Rage Cola. Just as *Rock War* showed early signs of success, Rage Cola had pulled out due to the behaviour of some contestants. Venus TV teetered on the edge of bankruptcy and *Rock War* almost got shut down.

Karen Trim, who'd made a two hundred and fifty million pound fortune from *Hit Machine* and other TV talent shows, swooped in to buy Venus TV. But Channel Six didn't like the idea of Trim owning the rights to all of their biggest shows and after a battle, Channel Six eventually bought Venus TV, in conjunction with celebrity chef Nick Cobb and a third investor who'd chosen to remain anonymous.

Dylan knew the story up to this point, but he'd not known that Karen Trim had a final sting in her tail. The article described how Venus TV had agreed to use a telephone voting system developed and owned by Karen Trim to collect votes for *Rock War*. After losing her battle to buy *Rock War*, the article explained that Trim had refused to allow the show to continue using her technology.

Unfortunately for Venus TV, Karen Trim's telephone voting technology was even more successful than the talent shows for which she'd developed it. When the new owners of Venus TV went looking for an alternative supplier, they found that pretty much every talent show in the world used Trim's system to collect phone votes and add the totals.

Trim had then played hardball, refusing to license her technology unless she was given a stake in Venus TV and a share in the profits from *Rock War*. Apparently, Karolina Kundt was on the verge of giving in to Trim's demands when they discovered QStat, a small New Zealand-based start-up company, that had developed voting tech for smartphone games.

Venus TV signed a deal with QStat and Karen Trim was thwarted again. Dylan had never liked Karen Trim, so he allowed himself a smile as he saw the three men pictured at the top of the article. They were in an office overlooking Auckland harbour, huddled around a laptop displaying QStat's logo.

The men on either side were geeky, twenty-something New Zealanders. The man in the middle was closer to sixty and wore a beige suit and huge rectangular sunglasses. The caption beside the photo read: *QStat founders, Matt and Leo Finn, pictured after concluding their NZ$1.25 million buyout deal, pictured with Channel Six (UK) executive Jack Smith.*

Something about the man in the centre caught Dylan's eye. Jack Smith seemed familiar, but Dylan dismissed it as a face he'd seen at a Channel Six launch party a few months earlier, or maybe one of the executives who occasionally visited the manor.

But somehow that didn't sit right. This man stirred thoughts from somewhere deeper in Dylan's memory. He stared at the face until the screen went into power save, then shot bolt upright when he finally realised who he was looking at.

'Shit!' Dylan shouted, feeling like his guts were being crushed as fragments fell into devastatingly sharp focus.

Dylan knew who the man was. He knew the identity of *Rock War*'s secret investor. He knew why the Pandas of Doom hadn't been voted out of *Rock War*.

Now he had to figure out what the hell he was going to do about it.

17. Cuddle Wuddles

There was mild chaos as the four members of Jet and their families left the curry house. Since the semi-final wasn't for two weeks, the contestants had been given a couple of days off and most planned to spend some of this time with their families.

Theo was meeting up with some guys he knew and going to a club. Adam was spending the night at home, because he was going to watch his girlfriend's soccer match the following morning, and Babatunde's parents were driving up to Northampton to take him to visit his grandparents.

That left Jay as the only one going back to the hotel. His mum made a big fuss, saying that King's Cross was a dodgy area and there was no way he was walking alone after midnight, so Jay ended up strolling with his dad, Chris.

'You OK?' Jay asked. 'You know, since you quit the force?'

Chris shrugged. 'Security guard isn't so bad. The money's crap, but it's way less stressful.'

'I guess,' Jay said, sensing that his dad was putting a sheen on things. 'I'm not a little kid, you know. You *can* tell me if things are rough.'

Chris smiled a little awkwardly. 'It's fine. I've got stuff to work through, but who hasn't?'

Before Jay could continue, he got recognised by a couple of drunk girls who wanted selfies. One of them held her shoes in her hand and Jay glanced down at her bust when she put her arm around his back.

'My boy, the celebrity,' Chris said, smiling as he got handed a pink Samsung to take a pic of Jay with one of the girls on either side.

'You were amazing tonight,' one of the women said. 'Bloody loved it when you took the microphone after you'd played. Instead of Theo gobbing off as usual.'

Jay smiled at the compliment as they headed off. But he was annoyed that the selfies had taken him off subject, when he was trying to get a sense of how his dad was really feeling. And now they'd reached the hotel lobby before he managed to steer the conversation back.

'Love you, son,' Chris said, as he hugged Jay. 'We'll spend some time together once this *Rock War* thing's over.'

'Look forward to it,' Jay said. 'I think the bar's still open inside if you wanted to hang.'

'Unfortunately I've got work in an hour,' Chris said. 'Graveyard shift at a freight depot. Two till two.'

'Well that sucks,' Jay said, as he hugged his dad back. 'Night, Dad.'

Contestants and families had mostly gone to bed, but the hotel bar was packed with *Rock War* staff and crew. Jay spotted Summer on a couch in the lobby. Her hair was still black, but she'd switched to jeans and a camouflage hoodie with a bright yellow smiley face on the front.

'All alone?' Jay asked.

Summer pointed to a publicist who was shaking hands with a journalist a few metres away. 'Just did an interview,' Summer explained. 'How was your curry?'

'Fiery,' Jay said, grinning as he sat at the opposite end of the sofa to Summer and reached for a clean glass and a water jug that had been put out for the interview.

'I never sleep after a show,' Summer said. 'My mind goes way too fast.'

'I know exactly,' Jay said. 'So you're OK? I thought you were limping a bit backstage.'

'I think it's just being in hospital so long,' Summer said. 'I've got an exercise sheet, and physio every Wednesday.'

Summer reached for her own water and used it as an excuse to shuffle into the middle of the couch. Jay read the signal and slipped his arm around her back.

They sat like that for ages, talking. Summer explained about her nan and why she'd run away from hospital. She told him how she was worried that her band mates – particularly Michelle – were jealous about the amount of media coverage she got.

Jay told Summer how he was worried about his dad, and how he'd avoided going home because he couldn't stand his younger brother Kai. They both cringed at the thought of facing their classmates when they got back to school.

'If I lose, they'll rip into me for that,' Jay said. 'And if Jet win it'll be even worse.'

Jay found girls pretty terrifying. But even though Summer was beautiful, and in the year above him at school, they'd always clicked. Jay entertained Summer with stories about stuff that had happened at the manor while she'd been in hospital, and things Theo had done before *Rock War*.

Summer was laughing and squeezing Jay's knee, and then she whispered in his ear. 'I'm sharing with Michelle. But aren't you in a single?'

'Sharing with Babatunde,' Jay corrected. 'But he's gone north with his folks.'

'Well we can't kiss here, in case there's press hiding,' Summer said. 'Soooooo . . .'

Jay beamed. 'You wanna come up to my room?'

'I *totally* do.'

Twenty-nine points and a make-out session with Summer . . . Jay had decided this was the best night of his life, but he had to play it cool, because they shared the lift with a drunk camera operator and Karolina's husband.

The hotel had over four hundred rooms, and getting to Jay's seventh-floor twin seemed to involve walking past most of them. Summer jokingly barged Jay into the wall. Jay grinned and shoved her back. Then Summer decided she wanted a piggyback, but she weighed more than Jay and he only managed a dozen steps before buckling.

'Gee up!' Summer giggled, poking Jay between the shoulder blades. 'You're the worst mule ever.'

Summer was moving in for a kiss when Dylan came out of a room a few doors down. He wore a green canvas parka jacket, stripy bobble hat and pulled a silver Tumi wheelie case.

'Dylan, buddy!' Jay said cheerfully.

Dylan was one of the most laid-back people Jay knew, but he seemed stiff and angry.

'Where you off to at this time of night?' Summer asked, sweeping tangled hair off her face as she found her feet.

'I thought you were heading back to the manor with us, tomorrow,' Jay added.

'I'll be there sooner or laters,' Dylan said. 'But there's something to take care of.'

Summer sensed that he was upset. 'It's almost two in the morning. Where are you going?'

'It's complicated,' Dylan said. 'I've got to get to Stansted for a five a.m. flight. My Uber is waiting downstairs.'

'Are you sure you're OK, mate?' Jay asked.

'Explain back at the manor,' Dylan said, as he started towards the lift. 'I've gotta run.'

Summer and Jay glanced backwards as Dylan jogged off.

'So not Dylan,' Summer said. 'You think someone's sick? His mum or something?'

Jay shrugged. He regarded Dylan as a good friend, but he never spoke about his home life. Jay wasn't even sure if Dylan had siblings, or if his parents were still together.

'I guess there's not much we can do,' Summer said.

Summer pulled Jay close for a kiss, and he was relieved that concern for Dylan hadn't knocked her off task. His room was a few doors past Dylan's and Summer put her hand on his bum as he fumbled with his key card.

When they got inside the room, Summer backed up to the doors of a built-in wardrobe. Jay stared into her eyes, catching his breath. Seeing all the little details, like the freckles under her nose and a spot below her chin where the make-up hadn't quite come off. With any other girl he'd have been completely terrified, but Summer made everything feel OK.

18. Nightmare Junior

The easyJet touched down at Edinburgh airport just after seven thirty. Dylan hadn't slept and his eyes drooped as the sun rose and his taxi cruised dead, Sunday morning streets.

'Well posh round here,' the driver observed, as they pulled up at a cobbled kerb overlooking Edinburgh's Bruntsfield Park.

'Keep the change, pal,' Dylan said, as he handed over a twenty and slammed the door.

A Lycra-clad couple jogged by as Dylan passed five-storey, sandstone apartment blocks. He went on tiptoes and peered over a fence into a line of parking spaces, built between the last house and a church.

The only car inside was a classic E-Type Jaguar, which had been parked long enough for moss to bloom on its grey weatherproof cover. A gate squealed, and Dylan eyed the security cameras as he crossed an immaculately restored mosaic path, towards the church's six-metre arched wooden door.

Disguised in the side of the arch, a more modest entrance had been cut through the thick stone. There was a letterbox and a riveted steel door, with a CCTV dome above. There was a single doorbell, but an engraved plaque listed the names of several companies headquartered here: Wilton Music, Napier Artist Management, Blade-Ingram Music Publishing, Blade Film Partnership, Glacier Films Group, Terra Licencing. Dylan noticed a new addition at the bottom: Glacier Media Holdings.

Dylan shuddered as his fingers hovered over an aluminium entry pad. His plan relied on getting inside. He wasn't certain of the code. But his dad's memory had suffered from decades of drug use and Dylan knew the two PINs he used for everything from his iPhone login to his Amex Centurion card.

But tapping 7071 did nothing. Then he noticed there was a green key at the bottom of the pad, and 7071 followed by the green brought a satisfying click from the lock. The air inside was warm. There was a swanky Pinarello racing bike just inside the door, the unmistakeable must of church, and multicoloured streaks projected through stained glass.

Dylan's dad had bought the church in the eighties, when his band Terraplane were topping charts and selling out stadiums. A no-expense-spared restoration transformed the building from near ruin to modern offices, from which the band's affairs had been managed for more than thirty years.

The nave had been sympathetically restored and turned into an air-conditioned venue for press conferences and film screenings. The U-shaped upper galleries were private offices for the band's five members and their manager, plus an open-plan area for admin staff. The basement had a modest recording studio, a decent-sized gym and held the band's archives, including its priceless analogue master tapes in a fireproof vault.

Dylan was confident he'd have the place to himself at eight a.m. on a Sunday, but still checked the major areas to be certain. After parking his case under a coat rack, Dylan wound up in the secretarial pool, which overlooked the nave. All twelve desks would have been staffed back in the eighties, but Terraplane hadn't played a gig in twenty years and some of the immaculately-clean workstations had turned into period pieces, with glass ashtrays, electric typewriters and chunky push button phones.

The place stirred memories of being small and bored, playing with the swivel chairs while his dad was in meetings. Dylan stuck his head in his father's office, and found it so derelict that boxes of files had been stacked around the desk. One wall had a long yellow stain where the roof had leaked. But his real target was Harry Napier's office at the far end.

Napier was a music industry legend. Former middleweight boxer and son of a Glasgow gangster, Dylan knew him as Uncle Harry, but to most of the music industry he was Nightmare Napier. While a lot of bands squandered fortunes and got ripped off by everyone from concert promoters to record companies, Napier mixed a sharp business brain and thuggish reputation to ensure that Terraplane always made money.

Napier's twenty per cent cut of everything Terraplane and several other highly successful bands earned, plus some very wise investments, had made the seventy-five-year-old one of Scotland's wealthiest men. The *Forbes* magazine Rich List said he was worth over four hundred million.

Uncle Harry's office was locked, but Dylan was more interested in the cabinets lined with suspension files outside. They were alphabetised and he hunted down the new name he'd noticed on the engraved plaque.

Glacier Media Holdings had an entire cabinet to itself. Dylan pulled a file at random, and got a bunch of Companies House documents, confirming that the company had been created earlier that year. The next batch were all expense documents. Then he eyed a file named *Venus TV*.

Dylan took the file out. The first thing he noticed were letters on the headed notepaper of Channel Six and Rage Cola. The folder was organised by date, with the oldest stuff at the back. The first sheet was a set of handwritten notes from a conversation between Harry Napier and Zig Allen.

Dylan flipped through pages. There were printouts of email exchanges between Zig, who wanted eight million for Venus TV, and Harry, who was offering three. Dylan's dad – Jake Blade – got a few mentions, but there was nothing about Dylan being a member of the Pandas.

So now Dylan was certain. His dad regularly forgot his birthday, and had never even sent a good luck text before his band appeared on TV. But why bother with a text, when you can buy a major stake in a TV talent show and then rig the voting so that your kid's band wins?

'Why can't I just have normal *bloody* parents?' Dylan asked himself aloud, then sighed as he went down on one knee. He tore out a couple of key pages in case his dad tried to deny everything, then slid the folder back into the rack.

It seemed ironic to Dylan that *Rock War* had been rigged in his favour, while he'd fallen out with his band and didn't want to win. But even if he had still wanted to win, he wouldn't want to do it by cheating mates like Jay, Summer, Babatunde and Noah. He was the only son of a multimillionaire, while Jay lived in a crap-hole and Summer had told Dylan how she used to steal toilet roll from school to save money.

Now he was certain, Dylan had to call his dad and confront him. But his hands were trembling and he knew a smoke would calm him down. He pocketed the papers, filled a cup from the water cooler and drank it before heading downstairs. As he reached the bottom, a great slab of a man shot out from behind a door.

'Gotcha, you robbing shite!' he roared, as he hooked Dylan's ankle and slammed him to the stone floor.

The guy was twice Dylan's size. He'd been using the basement gym and his shirt was wringing. He placed one knee over Dylan's chest and his sweat rained as he pulled back a huge fist.

'Cops won't do shit with a scally your age,' the guy said menacingly. 'But I'll bloody teach you.'

'I'm not robbing . . .' Dylan tried to explain.

Then he took the hardest punch of his life.

*

There had been no interlocking of naughty parts and only outerwear had hit the floor around Jay's bed. But there had been some amazing kissing, an ice cube and pillow fight and a beautiful moment when he woke up, nestled against Summer's back.

Jay watched her breathe and studied the circular scar in the back of her head. He could have happily watched forever, but his bladder had other ideas and he rolled gently off the bed and enjoyed his first pee of the day.

He could imagine Theo calling him hopeless for spending the night with a girl and not even trying to have sex. But it wasn't so bad: he'd only just turned fourteen, and he doubted that any of his school-mates had got this far with a hot older girl.

As he padded out of the bathroom, Jay caught a muffled version of his Imperial Death March ringtone. The phone was buried in his balled-up jeans. They were damp from melted ice cubes and there was a mist of feathers as he extracted his phone from the front pocket.

'Yeah,' Jay said, but it was a recorded voice.

'You have one voice message. To listen to your message, press one. To delete this message press—'

Jay pressed one, and he heard a woman's voice. Slightly fraught.

'Jay, it's Susanna from publicity. We're looking for Summer, but she's not in her room. A few people saw you talking to her late last night. If you know where she ended up, either let me know or tell her to call me immediately. And tell her not to speak to *anyone* else before she does.'

Summer had heard the ringtone and was shuffling up the headboard, stifling a yawn.

'They're looking for you,' Jay said. 'Susanna, sounds urgent.'

'Why are they calling you?' Summer said, as she reached over the side of her bed.

Her phone was in a little shoulder bag. She pressed the power button, but the screen stayed black.

'Right,' Summer said groggily as she grabbed her jeans. 'I only had six per cent battery when I left Alexandra Palace.'

'I've got fourteen,' Jay said. 'You wanna call her on this?'

'Then they'll know we spent the night together,' Summer said, as she pulled a T-shirt over her head.

'Nothing too inappropriate happened,' Jay pointed out, as he realised his jeans were soaked and decided on a clean pair from his overnight bag.

'But what will people believe?' Summer said, standing up as she zipped her jeans. 'I'll go call from my room.'

Jay hated being the youngest and least sexually accomplished member of Jet. He imagined how cool it would be, strutting into rehearsal with all his band mates thinking that he'd shagged Summer. He came back to earth as Summer pushed her feet into her pumps and scrambled towards the door.

'I hope it's nothing bad,' Jay said.

'Probably Michelle done something crazy again,' Summer suggested, as she swooped in and gave Jay a very quick kiss. 'I *know* I've not done anything wrong.'

19. Tiny Tina's Terror

When Dylan was seven, he'd attended a barbecue at Harry Napier's extensive Edinburgh home. In finest Scottish tradition, the caterers grilled under canopies, while the guests stood inside watching rain lash the windows.

There'd been a lot of kids around. Thumping up and down the stairs and mucking around by the patio doors, shoving other kids out into the rain. But Dylan was never the rough-and-tumble type, so he'd snuck upstairs to the library.

He found a leather chaise and an illustrated edition of Kipling's *Just So Stories*, but peace only lasted until Harry's wingnut-eared son, Dougal, charged in. As the burly teen mashed Dylan's face against a bookshelf, he got told that upstairs was off limits and that he had to be punished. This involved getting hauled into a bathroom, where Dougal pinched Dylan's nose and squirted foul-tasting perfume in his mouth when he opened up to breathe.

This trauma got reimagined through so many childhood

nightmares, that Dylan wondered if it had really happened. But as he squirmed on the church floor fearing a second punch, there was something unmistakeable about the jutting ears of the man attacking him.

'You're Dougal Napier,' Dylan yelled desperately. 'You sprayed Dolce and Gabbana in my mouth.'

It was too late to stop a slam to the ribs, but Dougal backed off right after.

'I've seen yous on that *Rock War*,' Dougal blurted. 'Sat through that shite with my girl last night.'

Dylan sat up slightly, clutching his stomach and wiping a bloody top lip on his cuff.

'I'm Jake Blade's son,' Dylan gasped. 'Remember the barbecue at your dad's house? You found me in the library. I guess you were about fourteen.'

'Cannae remember, but it sounds like something I'd have done. So why you here?'

'My dad asked me to pick up some files,' Dylan lied. 'And I could ask the same about *you*.'

'The gym,' Dougal explained, gesturing at his sweaty shirt and trackies as if it was obvious. 'It's only me ever uses it. But I don't get how you're Dylan Wilton off *Rock War*, if your dad is Jake Blade?'

Dougal clearly hadn't inherited his dad's brains. 'Blade is a stage name,' Dylan said, a touch patronisingly. 'It even says *Wilton Music* outside, on the name plate.'

Dougal nodded. 'Always wondered who that was.'

'So, my dad's waiting,' Dylan lied, as he rummaged down

his pocket for a tissue to wipe his bloody top lip. He found one, then went to grab his case from the coat rack.

Dougal blocked Dylan's path as he headed for the door.

'Let me out and we'll forget this whole thing,' Dylan suggested.

But Dougal was pulling his phone. 'I'm no' saying you're lying,' Dougal said, raising one hand apologetically. 'But my dad will have my balls if you're having me on, so I'm gonna call him to be sure.'

'There's no need,' Dylan said airily, as he sidestepped towards the door.

The hand became aggressive as Dylan tried to get past.

'Don't even *think* about it,' Dougal warned.

Dylan knew there was a fire exit up back, behind the cinema screen. But he didn't rate his chances of outrunning Dougal.

'Dad,' Dougal said, as the phone connected. 'Dad . . . I know it's Sunday morning . . . NO, I'm not in trouble. Will ya listen? I was down in the gym. There was a kid nosing around upstairs. I thought he was robbing, but he says he's Jake's son. I gave him a bit of a bloody nose . . . Dylan, that's right . . . No, I don't think he's hurt serious . . . Right. No probs.'

After another pause, Dougal pocketed the phone.

'My dad's sending a car. He says he has to talk to you.'

*

Summer had left in a rush, and Jay noticed one of her trainer socks on the carpet as he sat on the corner of his bed, speaking into the hotel phone.

'Full English, no baked beans. Eggs . . .? Scrambled, I guess. Toast white, and pineapple juice. How long will that take . . .? Fabulous.'

Room service would take twenty, so Jay found the remote and put the TV on. Then he reached across and grabbed his phone, which he'd now put on charge. He was about to check messages when he heard *Rock War* mentioned on the TV.

It was UK24 News. Presenter Matt Blenkinsopp, a member of parliament and two micro-celebs sat around a big oval table, piled with Sunday newspapers and coffee cups. The presenter was warbling on. 'Fifteen million viewers for *Rock War*,' he commented, shaking his head. 'When I think of all the great dramas made by the BBC, and the comedies. I just find it rather depressing that this show gets more viewers.'

The camera cut to a jolly woman, with multi-chins and a lot of make-up. 'I disagree, Matt,' she said. 'My daughters both sat up watching it last night and it was *great* fun. Some of the contestants are rough around the edges, but I think that sense of reality is why the show has caught on in such a big way.'

'So, who do your daughters like?' Matt asked.

The woman smiled. 'They're eight and eleven, so they still like their boys squeaky clean. So it's Half Term Haircut for the win. But they were both voting for Summer's band last night.'

'But this show can't stay out of the headlines,' Matt said. 'And it's Summer's band, Industrial whatever-it's-called, that appear to have set off the latest storm this morning.'

Jay gasped as the screen showed the front page of the trashy *Sunday Courier*. It had a picture of a middle-aged woman dressed in a train guard's uniform. But there was a red bulge where her right eye belonged and the headline screamed:

COURIER EXCLUSIVE: ROCK WAR GIRLS RIPPED OUT MY EYEBALL

The hotel TV was titchy, but Jay could just read the sub-headline: CCTV *shows girl rockers in horror attack on train guard*.

Jay grabbed his phone and Googled *Rock War Train Guard*. There was a link to the *Courier* website, followed by a line that read *click to see 179 related stories*.

The video was at the top of the page and he skimmed the article while the site forced him to watch a thirty-second ad for fabric softener and close a pop-up asking him to subscribe to online newsletters.

Jay realised the incident had taken place in the Easter holidays, as Industrial Scale Slaughter travelled to London to take part in a battle of the bands called *Rock the Lock*. It was the day he'd first met the girls, and while it was only six months past, that felt like it was a lifetime away.

The article had several quotes from a train guard called Tina Manning. It described how the girls had '*descended on her like a pack of wolves, punching and shoving the petite 4ft 10inch train manager*'. Tina had apparently had to take a week off work after the incident.

Jay thought a week seemed pretty brief for someone who'd

had their eye ripped out, but further down the article made clear that Tina wore a glass eye, and it was this that had been knocked out during all the pushing and shoving.

Finally, the teen stereotype in the onscreen ad marvelled at how soft his rugby kit now felt, and Jay turned his phone sideways so that he got a full-screen image. The video was blurry, with a timecode running in one corner and a graphic that said *Courier Exclusive* at the bottom.

In contrast to the dramatic headlines, the silent video began with Summer, Lucy, Coco and Michelle sat around the table in a near-empty First Class carriage, while Tina the train guard stood in the aisle giving them a lecture.

After a few seconds, Michelle stood up, looking riled. Then Lucy seemed to lose her temper with Michelle and grabbed her. The train guard backed off and spoke into her radio, as Lucy gave Michelle an almighty shove out into the aisle.

A platform started appearing out of the window as Coco and Summer got up to run away, but a larger, male train guard had arrived to block their exit. Realising that they were trapped, Lucy and Michelle stopped fighting each other and lunged at Tina, sending her backwards over a pair of empty seats. The footage was grainy, but Jay guessed that this was when Tina 'lost' her eye.

The male guard didn't seem keen to get stuck in as the girls grabbed bags and guitars and made a dash. As the girls ran out of the grainy shot, the male guard stepped forward and gave Tina a hand up.

Jay almost admired the way that the tabloid turned a video

of some pushing and shoving into such a sensational headline. But he was worried for Summer, who'd be in a state over how her nan would react when she found out.

As Jay's phone cut to another pop-up advert, the TV showed the presenter and guests continuing to debate *Rock War*'s latest scandal. The director cut to a tight shot of presenter Matt, who was peering over the top of his glasses.

'We've just received a further development on this Train Wars episode,' Matt said, switching from his chatty voice to full-on newsreader. 'A spokesperson from British Transport Police has just issued the following statement. *British Transport Police have received information from the* Sunday Courier *newspaper, which may help identify the perpetrators of a serious assault on train staff that took place in April. British Transport Police have a zero tolerance approach to assaults on railway company staff. We take these matters very seriously and will use the information provided in furtherance of our investigation.*'

Jay looked down at his phone as a Facebook message came through from Babatunde.

What should Industrial Scale Slaughter sing in the semi-final? Jailhouse Rock, or Folsom Prison Blues? ☺

U not funny, Jay messaged back.

20. The Great Bamboozling

Dylan didn't know what to feel as home came into view. Rock War Manor would have fitted into the smallest of its four wings. As an only child, he stood to inherit the whole place, but he hated living on such an inhuman scale and often wondered who but his dad would ever be crazy enough to buy it.

The chopper touched down in front of a hangar, its roll-back doors cut into a hillside to avoid spoiling the view from the house. The co-pilot opened the sliding passenger door, blasting Dylan with cold and noise as he undid his harness and grabbed his luggage.

'Cheers,' Dylan said, ducking the blades as he set off at a dash.

There were two more helicopters parked in the hangar: a ten-passenger-long ranger, which could make it to London without refuelling, and a fragile-looking Huey. It had clocked three thousand hours in the Vietnam War and still wore US

Marines insignia. Dylan's dad had flown it in a few air shows, but had lost his pilot status after a drug bust.

You could ride a golf buggy or Segway through the James Bondish tunnel between the hangar and the main house, but Dylan chose to walk. The skylights were frosted over, but there was just enough light to see weird artworks, purchased by a mother he'd not seen in more than three years.

'Young man,' a sharp Scottish voice said, offering a hand to shake as Dylan emerged up carpeted steps, into the nineteenth-century splendour of the manor's main entrance.

'Uncle Harry,' Dylan said, awkwardly. 'You got here before me.'

Harry was past seventy, but his handshake remained brutal. 'I was here already, as it happens,' he said. 'There's been a lot of planning going on these past weeks. And the beauty of this place is, nobody sees who comes and goes.'

Dylan's father, Jake Blade, strolled out of a side room. His long grey curls were tied back, and he wore a plaid shirt and jeans browned with auto grease. Dylan got a familiar whiff of marijuana smoke and motor oil as they hugged.

'Long time no see, laddie,' Jake said. 'Pushed up a couple more centimetres, I reckon. Be taller than your old man soon.'

'Working on a car?' Dylan asked, more out of habit than any genuine interest.

'Dino GT,' Jake confirmed. 'Just got the rebuilt engine back from Marinello.'

Dylan patted his stomach. 'You've lost a bit round the middle, Dad.'

'Personal trainer,' Jake explained. 'Harry fixed me up with a guy. Get him working on you too, if you like. Have you nicely muscled up for your female admirers!'

One reason Dylan had always been flabby was the food at home. He got a stir of childhood nostalgia as his dad led him through to a large drawing-room with a whiff of smoked paprika in the air.

'Cajun chicken stew,' Jake explained. 'Chef Maureen said it was your favourite.'

The fireplace was ablaze and the staff had set a round table with three places, and the stew on a hot plate in the centre. There were also fresh-baked cornbread muffins and a tray of mac and cheese.

It was oddly silent as Dylan, Jake and Harry stood around the table ladling out stew. Harry broke silence as the trio settled into chairs.

'So kiddo, I'm dying to ask how you rumbled us?' Harry asked.

Dylan didn't want Bev getting fired, so he kept his answer vague. 'It's a pretty tight-knit crew at the manor. We didn't play well, everyone said the numbers were against us. When Brontobyte got the boot, I smelled a rat.'

Harry nodded as he gobbled mac and cheese off a spoon. 'But how'd you get from that to sneaking around in my office?'

'QStat,' Dylan said. 'I found out they were doing the voting. When I Googled them, I saw the story about the deal, and the picture of the two geeks with the Channel Six executive. Only, he didn't work for Channel Six. It was Uncle Noel.'

Jake was proud of his son's smarts. 'Noel Brangan lashed up a broken exhaust on our VW camper, driving us to Terraplane's first gig,' Jake told his son. 'And he's been fixing our problems ever since.'

Harry shook his head as he broke a muffin. 'This bastard internet,' he growled. 'And you kids are all so smart with it.'

Jake was shaking his head. 'Noel should have kept his face out of the paper.'

Harry grunted. 'He's getting bollocked, for sure. But Noel's a background guy. Who apart from Dylan could have pieced this together?'

Jake looked at his son. 'Dylan, I know your pride is dented. You thought you were getting through *Rock War* all on your own. But there's no shame in taking a hand up. *Everyone* does it.'

Dylan tutted. 'I'd rather not win *Rock War* than win it by cheating.'

Harry shook with dry laughter. 'Teenagers,' he scoffed, making a big hands-in-the-air gesture. 'It's all good and bad, black and white. Save the planet, don't eat meat, drive electric. But there's a *real* world out there, sonny. Shades of grey. Sharks who'll rob all your money, screw your girl, then dump your ass in the kerb.'

'Harry's right,' Jake told his son. 'You've seen pictures of where I grew up. Tin bath once a week, spaghetti hoops on toast and dirty old plimsolls, worn till my toes burst through.'

'This was *my* thing,' Dylan steamed. 'I didn't want to be the rich-kid son of Jake Blade Superstar. Why did you have to interfere?'

Jake wagged his fork. 'Because you're my son.'

Dylan's hands shook. 'Why do you never get it?'

'What?' Jake asked.

'Being a dad,' Dylan said. 'Like, when I was nine and I wanted Scalextric. You got one of your people to order up sets, and spares, and twenty cars and a fancy lap board, and then you just dumped it in my room. But what I actually wanted was one normal set, and maybe that you spent a few hours sitting on my floor playing with me.'

Jake rocked his chair back, wounded and unsure what to say.

'It's not *purely* about you, Dylan,' Harry said. 'When your dad said you were going into this competition, we didn't think much about it. But I sniffed blood when Rage Cola pulled out. Karen Trim was interested, so I knew there was money to be made. Your father and I snapped up our fifty per cent of Venus TV for less than two million. We've already earned four times that, selling the format overseas, and now the networks are talking high eight figures to bring *Rock War* to the US. Then there's all the recording rights and merchandising. We've turned two mil into seventy mil in the space of four months.'

'And that's *your* money in the long term,' Jake said.

'Give it to the bloody refugees,' Dylan said, holding up his arms to point out their grand surroundings. 'It's not like we're short of cash.'

Harry huffed. 'It's the schools, you know, Jake? They pump these kids full of left-wing drivel.'

Dylan had a thought. 'So you invested, you're making all this money from *Rock War*. Why bother fixing it? Surely it's better commercially if Jet or Half Term Haircut wins.'

'I wanted to do this for *you*, Dylan,' Jake said.

'Show the kid the other thing,' Harry said. 'The picture on your phone.'

'It's just a mock-up,' Jake explained, as he opened the gallery on his mobile and showed his son a poster.

The poster had the Terraplane band logo at the top, then below that *2017–18 The Resurrection Tour*. The next bit was harder to read, so Jake zoomed in to the part where it said, *Supported by* Rock War *UK winners, Pandas of Doom.*

'Imagine it, Dylan,' Jake said, beaming. 'Father and son, on the road. You'll be playing to stadiums packed with sixty to a hundred thousand people. The USA, Brazil, Japan, Australia.'

Dylan shuddered at the thought of touring the world with Max. 'Dad, you *always* take the piss out of the Rolling Stones. You always said Terraplane would never embarrass themselves with old songs banged out by granddads.'

'I've done well thanks to our man Harry managing the financials,' Jake explained. 'I make more from Edinburgh property than I do from music these days. But Dave Ingham and the other three need money. And my therapist says it might be healthy to head out on the road, instead of rattling round this house.'

'These stadium tours are money machines,' Harry told Dylan, as his eyes went starry. 'Eighty thousand tickets at a hundred and fifty dollars a pop. That's twelve million dollars *every* night. We book eighty stadium gigs over nine months and gross over a billion dollars.'

'Everyone's downloading,' Jake said. 'The money used to be in CD sales, but now it's in gigs.'

'There are also financial advantages if the Pandas form part of the tour,' Harry explained. 'In order to avoid tax, we'll set up an overseas trust and you'll be paid twenty million dollars for your part in the tour. Leo, Eve and Max would get two million each. And the Pandas will get the kind of global exposure that other bands can only dream of.'

Dylan gasped. 'When you say, *I'd make*. Is that *my* money? Like, I get to do whatever I want with it?'

'For tax purposes, the money *has* to be yours,' Harry said. 'Legally there has to be a financial guardianship in place while you're a minor. But on your eighteenth birthday, it's all yours.'

'So I can buy an aeroplane, snort drugs off titties and drive my Ferrari through a shopping mall?'

Harry smiled. 'Let's hope you're more sensible than that.'

'But the Pandas are *way* less popular than some of the other bands in *Rock War*,' Dylan said. 'My band mates know I'm your son, but it's never got into the media because I'm basically a boring-assed keyboard player in a band nobody has paid much attention to. But if we win against all odds, the whole world will start digging.'

Harry shrugged. 'Son, I've been manipulating the media since before you were born. People will work out who your parents are sooner or later, but that's no biggie. If they find out that your father is the secret investor in *Rock War*, we'll say he did it to save the show and keep you in the competition. Then I'll provide reams of statistical data, and dozens of sworn witness statements, proving that the voting process was completely kosher.'

'But it *isn't*,' Dylan pointed out.

A nasty look flashed across Harry's face. 'Anyone messes with me will get to find out why I'm known as the Nightmare. With *Rock War* going global, there's plenty of good jobs for people who keep on message.'

'So are you in, son?' Jake asked. 'You going back to that boarding school you hate so much? Or you up for a wild ride with your old man?'

Dylan had arrived expecting to give his dad a lecture. Telling him how there was no way he was prepared to win by cheating, and that he'd expose the scandal if they tried. But now his head spun with thoughts of big bucks, bigger breasts and no more boarding school.

'It's a lot to think about,' Dylan said. 'And I didn't sleep at all last night, so my head's a blur.'

'What's there to think about?' Harry growled. 'If this ain't a no-brainer, I don't know what is.'

'I think I need to go lie down for a bit,' Dylan said.

Harry reared up from his chair, but Jake gave him a *calm down* gesture, and smiled as Dylan backed away from the table.

'There's no rush, son,' Jake said soothingly. 'You go freshen up and take a nap. Harry's heading off to play golf back in the smoke, but I'll be tinkering in the garage when you feel ready to talk.'

21. No Further Questions

Jay almost clattered a room service tray as he darted from his room. Twelve flights of fire stairs went as fast as he dared, and he emerged into a second-floor hallway lined with garish carpet. He passed a banqueting room hosting a fiftieth wedding anniversary and got a flash of recognition from tween sisters in party dresses.

There was a line of press trying to get into the Churchill conference room. Jay kept his face low, as he cut down a side entrance. When he opened a door, Jen the publicist growled at him.

'You're supposed to be on the coach back to the manor. Have you even checked out of your room?'

They were in a private lounge, behind the conference room. There were quite a few people around, and Jay went on tiptoes to try and spot Summer.

'Are you listening to me?' Jen said, grabbing Jay's arm. 'Did you get the message about the no-comment policy? You shouldn't be anywhere near the press right now.'

'Summer texted me,' Jay said, as he spotted her by a set of double doors on the opposite side of the room. 'I won't talk to anyone but her.'

Jen would have liked to kick Jay out, but she didn't want a scene so she let him break free, stepping past Karolina and a pair of Channel Six bods dressed for golf.

'Three minutes,' someone shouted. 'We need to keep the chatter down in here.'

'Hey, you,' Jay said, smiling as he stepped up to Summer. The publicists had made her dress in nice-girl clothes: lemon jumper, white leggings and ballerinas with little bows on. 'I came down as soon as I got your text.'

'It's horrible,' Summer said, shuddering and looking ashamed. 'Did you watch it?'

Jay nodded. 'The headlines make it fifty times worse than it is. Did you speak to your nan?'

'She's not too bad,' Summer said. 'I guess after almost getting myself killed, this is pretty mild.'

'So what's going on?'

'I'm just keeping my head down,' Summer said, looking around suspiciously. 'It's all being handled—'

A woman interrupted. She was tiny, with a face consisting entirely of sharp angles. 'You must be Theo's brother, Jay,' she said, offering her hand. 'I hope he's keeping out of trouble?'

'We all live in hope,' Jay said, smiling slightly.

'This is Megan Seebag, our lawyer,' Summer explained.

Megan gave Summer a serious look. 'Remember what I said?'

Summer nodded. 'Sit up straight, don't laugh or smile, because that's the picture they print and we'll end up looking cocky. We don't speak, even if the press tries to goad us.'

Megan cracked a rare smile. 'Almost word perfect. I'm just waiting for a microphone check, and we'll be up. Try not to look scared.'

But Summer did look scared as Megan headed off to speak with Coco. 'They said it's zero tolerance,' Summer told Jay warily. 'I'll probably have to go to court.'

Jay shrugged. 'It'll just be a fine, or community service. It's your first offence, right?'

Summer smirked slightly. 'Yes it's my first offence. Who do you think I am?'

'It'll all be grand,' Jay said, as he opened his arms for a hug.

Summer squeezed him really tight. 'It sucks less when you're around,' she told him.

Jay loved Summer's smell, but was alarmed when his chin caught an H&M tag spearing the back of her top.

'One of the publicists will have scissors or nail clippers,' he told her.

Jay settled on a plastic chair as Summer rushed across to Jen, who began a frantic handbag rummage. He watched Megan head through a heavy curtain into the conference room. Coco and Lucy had also been decked out in pastels, while Michelle didn't seem at all impressed with her lacy-collared blouse.

Freed of her label, Summer was last through the curtain and drew a barrage of camera flashes. The room had been booked at short notice, and was crammed to the point where journalists had arms pinned to their sides and an overflow snaked out into the hallway.

Megan sat in the middle, with two members of ISS on either side.

'Summer, are you ashamed of what you've done?' someone shouted.

Summer shuddered and stared silently at her knuckles. Her mouth felt like it was full of sand.

'I will read a short, prepared statement,' Megan began. 'I am Megan Seebag, senior criminal solicitor with Buick Partners. I would like to remind everyone in this room that all of my clients are under eighteen. Anyone breaching the rules regarding reporting of allegations made against minors can expect the full weight of Buick Partners to come down upon them.

'My clients have submitted individual statements to British Transport Police. They have admitted their role in non-payment of fares totalling approximately one hundred and eighty pounds. They have also admitted their role in the incident which was filmed on CCTV and reported in the *Sunday Courier* this morning. The girls have issued their sincere apologies.

'I have now passed the written statements to British Transport Police. The investigating officers have agreed that the statements contain all of the necessary information and that they have no further requirement to interview any of my clients. The documentation relating to this incident will now be passed on to the Department of Public Prosecutions, who will consider whether to pursue a court case against my clients.

'The decision to prosecute typically takes four to six weeks. Therefore we do not anticipate any furtherance of this matter until *after* the *Rock War* final takes place on Saturday December 24th. Karolina Kundt, the chairperson of Venus TV, has also authorised me to state that since this matter took place before Industrial Scale Slaughter were selected to take part in *Rock War*, it will have no effect on their participation in the semi-finals in two weeks' time.'

There was a roar of questions as Megan lowered her papers.

'Will any of the girls be personally apologising to Tina Marshall?'

'Do you think seeing you assault a train guard will affect your chances of winning *Rock War*?'

'If the girls are so sorry, why didn't they own up before the *Courier* found the video?'

As questions continued, Megan stood, scowled and gestured towards the girls to start heading off stage.

'No further questions,' she said firmly.

22. Cold Ma

Dylan pottered out of the sauna, ditched his ice bucket and towel, then settled into a lounger beside an indoor pool. He'd slept through the early part of the afternoon and the steaming pool, complete with waterfalls and lush tropical borders, usually relaxed him. But his brain had other ideas.

One of the kitchen staff came by with an order of steak baguette, fries and vanilla Coke, but he just picked a couple of pieces of meat out of the bread and stared guiltily at his bare, flabby, stomach. His dilemma was straightforward, the solution less so.

Dylan loathed boarding school. Hated the cricket whites and rugby stripes. The noise, the masters who always knew best, the bullies and the itchy wool trousers. And if he didn't win *Rock War*, he'd be back there eating soggy veg and sleeping with his feet sticking off the end of a crappy single bed inside a month.

The prospect made Dylan ache. But so did the idea of

screwing over Jet, Half Term Haircut and Frosty Vader. If he'd liked his band mates he could have consoled himself with the thought of helping *them* out. But even if Max and Eve's dad let them go on some eight-month world tour, it would be a nightmare being stuck with them.

Dylan felt like talking to someone. The lifelong buddy who shared all his secrets, or a mentor full of wise advice. He stuffed another piece of steak, winced as it passed his swollen top lip, then grabbed his phone and rolled through contacts.

There were a bunch of *Rock War* kids, some guys he'd known from primary school who'd probably forgotten he even existed. His dad's brother and his aunt, who lived in Edinburgh and spent an hour showing new additions to their collection of shire horse ornaments whenever you visited. These weren't people you could have a heart-to-heart with. But one entry gave him pause for thought:

Mum.

She had joint custody, so she'd had to sign a form when Dylan entered *Rock War*, but that all got done by email. And they usually spoke at Christmas, but come to think of it, they hadn't this year.

Dylan's thumb hovered over the dial button for a few seconds and he almost chickened out as he heard weird connecting-to-a-foreign-land noises. He wondered about the time difference. Seven hours back made it around eight a.m., which wasn't too bad . . .

'Hello?'

'Mum?' But Dylan's mum had a New York accent, and this was pure California.

'This is Belle Winterton, personal assistant to Kaitlyn Haverford-Blade,' she said stiffly. 'May I ask why you're calling her private number?'

Dylan tutted and mocked Belle's manner. 'I wish to talk to Miss Kaitlyn Haverford-Blade.'

'I'm afraid Kaitlyn is redirecting all of her calls to me while she takes some personal time at the cabin with her husband and the boys. Perhaps I could be of assistance?'

'I doubt it,' Dylan said. 'Since you're *not* my mother.'

'I'm sorry, I don't understand.'

'I'm Dylan. I want to talk to my *mother*.'

'Do you have the right number?'

Dylan felt like bashing his phone against the table. 'How long have you had this job?'

'A little over eight months.'

'And in that eight months, has your boss mentioned that she was married before? That she has a son – that's me, by the way – who lives in Scotland with his father?'

'I knew she was married to Jake Blade, but she never . ...' Belle realised she was digging herself a hole and suddenly became more positive. 'Dylan, I'm sure she's mentioned you *lots* of times. But there's been so much going on with the show in Tokyo and the Art for Autism campaign . . .'

Now Dylan felt ridiculous for even thinking that his mother would want to hear his problems. He imagined her at her cabin. Riding bikes through the woods with the hubby who was sixteen years younger and his four- and six-year-old half-brothers, the younger of whom he'd never even met.

He had a lump in his throat as he spoke. 'Just forget it,' he said. '*Don't* tell her I called.'

'I have a number I can call at the cabin,' Belle said. 'I'm sure Kaitlyn will call you . . .'

'Forget it,' Dylan said, ending the call as a tear streaked down his face.

He stuffed a massive handful of chips in his mouth and scowled at his phone, which rose with his chest as he took short, angry breaths.

It hurt having a mum who acted like he didn't exist and a dad who sent him off to boarding school and took more interest in rechroming the grille of his '54 Alvis drop head. But it had helped Dylan to realise who mattered in his life.

He was going to tell his dad to stick his *no-brainer* decision up his arse and tell everyone what was going on if the voting wasn't fair in the final two rounds. The friends he'd made at the manor weren't perfect, but most of them were decent people and they deserved fair treatment.

Maybe he was naïve and idealistic, like Uncle Harry said. His dad would be pissed off and boarding school would be three more years of shit, but living a life based on a massive lie would be worse.

As another tear bulged, Dylan stood up, grabbing his phone and the last piece of steak from the untouched baguette. He took a folded white robe out of a heated cabinet and slipped it on before padding towards his bedroom, feeling guilty about all the starving people in the world and the minimum-wage cleaner who'd pick up his plates and mop the damp footprints he was leaving along the hallway.

The house was massive, but one relic of early childhood was that Dylan's room was directly opposite his father's. His tears were slowing, but his dad could be really moody and Dylan didn't relish the looming confrontation. He was sure his dad would be down in the basement garage, but knocked to be sure.

'Dad?'

The suite was dominated by a huge, mahogany four-poster. There was a stuffed zebra in front of a triple-bay window, which was being ridden by a suit of armour. There was a table covered with framed photographs, and Dylan was pleased to see several pictures of his younger self, amidst shots of his long-dead grandparents, his father sat in a vintage racing Bugatti, and a famous shot of Terraplane taken for the cover of *Rolling Stone* magazine.

But his interest lay in the bathroom. The staff made up rooms just like in a hotel, so the black-marbled space was pristine, with fresh towels and strong scent from a huge vase of lilies in front of the walk-in shower.

A sliding door at the far end opened into a walk-in closet, but Dylan's interest lay in the marble-faced unit beneath the sink. He'd discovered the hidden drawer back when he was short enough to spot its concealed catch without ducking.

After doubling back to bolt the door, Dylan went on one knee and flipped the lever. The drawer that gently rolled open was cut into the cabinet in such a way that it just seemed like a join in the stone. The inside was eight centimetres deep, with a U shape cut out of the back, allowing space for the washbasin pipes when it was closed.

'Naughty daddy!' Dylan told himself, as he looked down, grinning.

The left-hand side was dominated by three large bags of grass, amidst many smaller ones. In the centre were bottles filled with unlabelled pills and a bag of mushrooms. The right-hand compartment looked empty by comparison, but there were at least fifty one-gram bags of cocaine, and a dozen larger bags with a slightly yellowish powder.

Dylan didn't want his dad to know he'd been robbed, so he grabbed three little bags of grass and moved the rest around to fill in the gaps. Then he grabbed one of the little bags of cocaine and held it up to the light.

The white powder scared him, but he'd been curious for ages and while he'd heard stories of people seriously messed up on Terraplane tours, his dad had dabbled with drugs for years, and claimed that people only got addicted if they were total idiots.

After the latest snub by his mum, facing an awkward convo with his dad, and Yellowcote boarding school on the wrong side of Christmas, life felt shitty and this could take the edge off for a bit.

He thought about crossing the hall to his own room to be extra safe, but the bathroom was locked and his dad always worked in the garage until at least six. There were a bunch of metal snorting tubes rolling around behind the mushrooms. He took a gold one out and was surprised to find it had been engraved, *To Kaitlyn, Happy 21st Birthday.*

Dylan tapped a quarter of the white powder on to the countertop and clumsily used his little finger to push it into a wonky line. He leaned forward to snort, and felt weird imagining this same tube being up his mum's nose more than twenty years earlier.

He stayed still for almost twenty seconds. Scared that he was crossing some line. He came close to flicking the powder with the sleeve of his robe and retreating back to his room, but then he thought about his mum again. He relived the imaginary scene, with the sun setting, his half-brothers riding their little bikes towards his mother, standing in the doorway of a log cabin . . .

'I hate that bitch,' Dylan told himself, as his eyes welled up again.

Then he took a snort of cocaine.

Twelve Days Later

23. Sensitive Soles

'Howdy-do, *Rock War* fans,' Noah said, as he sat on one of the beanbags in Rock War Manor's ballroom. 'So here's another vlog for my gillions of fans.'

His band mate Sadie was next to him, but she'd rolled backwards off her beanbag, so all his camera picked up were her black leggings and unmatched socks sticking in the air.

'It's only two days until the semi-finals. But the atmosphere here at the manor has been awesome. Everyone's rehearsing hard, but there's no bitchiness or anything, even though all the bands are competing.

'We've got to play two tracks. One is a free choice, and since we're doing the show in Manchester, all the bands have to do a song by a Manchester band. If you're a loyal viewer, you'll have watched the draw live on 6point2 last night and seen that we got The Smiths. Jet got Oasis, which is the one *everyone* wanted. Industrial Scale Slaughter got Joy

Division. I can't remember . . . Sadie, do you remember who the others got?'

'I totally do,' Sadie said, as she waved her legs in the air. 'But I'm not telling.'

Sadie jabbed Noah's head with her big toe, but immediately regretted it. His arms were pumped from pushing his chair and he grabbed her around the knees and clamped both legs to his chest.

'One thing I've learned about Sadie is that her feet are really ticklish!' Noah told the camera.

'If you dare, Noah . . .'

Noah gently ran his forefinger along Sadie's sole and she bucked like a wild horse.

'I *will* kill you,' she squealed. 'No, stop it . . . You git!'

Noah let Sadie go and she bolted away, giggling until she trod on an Xbox controller and sprawled into more beanbags.

Noah gave the camera the straightest face he could manage. 'Where was I, before I was so rudely interrupted?' Then he snapped his fingers and spoke triumphantly. '*Now* I remember what this vlog was supposed to be about!'

Sadie stepped behind Noah and started wiggling her bum and doing random ballet-style moves. Noah could hear, but realised the video would be funnier if he acted clueless.

'Last night my dad rang to ask how I was,' Noah began. 'Apparently, he found a betting shop offering odds of six to one on Frosty Vader winning *Rock War*. He doesn't normally gamble, but he went in and put on a five hundred quid bet! So, thanks Dad, no extra pressure. The good news is he gets three grand if I win, the bad is that my mum found out and she's *fuming*.'

Noah grabbed a webpage printout and held it close to his camera as Sadie looked bored and strolled out of shot.

'I hope you can read this OK,' Noah said. 'I printed it from BetForce.com and these are this morning's odds for the five remaining bands to win *Rock War*:'

CATEGORIES >> ALTERNATIVE BETS
ROCK WAR – ODDS TO WIN FINAL

Half Term Haircut	2–1 Favourite
Industrial Scale Slaughter	5–2
Jet	5–2
Frosty Vader	5–1
Pandas of Doom	8–1

'I reckon if you'd looked a few days ago, Half Term and Industrial Scale would have been *joint* favourites. But, even though that video of the girls on the train was all a bit handbags-at-five-paces, that train guard woman keeps going on TV slagging them off and it's definitely dented Summer's good-girl image.

'All five bands spent time in the studio on our rehearsal week, recording a couple of tracks. Dylan helped Half Term Haircut make a recording of "Puff" and put it on YouTube. That song's so catchy it got half a million views in one day. So Karolina authorised it to be released as a download, and darn tooting if it isn't number four in the iTunes chart. Some radio stations are even starting to play it.

'Jet are third favourites. Jay and Summer seem to have gotten *uber* close in a kissy kind of way. I've heard Jet in rehearsals and Theo's performance is *so* much better than a few weeks back.

'Now my dad got six to one, but my crew, Frosty Vader, were only five to one when I printed this off before brekky. Maybe the odds are narrowing because we've been awesome in rehearsals. And if you ask me, the three favourites are going to cannibalise each other's votes and Frosty Vader shall come storming through F-T-W! Or at least, I think we've got a decent chance of upsetting the three favourites and making it to the final.

'Last, the Pandas are at eight to one. I think *everyone* was surprised when they beat Brontobyte and stayed . . .'

As Noah tried to finish his sentence, Sadie sprinted in from the right with a giant cushion clutched to her chest. She charged into Noah, whacking him backwards off the beanbag. As Noah flailed, Sadie scrambled up and stuck her face into his camera.

'And *that*, my feathered friends, is what happens to people who tickle my feet!'

24. Bait and Snap

While four bands stayed at the manor, squeezing in a final rehearsal, Jet travelled up to Manchester a day early to do a couple of interviews at Salford Media City. Jay was on the pastel set of Channel Six's *Mags at Midday*, with his band mates sitting to his right.

'So the semi-final looms large,' Mags said, with her famous Jamaican lilt. 'How are you boys feeling?'

Jay shrugged as a computer-controlled camera swung eerily from the gantry above for a close-up. He looked slightly stiff with his top shirt button done up, but it was hiding a massive love bite Summer had given him the night before.

'Every round is tougher,' Jay said. 'At the start of Battle Zone it was one band out of ten dropping out. But only three out of five are gonna make the final.'

Mags's arms were covered in bangles that shuddered as her chunky frame laughed. 'And you got DeAngelo Hunt to cough up that half million dollars for the Red Cross.'

'I'm proud of that,' Jay said, smiling. 'My brother Theo's not DeAngelo's biggest fan, but credit to the guy for coughing up.'

Babatunde scoffed. 'He had to pay! He was getting bashed up on Twitter!'

'What's half a million to a guy making twenty on every movie?' Adam added.

'Karen Trim is still not coughing up her half million?' Mags asked.

Jay shook his head. 'I guess she's short of a few quid. After all, *Hit Machine*'s getting less than half *Rock War*'s viewing figures.'

The show had a closed set, but there was some laughter from the crew and Mags did a little clap.

'You boys got a history with that lady,' Mags said joyously. 'Now Theo, *you* have a reputation for trouble. And I know I told you I won't have misbehaving on my show. But that don't mean you ain't gotta say nothing!'

Theo cracked a smile. 'I guess I was dazzled into silence by your beauty, Mags.'

'Oooh, I like you, Theo,' Mags said, howling with laughter. 'I might just have to give you a hug as you step off my set. Well it's been great having you boys on the show. You've got *my* vote on Saturday night for sure. If you win, are you going to come back on the show and play me a song?'

'Sure,' the boys said in unison.

As promised, Mags jumped up and engulfed Theo in a hug as the camera panned back and *Mags at Midday* cut to a commercial.

Jen the publicist was poised in a hallway outside the studio, wearing a big smile. 'Awesome, guys,' she beamed. 'Light and funny. Keeping things positive, good rapport with Mags. It's almost as if you actually *listened* to me during your media training.'

'We getting fed now?' Babatunde asked.

Jen nodded as she fiddled with a taxi booking app on her phone. 'That was the last interview for now, though I'm trying to get you a phoner on Radio One this evening. So don't go disappearing on me, or start drinking the minibar in your room.'

They headed up two flights from the basement studio, past reception, and stood at the kerb in a small parking area, waiting for a taxi to their hotel.

There was a scruffy Peugeot van parked two rows across. It had the tailgate raised, and two guys shielding behind it. One wore a tactical vest and had a camera with a big zoom lens, while the other, who looked a proper villain, swaggered towards the band.

'You them boys off *Rock War*,' he shouted loutishly.

The photographer clicked as the boys looked over.

Then the guy shouted, ''Ere, Theo? You're Theo, right? I hear your mum's a proper slag!'

Jay's heart shot into his mouth. It was *his* mum too, but he was more worried about Theo's reaction than the insult.

'Cool heads,' Jen mouthed to Theo, as she clutched the sleeve of his jacket. 'Do *not* react. Don't even give them the finger.'

The guy realised Theo wasn't biting and changed tack. 'Babatunde,' he shouted. 'Shouldn't you be in the jungle, eating bananas with the other baboons?'

The photographer snapped more pictures, but all he got were the four band mates looking stone-faced at the pavement.

'You fly off the handle and you give those lowlifes a photo to sell,' Jen told the boys.

The publicist glanced behind, thinking about taking the boys back into reception. But their ride was rolling into the parking lot, and she heaped more praise as she shepherded the lads into a seven-seat Mercedes.

'Racist ass wipe,' Babatunde snarled, smacking an arm rest as he settled into a leather seat. 'Can you believe that?'

'If I catch him without his camera . . .' Theo warned.

The Ogel Hotel was barely five minutes from the studio. It was just past one on a school day, but word had leaked on where the *Rock War* contestants were staying and eight school-aged girls stood by the rotating door at the main entrance. They acted shy as Jet stepped out of their taxi, snapping with their phones as they huddled up and almost backed themselves into an infinity pond.

Adam eyed a blonde with curves how he liked them. 'Shouldn't you be at school?' he asked, as Jen watched cautiously.

The girl looked down, then up again. 'Shouldn't *you?*' she asked, setting off high-pitched giggles amongst her girlfriends.

Theo spotted a geeky older girl holding a picture of Owen

from Half Term Haircut. 'You like *him?*' Theo teased. 'You should smell the crapper in the rehearsal blocks after he's used it. It's like rotting dog carcass, or something.'

'Gross,' the girl said, but was clearly flattered by Theo's attention.

Jay stayed back, shyly, but one girl broke out of the gaggle and asked if she could take a selfie.

'I saw you kissing Summer on *Rock War Update*,' she said, as Jay closed up and stared into an iPhone cover shaped like a McDonald's French fry packet. 'Did she give you that massive hickey on your neck?'

'Let's move inside, guys,' Jen said firmly, as Jay realised he'd unconsciously freed his shirt button inside the taxi.

'You what?' Babatunde said, turning towards Jay and grabbing his collar. 'Jesus, guys, look what Summer gave him!'

As Jay squirmed, Theo and Adam leaned in to inspect Jay's neck.

'Photograph this and Tweet it,' Theo told the girls, as he grabbed Jay's arm to stop him wriggling. 'Hashtag, *Jay's got a monster hickey.*'

Several of the girls snapped pics of Jet, with Jay restrained in the centre and the other three lads pointing at his exposed neck.

'Guys, stop larking about,' Jen said firmly. 'You want lunch, don't you?'

'Good to meet you, ladies,' Adam said, giving his favourite one a wink before going inside. Theo cheekily snatched the picture of Owen and flicked it behind into the shallow pool.

The girl laughed and got him to sign the driest part after she'd fished it out.

The lads' luggage had already been delivered to their rooms, but Jen had to get key cards from reception. Jet got evil eyes from a doorman as they splayed over fancy lobby chairs and Theo put his filthy boots on a glass tabletop.

'Excuse me, young fella,' said an elderly man, holding up a tape recorder as Jay rebuttoned his shirt. 'I'm from the local newspaper here in Manchester. I know you've only just arrived in town, but I wondered what your first impressions of our city were?'

Jay looked behind, hoping Jen would swoop and tell the elderly journalist to buzz off. But she was marooned at the reception desk and the hotel's security team were noisily arguing with a teen truant who was demanding to come in and use the toilet.

'It's just for the local paper,' the man repeated, as he jiggled an ancient mini-cassette recorder that seemed mostly held together with duct tape and elastic bands.

'Manchester's fine, I guess,' Jay said, still grumpy from the hickey humiliation.

'Is there anything you don't like here?' he asked sweetly.

'You need to talk to Jen if you want an interview,' Jay said.

'A couple of sentences,' he begged. 'One *teensy* line to stop my editor from busting my balls.'

Jay smirked. 'So like, all the women in Manchester are ugly and it smells like sewage, that sort of thing?'

'Exactly,' the old man purred. 'I *know* you're joking. I'm just doing a little piece for the local rag.'

'Not sure about your Manc' football teams,' Babatunde said. 'City and United are no match for the mighty gods of Northampton Town.'

'These chairs aren't too comfortable,' Theo added, smirking. 'And this hotel seems to exclusively employ women with *terrible* fake tans.'

'What about the city sites?' the man asked, as he moved his recorder closer to Theo. 'What have you seen so far?'

As the recorder got close, Theo jumped up and put his lungs into a full roar. The old guy was so shocked that he stumbled backwards into a glass table and sent a vase of dried flowers flying. After trying to save himself by grabbing the arm of a chair, he wound up lying on his side on the floor as the four members of Jet killed themselves laughing.

'What the hell?' Jen asked, as she rushed over, getting between the boys and a woman who'd sprung from cover with a Nikon.

'Why'd you do that, nutter?' Jay asked Theo, shaking with laughter as one of the doormen helped the old guy off the floor.

Theo shrugged. 'I've put up with enough crap already this morning.'

25. High Wire

Manchester had once been Britain's clubbing capital. DJs who'd go on to became global superstars played music until sunrise for vast crowds, high on Ecstasy. But when residents complained, kids overdosed and the drug dealers started a shooting war, the cops closed most big clubs down and the party moved to Ibiza.

The Sandpit was the sole survivor of Manchester's legendary nineties club scene and the last of the venues that Zig Allen had picked for *Rock War*. Originally a factory that made light trucks and double decker buses, the huge space had a decrepit air. One end had already been bulldozed and replaced with luxury apartments, while the main stage had a temporary circus-tent-style roof, which had been designed with a five-year lifespan when it was put up twenty years earlier.

It was Friday noon and Jay sat amidst mildewed stacking chairs a few metres from the stage, waiting for his sound check and a late-running rehearsal. The crew were having nightmares, because the acoustics were horrible and the roof over the stage leaked. An extra generator truck had been brought in, but things still kept fusing because of the damp.

While a woman in neon leggings bounded about on a circus net directly above Jay's head, he felt a little buzz in his pocket and was pleased to see a message from Summer:

> Just dropped our bags at Ogel. Now heading to rehearsal. Can't wait 2CU!
>> Bring a book. Rehearsals way late. Bored off my head and lighting rig not even up yet.
> Find a spot where we can cuddle. I missssssed U!!!!
>> Way ahead of U on that ☺

Up on stage, one of the road crew was shouting, 'If it rains tomorrow night, we're all getting electrocuted.'

Karolina was a few metres in front of Jay, trying to impress a tanned American who bore an uncanny resemblance to Barbie's Ken. 'Season two is going to be arena based,' Karolina told him. 'Moving the show every week has been hellish.'

'That's what we'll do stateside,' the big Yank said. 'Assuming we can strike this deal.'

There was a huge crash back behind the stage, followed by swearyness. Dylan and his band mate Leo sat close to Jay and the trio laughed so hard that they didn't hear Jen the publicist approaching.

'Nice work,' Jen snapped, as she threw the first print of the *Manchester Evening Mail* in Jay's lap. 'What did I tell you guys about being careful? I take my eye off you for three seconds to sort out your room keys . . .'

The paper was folded open to page three, where the headline read: '*Manchester girls ugly' says TV rocker Jay*. The picture below showed the elderly journalist sprawled on the hotel carpet, as Theo loomed menacingly and Babatunde clutched his chest, laughing.

Dylan read aloud over Jay's shoulder. '*Jet's youngest member insulted Manchester's women and said that the city smelled like sewage. Moments later, the* Evening Mail's *veteran correspondent, Ted Lund, seventy-one, was knocked to the ground by the leering Theo Richardson, the 17-year-old singer and powerfully built South East Counties boxing champion.*

'*Lund – who received an MBE for services to journalism and was injured while reporting on the Falklands War – also witnessed Richardson snatch a photograph from an autograph hunter and throw it into a hotel fountain.*

'*Fourteen-year-old Kelly from Salford was reduced to tears following Theo's loutish behaviour. The boys then held court in the hotel lobby, noisily insulting Manchester football teams and claiming that the local women had horrible orange fake tans.*'

'Ooopsy,' Leo said, giving Jay a friendly pat on the shoulder.

'You were there,' Jay told Jen, gasping and slapping the page. 'Most of this is made up. The reporter knew I was joking and that girl *laughed* when Theo drenched her photo.'

Jen tapped the picture of Theo snarling and the elderly reporter with his legs in the air. 'If you give the press ammunition like that, who will readers believe?'

'He didn't physically touch the old geezer,' Jay pointed out. 'And why are you moaning at me? Why don't you go find Theo?'

'Theo listens to you,' Jen said, as her phone buzzed.

'To me?' Jay said, bursting out laughing. 'Give me a break.'

Jen ignored Jay's remark and tapped her phone screen. 'BBC Manchester radio wants you guys to go on air and defend your comments,' she groaned. 'And apparently one of the tabloids is going to run this story nationally tomorrow morning and they want Theo to supply a quote.'

'Good luck finding him,' Jay said, smirking.

'Where did he go?' Jen asked.

'He travelled here in the same taxi as me,' Jay explained. 'But he got bored waiting for rehearsal. Him and Adam are hooking up with some random chicks that have been texting them.'

Jen stamped her leather boot. 'Two more weeks of this,' she told herself. 'Then it's Eilat with my fiancé.'

Dylan shook his head as Jen stormed off. 'She's not the only one looking forward to the end of all this craziness,' he said. 'Don't worry about the press, Jay. All that article shows is that if you don't give them a story, they'll make one up.'

Jay nodded. 'But who the hell wants to go back to school? The press might be a pain, but the manor has been the best time of my life.'

'Agreed,' Dylan said.

'They do good puddings at Yellowcote,' Leo noted.

Dylan laughed and nodded. 'Our boarding school sucks, but the steamed marmalade pudding is killer.'

'No point sitting here watching this chaos any more,' Jay said, as he stood up. 'Gonna head out back and meet Summer when she arrives. You coming with?'

'May as well,' Dylan said, as he felt for his cigarettes in his pocket. 'Grab a smoke if nothing else.'

*

Rehearsal had been scheduled from eleven until four, but it was three before the lighting rig was even in place. Press interviews and family meet-ups got cancelled or pushed back as the rehearsal dragged past eight p.m. Now that there were only five bands left, the two-hour semi-final show had been padded out with a special guest appearance by US rockers the Black Swans.

The all-girl trio were one of Noah's favourite bands, but his opinion of them plunged as they fussed over every detail in rehearsal, demanding that lights be moved, complaining about the sound system, the way Lorrie introduced them and the pronunciation of the name of their new album. Then they insisted on four runs of their whole set, even after Joseph the director explained that most of the crew had already been working since six a.m.

It was five past nine when Joseph finally called a wrap on the rehearsals, but Noah had to stay back and practise a secret extra with Sadie. In the first *Rock War* knockout round, Noah had stunned the audience by stage-diving in his wheelchair.

Much of the audience had assumed he was hurt, until three members of the road crew pulled him out of a foam-filled orchestra pit.

This wheelchair dive got replayed at the end of *Rock War*'s opening titles every week and in most promo reels for the show. Noah had immediately agreed when Karolina suggested an enhanced version of the trick for the semi-finals, but he felt less sure as he sat in the centre of the stage, listening to instructions from a burly stunt co-ordinator.

'Sadie, as soon as you stop playing, your job is to get behind Noah's chair and connect the hooks that come down from the ceiling.'

The stunt director signalled to the control room and a pair of steel wires descended from above the stage.

'Clip and lock, like this,' the stunt co-ordinator explained. 'You do it.'

Noah looked behind nervously as Sadie got the knack of attaching two climbing shackles to a special harness sewn on the back of his chair.

'Noah has another harness under his shirt, holding him into his chair. Once the hooks are attached, step back and cross both arms across your chest like this.'

Sadie smirked as she copied the gesture.

'Any other gesture and the stunt will be aborted. After an abort the wires will drop from above and if they're attached to the chair they'll just trail behind as Noah wheels himself off stage.'

Noah and Sadie both nodded as the stunt co-ordinator

squatted in front of Noah and checked that his harness was on tight.

'Noah, once the hooks are on, you check your harness is locked, then you make the same gesture as Sadie with your arms. You'll get pulled into the air, then when you halt at the top of the zip line, you give the button in the centre of your harness a good whack and down you'll go. Any questions?'

'Sounds OK,' Noah said, anxiously.

'It was nice knowing you, buddy,' Sadie said, as she put a fond hand on her best friend's shoulder.

'OK, from the top,' the stuntman said, speaking to the director's booth through his radio mic. 'Wires up, and then down on my mark . . . And go, Sadie.'

Sadie took two steps from the position where she'd finish playing Frosty Vader's set, then grabbed the steel cables from above and hooked them to Noah's chair.

'Now signal,' the stunt co-ordinator reminded her. 'Good, and Noah's signal means we can fire the winch and . . .'

Noah didn't hear the next part because the wires he was attached to shot up at a steep angle, firing his chair deep into the tent's roof. He felt sick as he made the mistake of looking down, and dithered at the top, long enough to hear a shout of, 'Free the harness.'

Noah hit the button on his six-point harness and shoved himself face first out of his chair.

'Jeeeeeeeeeeeee-sus!'

He plunged twenty-five metres, landing face down in the giant circus net strung over the empty auditorium. It hurt his chin and shoulder slightly and he was alarmed as he bounced back a few metres and flipped, eventually settling on his back.

When he opened his eyes, a pair of athletic stunt women were peering down at him.

'How was that?' one asked, in a heavy Romanian accent.

'Fun,' Noah said, as he cracked a big smile. 'Let's do one more.'

26. Sex 'N' Drugs

The Sandpit's heating wasn't up to much and Jay was still warming up as he crossed reception and headed up to the Ogel's ninth floor with Summer. He nestled in behind to kiss her neck, but she flinched.

'Your nose is like ice,' she gasped, tipping her head back and shuddering.

Jay made to kiss her again, without his nose touching, but she took a half step forwards and made a little *nah* sound.

'Did I do something?'

Summer turned around as the elevator passed the eighth floor. 'It was a crap day, waiting around in the cold, and my leg is throbbing.'

'You wanna come to my room? I've got Netflix and the Wi-Fi seems OK.'

Summer kissed him, then shook her head. 'I've got some Ibuprofen. I'm gonna soak in the bath, give my nan a quick call, then hopefully sleep for about ten hours.'

Jay hid his disappointment as they stepped out of the lift. Their rooms were in opposite directions, so they hugged goodnight and headed off. He was nowhere near sleepy, so he was relieved when he heard a racket coming out of Adam and Theo's room across the hall from his own.

'What up, Jay-Jay?' Babatunde asked, as he opened the door.

There were at least fifteen people crammed into the darkened room. Michelle and Lucy from ISS, half of Half Term Haircut, Theo and Adam plus Otis from Frosty Vader. Besides the familiar faces, there was a bunch of girls, some of whom Jay had seen hanging around in the hotel lobby, or at The Sandpit.

'Beer, bruv?' Theo said, passing Jay a can.

As Jay took his first swig, he looked around for a place to sit. Adam was on one of the double beds, getting the rock star treatment from a girl on either side. There were bodies on the sofa, the desk, and one of the Half Term Haircut guys apparently having a meaningful conversation with a geeky girl in the shower cubicle.

'Am I orange?' a girl yelled, right in Jay's face. 'I'm from Manchester. What you got against Manchester, Jay Thomas?'

She was older than Jay. Pale skin and too-bright make-up, laddered tights and battered retro Nikes setting off a moderately sexy bad-girl vibe.

'What's your problem?' Jay said, pushing her back slightly.

'What's yours?' she asked, then she grabbed his head and started kissing him.

A few people laughed as Jay backed off in shock.

'Leave my baby brother alone,' Theo said, sounding a touch drunk. 'I was there. He never said nothing about Manchester.'

Flushing bright red, Jay straddled outstretched legs and sat on the floor with his back against a TV console and a view of Adam's hand wandering inside a girl's skirt. Some awful MTV type channel was blaring out of the screen above his head and he started thinking about going back to his room when he got handed a shot glass full of green stuff.

'What's this?'

Nobody answered, but he drank it anyway. Then Babatunde topped up his glass. Michelle was jumping on one of the beds and demolished a light fitting, and someone in the next room started thumping on the wall, then came out into the hallway threatening to call hotel management.

'You bang that wall again,' Theo roared, as he confronted the balding man. 'You bang that wall again and I'll stick your damned head through it.'

A big cheer went up as the man retreated into his room. Jay spent ten minutes dwelling on a second beer, feeling bloated.

'I'm turning in,' Jay told nobody in particular.

He wobbled from three and a half drinks as he stepped over legs and made it into the hallway. His key card wouldn't stay still as he tried getting into his room. When he finally got the door open, he heard a gasp.

The room had two double beds. The only light came out of the bathroom, but it was enough to see Babatunde, naked but for his hoodie, with a girl lying beneath.

'Give us a half-hour,' Babatunde shouted breathlessly.

Jay backed out fast as his face flushed with embarrassment. He didn't want to go back to the party in his brothers' room, so he stood around in the corridor feeling like a failure. Babatunde was shagging, Adam had two girls all over him and Theo would doubtless find some willing outlet for his lustful urges before the night was over.

Summer definitely wouldn't appreciate him knocking when she'd told him she was tired, and he didn't know what room Dylan was in. Jay had just decided to kill half an hour sitting in the hotel lobby when the scary girl who'd kissed him stumbled out.

A glimpse inside showed that the music had been turned down, but the hormones seemed to be at max volume. Michelle was making out with Steve from Half Term Haircut, Adam's threesome seemed to involve a rapidly decreasing amount of clothing, Theo had vanished and Lucy was making out with a girl with braces.

'What's wrong with me?' the scary girl asked, pulling in her stomach so that her breasts looked bigger.

'Nothing,' Jay said, as he realised that her sense of rejection mirrored his own. Then to cheer her up, 'There's three girls for every guy in that room.'

The girl stepped up close, wobbled her head drunkenly and placed a finger on Jay's chin. 'I like your dimple when you smile.'

Part of Jay wanted to tell her that Summer was his girl. But his room was out of bounds, there was booze in his veins and she had a whiff of fresh sweat and perfume that turned him on.

'Where's your accent from?' Jay asked. 'It doesn't sound like Manchester.'

'Lived between Dublin and LA mostly,' she said. 'My dad works for Channel Six.'

'Right,' Jay said, as someone retched outside on his brother's balcony. 'Have you got a name?'

'Moirin,' she said, as she got teasingly closer and broke into a smile as Jay's breath shuddered. 'You're not like your brothers, are you? You're innocent.'

The phrase made Jay hate himself a little. Not tough, not sporty. Still a virgin . . .

'I really like, Summer,' Jay stuttered, as Moirin got kissing close.

'I've got a boyfriend,' Moirin said, matter-of-factly. 'But he's seven thousand miles from here and I don't want to sit in my room alone.'

'Me neither,' Jay said, as he wondered how old she was. Older than him for sure. Older than Summer. She put her hand around Jay's waist and started to kiss. Her mouth was boozy and stale. She grabbed his bum and squeezed her chest against him. Jay hated cheating on Summer, but Summer was a six-course tasting menu in a fine restaurant. Moirin was like a KFC family bucket to a guy who'd spent a month on bread and water.

She shoved Jay back against the wall and pushed her tongue into his mouth.

'I'll get in trouble,' Jay blurted when he came up for air.

But he was turned on and went back for more.

She licked inside Jay's ear, then whispered, 'I'm staying on the fifteenth floor. Are you coming or what?'

She stepped back. The bum and the boobs. Pale white legs with laddered tights. Chunky hips and fat moist lips. His body trembled with excitement.

'For sure,' Jay gasped.

27. Matching Robes

Two floors down, Eve lay on the bed in her single room. Her face was lit by a laptop showing *Parks and Recreation* on Netflix and she doodled flowers in the Ogel-Hotel-branded notepad on her knee.

'You home?' Dylan asked, as he knocked.

Eve slid on a hotel robe as she walked to the door. Dylan wore a matching robe with boxers and T-shirt underneath. His hair was wet from a shower.

'You OK?' Dylan asked.

'Better now I've warmed up,' Eve said, as she stepped back to let Dylan inside.

'I guess The Sandpit will be warmer tomorrow, with a few thousand people jumping up and down,' Dylan suggested. 'I just saw your message as I stepped out of the shower.'

'Is everything all right with you?' Eve asked. 'You hardly speak in rehearsals these days.'

Dylan found this pretty ironic, seeing as Eve was about the

shyest person he'd ever met. He was also curious about her sudden interest, because they'd barely spoken since their break-up.

'I'm good,' Dylan said, flicking back wet hair. 'I keep my head down in rehearsals because you can't fight Max on every single thing. I know he's your brother, but . . .'

Eve laughed gently. 'Max is a domineering prick.'

'Pretty much . . . You know, I've been meaning to talk to you for ages. I still feel crappy about breaking up with you. I wish I'd found a better way to do it.'

'Is there any good way to break up?' Eve asked, shrugging. 'I was at a girls' boarding school, and you and Leo were the only boys I knew who weren't related to me. You were at a boys' school and I was the only girl you knew.'

Dylan smiled. 'We engaged in a weird little experiment.'

'No regrets,' Eve said, as she reached into the pocket of Levi's balled on the floor. Dylan choked when he saw the little packet of white powder.

'Dropped out of your pocket when we climbed up to the stage,' Eve said.

Dylan shook his head. 'That's not mine. Probably one of the roadies . . .'

Eve opened her robe, displaying marks on her belly where she'd cut herself. 'Don't bullshit a bullshitter. I *saw* it fall out of your pocket. You're lucky it was me standing behind, not Max, or one of the crew.'

'Fine,' Dylan said, grudgingly. 'It's just a little cocaine I whipped from my dad.'

'Right,' Eve tutted. '*Just* cocaine!'

'I thought you were cool. You've smoked joints with me.'

'A few puffs and I never liked it,' Eve said. 'Plus anyone who says weed is harmless should meet my uncle Cam. He was a massive stoner and now his memory's shot and he can't hold down a job.'

'You won't snitch, will you?' Dylan asked. 'I covered *your* ass when you cut yourself.'

'You know what I see?' Eve asked, as she twirled the packet between her fingers. 'You've always been chilled out, Dylan. Bit fat, bit of a stoner. Smart but lazy. But beneath the don't-give-a-damn exterior, I see a fifteen-year-old who's smoking too much weed and starting on cocaine. You have plenty of money and access to your dad's stash.'

Dylan sighed. 'It's not *that* big a deal.'

'Rich kid and drugs,' Eve said sharply. 'It rarely ends well.'

Dylan tutted. 'You're lecturing *me*, with all your antidepressants and therapists.'

'I have plenty of problems,' Eve admitted. 'But you don't even seem to realise that you *have* a problem.'

'It's one tiny bag of cocaine,' Dylan said. 'You're being melodramatic.'

'You're a nice guy, so I hope I'm wrong,' Eve said, as she flicked the bag of powder through the air. 'Take it.'

It landed by Dylan's pool shoes and he snatched it up. He tried thinking of something else to say, but Eve irritated him and he wanted out.

'Thanks for picking it up,' he said finally.

Dylan's room was four doors down. He'd still see Max and Leo at school after the Pandas broke up, but in all likelihood he'd never see Eve again and he liked the thought of having the awkward remains of their relationship out of his life.

Leo dozed with one hand in a Pringles can as Dylan stepped back inside their room.

After flipping the bathroom light and bolting the door, Dylan smiled at the bag Eve had returned. He found the little engraved straw in his wash bag, tapped white powder on to the counter beside the sink and inhaled in one long snort.

There was a slight burn, followed by numbness as the drug kicked in over several minutes. But this time Dylan felt like his whole nose was fizzing. There was a weird fullness in the back of his mouth. He caught the taste of blood as he realised he was going to sneeze.

The first sneeze sent blood firing out of his nose. Red mist hit the mirror and sink, and sprayed the front of his white hotel robe.

'Oh, shit!'

Two more bloody sneezes misted the floor as Dylan stumbled back and wound up leaning against the toilet cistern.

'Oh my god,' Dylan gasped, before one final sneeze left him doubled over the toilet with his nose and top lip going increasingly numb as strands of snot and blood dangled over the toilet bowl.

'Dude, are you OK in there?' Leo asked, from outside the locked door.

'Bit of a nosebleed,' Dylan gasped, as he wiped his mouth on his sleeve. 'Go back to sleep.'

28. Nil Points

While the contestants got regular rooms at the Ogel, the three legends on *Rock War*'s judging panel got suites on the top floor. Earl Haart was sixty-two years old. A tailored suit and twenty minutes in make-up made him handsome on TV, but all the flaws were on show as he stumbled out of bed in his boxers. It was 6:45 on Saturday morning and a swollen prostate made this his fourth trip to the bathroom since he'd turned in at one.

The suite had a kitchenette and Earl grabbed a water from a giant American-style fridge and downed half the bottle in four gulps. A peek between curtains showed it was still dark, with rain streaming through the gutter outside his window. He was booked on a Christmas morning flight to Sydney and the 35-degree family vacation couldn't come soon enough.

Earl knew he wouldn't get back to sleep. He'd decided to grab some room service and read the news on his iPad when his eye caught the door leading to the adjoining room. He had no idea if it was locked. He was pleased when it budged, but alarmed by the squeal as it opened.

The room was dark, so the only light was a shaft through the doorway. The days when his daughter bounced off the walls at seven a.m. were long gone, but he realised he'd not checked on her when he got back from drinking with the crew in the hotel bar, and he found watching his only child sleep as soothing now as he had when she was tiny.

The suite had a giant emperor-size bed. His daughter had managed to spread her crap everywhere, and there was a half-eaten room service pasta in the middle of the floor. There was also a boys' maroon Adidas Hamburg training shoe in the middle of it. And the shaft of light glinted off a pair of torn silver condom wrappers.

The plastic water bottle crackled as Earl's hand clenched. He let the door shut quietly and stepped up to the bed. Jay was asleep on his back, hair matted with sweat and lipstick all over his face. Earl shook for several seconds before tipping his water bottle over Jay's face.

Jay shot up, gasping. Earl's flabby chest and grey body hair were barely visible in the dark, and Jay was completely disorientated.

'You horny little bastard,' Earl shouted, as he grabbed the skinny arm hanging over the side of the bed and used it to drag Jay on to the floor.

Earl tried to slap Jay across the face, but he was sluggish, so Jay managed to twist around so that the blow just caught his shoulder. Moirin flipped on a bedside light and scrambled across the bed screaming.

'Daddy, don't be ridiculous.'

'Ridiculous,' Earl roared, as he glowered at his daughter. 'You stay out of this. Put some bloody clothes on.'

Earl gave Jay another whack, as Moirin dived on her father's back and shoved him out of the way. This gave Jay enough time to crawl free, as Earl stood up with his naked daughter clamped to his back.

'Daddy, it's 2016,' Moirin shouted. 'You're acting like a caveman.'

'I'll cut your dick off!' Earl shouted, as Jay grabbed his jeans and bolted for the door. 'She's under age!'

'He's even more under age,' Moirin shouted, as she put her legs down and tried to stop her father going after Jay. 'You're pathetic.'

As Jay bounded out the door, Earl managed to throw his daughter on to the bed. 'You are in serious trouble, missy,' he roared.

Jay noted the extraordinary softness of the penthouse floor's carpets as he sprinted naked down the hallway, with his jeans trailing behind.

'Get back here.'

As Earl charged in his boxers, Jay reached the lifts at the end of the hallway. The one at the far end was waiting and Jay gasped as he scrambled in. The control panel threw him. Instead of a row of buttons, the only options were P for Penthouse and L for Lobby. As Jay jabbed L and desperately tapped the *close door* button, he realised that he'd stepped into the swanky glass penthouse elevator that he'd seen running up the side of the hotel tower when he'd arrived the previous lunchtime.

But being naked in a glass elevator was only second on Jay's list of problems. The doors finally responded to his rapid pounding of the *close door* button. But Earl got his fingers between, just as it was about to close.

Jay instinctively grabbed two of Earl's fingers and yanked them back, hoping it would make the aging rocker pull out, but the lift doors started to open and Earl charged in.

'Daddy, stop,' Moirin yelled, as she sprinted down the hallway in a robe.

Jay got slammed against the back of the lift. 'She's my baby,' Earl shouted.

Jay failed to break free and stop the doors closing, and Moirin slammed helplessly against the outer doors as they headed down. Jay launched a knee at Earl's groin, but Earl was much heavier and hooked his ankle while his leg was raised.

Jay thumped the floor of the lift and backed up to the glass side, shielding his face. With nowhere to go, Jay expected a beating, but Earl looked down at a skinny, naked, fourteen-year-old who'd acted exactly how he'd have done at that age.

'Balls!' Earl roared, as he stamped and backed up to the opposite side of the elevator. 'Put your damned pants on. There's bound to be photographers in the lobby.'

'I'm sorry,' Jay said meekly, as the lift beeped out the floors.
6 – 5 – 4 – 3 –

Earl fought for breath as Jay hurriedly threw a leg into his jeans.

'Lucky for you I'm not a violent man,' Earl said, as his finger wagged. 'But you stay away from Moirin.'

Jay was buttoning his jeans as the express elevator slowed down. He sighed with relief as he stumbled barefoot and shirtless into the hotel lobby, while Earl pressed the P button to ride back up.

There was a queue at the check-in desk, and several members of the *Rock War* crew were heading out to The Sandpit to start work. Shorty the cameraman was among them and cast a curious eye over Jay's state of undress.

'Everything OK, pal?'

Jay fake-smiled. 'Guys upstairs played a prank,' he said weakly.

When billionaires and world leaders stay in hotels they book the entire place to ensure privacy. *Rock War* didn't have that kind of budget, so although security could keep fans and identifiable press out on the street, a member of the press only had to book a room for the night to get unrestricted access to all the hotel's public areas.

Jay needed one of the regular lifts to get back to his ninth-floor room. He hadn't seen any cameras, but his shirtless appearance was sure to attract attention sooner rather than later. He'd have walked up, but didn't fancy nine floors on bare feet.

The first lift that arrived was filled with a Chinese tour group heading up from the basement breakfast room. Moirin came out of the second penthouse elevator, dressed in her robe, as he was about to board the second.

'Where's your dad?' Jay asked warily, as Moirin handed over a plastic hotel laundry bag, into which she'd stuffed the rest of Jay's clothes and his phone.

'I guess we passed in opposite directions,' Moirin said.

'Are you in a lot of trouble?'

Moirin smirked. 'I can handle Daddy. Must remember to lock the connecting door next time though.'

'You want my number or something?' Jay asked.

'I've got a boyfriend back in LA,' Moirin said, as she went up on tiptoes and kissed Jay's cheek. 'So let's just leave it at that, yeah?'

The penthouse elevator was closing, so Moirin held it with her foot.

Jay felt a sudden surge of anxiety. 'Was I terrible?' he blurted. 'In bed, I mean.'

Moirin burst into giggles. 'You were a solid three out of five,' she said. 'Practice will make perfect, and you're a really nice guy.'

Jay had a sense of gravitas as he watched Moirin vanish behind the elevator doors: a fleeting acquaintance who he'd remember forever. He'd been absorbed in the moment, but when he looked behind into the lobby he was pretty sure he recognised at least one photographer, sat at a table in the Starbucks next to reception.

A lift arrived and Jay slipped his Adidas on as he rode up to the ninth floor. His brain was a tangle of pride, guilt, exuberance and remorse, all moving too fast for a single emotion to bed down. He ditched the now empty laundry bag as he stepped out and heard his phone ping in his back pocket. It was a message from Summer.

Amazing sleeepz. Sorry I was boring last night but I feel so much better. You up yet? Wanna do breakfast downstairs?

29. Closed Circuit

The Ogel's breakfast buffet was close to full as Summer brought seconds to a table shared with Jay, Lucy, Leo and all of Frosty Vader. She put a bowl of fruit down and Jay hovered over a strawberry with his fork.

'Go for it,' Summer said cheerily, as she sidled up.

Two things played over in Jay's mind: Moirin's naked body, jarring with the image of everything he stood to lose if Summer found out.

'Remember the chocolate-covered strawberries at the hotel in Newcastle?' Sadie asked.

'*Sooo* good,' Summer said fondly. 'That snooty waiter told me off, because I tried to sneak four out in a napkin.'

'So who's up to what today?' Noah asked. 'Our call's not until four. We could go see an early film.'

There was a murmur around the table that a film was a good idea, so Sadie got her phone out to try and work out where the nearest cinemas were. At the same time, Tory – who was an intern assigned to the publicity department – squatted down between Jay and Summer.

'Jen wants me to take you for an interview,' she told Jay. 'I assume you saw your Manchester comments made the tabloids this morning?'

'No, but Jen said they were gonna run it.'

At the same moment, Sadie downed her phone, complaining that there was no signal in the basement.

'Channel Six News wants to do a recorded interview with you for their lunchtime bulletin. Few comments on the Manchester thing, and some questions about tonight's show.'

'Do I really have to?' Jay moaned.

'You can bring one of your band mates along if it helps.'

'Summer?' Jay asked.

'You two are box office,' Tory said brightly, after a pause. 'You can have fifteen minutes to finish your breakfast. They're filming out front with all the crazy fans. So the piece will be you and Summer, and then they'll cut in some clips of fans talking about tonight's show. It's for Channel Six, so they're on our side.'

'I'd better quickly go fix my hair,' Summer said, as she pushed her chair back. Then she looked down at Jay. 'And you've got bacon grease down your shirt.'

Jay glugged his tea and headed off behind Summer. They went in different directions when they stepped out on the ninth floor. As Jay approached his room, Adam leaned out of the door opposite, shirtless and angry. 'Get your arse here,' he said furiously.

'I've got an interview,' Jay said. 'I'm just changing my shirt.'

'It can wait,' Adam said.

Theo and Adam's room was a disaster zone. The flat screen had come off one of its hinges, the curtain rail was down, the carpet was covered in all kinds of crap and there was a vague smell of vomit. Theo lay on his bed in socks and briefs.

'Sit,' Theo said menacingly, pointing to the end of his bed as he sat up.

'I've got an interview,' Jay repeated.

'Moirin Haart,' Adam shouted, making Jay jump as the door closed. 'Of all the girls, you have to pick the daughter of one of the three guys who can vote us off *Rock War*.'

'I'm actually kind of impressed that you sealed the deal,' Theo admitted, clearly less angry than Adam. 'But minus several million points for getting caught.'

'After all the work we've done,' Adam moaned. 'Moirin's not even that good-looking.'

'She told me her dad worked for Channel Six,' Jay explained. 'She didn't say it was Earl Haart. And how the hell did you guys find out?'

'Twitter,' Adam explained.

Jay had a little brain explosion. If it was on Twitter, Summer would know *very* soon.

'How is it on Twitter?' Jay asked. 'Are you sure?'

'There's a video of you being chased naked down a hallway by Earl Haart.'

'Ahh,' Jay said awkwardly.

'It's trending,' Theo added.

'Just my luck,' Jay said, burying his hands as he remembered that none of the gang had been able to get internet in the basement breakfast room. 'I didn't see a photographer up there. Though I didn't look backwards.'

Theo shook his head. 'It's direct from the hotel CCTV.'

'How could that get online so fast?' Jay gasped.

'I guess some minimum-wage security guard saved a copy and pocketed a few quid from one of the press hanging around outside,' Adam said.

Jay couldn't stop shaking. 'You've *got* to be kidding me.'

'See for yourself, dickhead,' Adam snapped, as he pulled his phone. 'And for the record, if this was down to me, I'd be hanging you off the balcony by your ankles right now. But Theo says he owes you a *get out of jail free* card.'

Jay managed to half smile at Theo, before crashing back on the bed. 'I'm totally screwed. You think Summer will take it better if she hears from me first?'

'I don't give a shit about your little girlfriend,' Adam said. 'What about Jet? If we get kicked off because Earl gives us a shit score . . .'

Theo smirked. 'You could give Summer the old *I tripped, fell and landed with my dick inside her* line?'

'This sucks,' Jay squirmed, as tears welled in his eyes. 'But like . . . I don't know. You guys always have loads of girls. You're always winding me up about being a virgin . . .'

'Don't make this our fault,' Adam said, making Jay flinch as he bunched a fist.

Adam was a year older than Jay. He was muscly like Theo,

but he was usually the cool head who kept Theo under control.

Jay looked accusingly at Adam. 'You've got a girlfriend, you cheated on her with *two* girls last night.'

Adam shook his head as Theo explained. 'Kid, it's not the cheating, it's the getting caught that counts.'

'So what are my options here?' Jay asked. Then after several seconds' silence: 'What do I say to Summer?'

'Short term, you're doomed however you play it,' Theo said. 'Maybe you've got a shot of winning her back long term, but when she finds out she's gonna be mad as.'

Jay stood up and started looking around for Adam's case. 'You got a clean T-shirt?'

Adam's Hollister polo was a size too big, but Jay pulled it on and raced off back towards the lift, where he'd arranged to meet Summer. He thought she might have misunderstood and gone down to the lobby already, but he heard a door further along the hallway and saw Lucy come out of her room.

'Have you seen Summer?' Jay asked warily.

'I'd strongly suggest you stay away from her,' Lucy growled.

'Is that Jay?' Summer asked, from inside the room. Her voice was wobbly, as if she'd been crying.

Jay dashed towards the room, but Lucy blocked him. 'Piss off, worm.'

'Summer, I'm sorry,' Jay pleaded. 'I'm completely dumb. I'll do *anything* to make this up to you.'

Coco tried to stop Summer from leaving the room, but she made the hallway after a little tussle. Her hair was all mussed and her face streaked with tears.

'You're *really* sorry?' Summer said, stifling a sob as Lucy, Coco and Michelle formed a wall in the hallway behind her.

Jay told himself that Summer was a decent person. There had always been a spark between them and maybe there was a chance she'd forgive him.

'I got really drunk,' Jay explained. 'And my brothers both had girls, and I couldn't even go back to my room because Babatunde had a girl in there. And they're always laying into me for being a geek and being crap with girls. And Moirin started kissing me. And she made me feel *so* horny.'

'Everyone's fault but yours,' Coco scoffed. 'Just like every guy ever . . .'

'Of course it's my fault, Summer. But I just did one, really, really, stupid thing and I'm *begging* you to forgive me because I think you're *completely* fantastic.'

Summer seemed less angry as she stepped away from her backup crew and looked into Jay's eyes.

'Don't kiss the dirt bag,' Michelle pleaded, covering her eyes in horror.

Jay couldn't believe his luck. But there *had* always been a spark, and Summer was a sweet, caring person. He'd just got the first taste of relief when Summer chinned him with a right hook.

'You randy little . . .!' Summer screamed, as she followed with a slug in the gut, then brought her knee up as Jay buckled, viciously smashing his nose. A two-fisted finale sent Jay collapsing to the carpet, then Summer took a step back and gave an almighty kick to the hands covering his head.

Jay was seeing stars and Summer stepped back to take another shot.

'Please,' he begged.

'Scrawny little idiot,' Summer yelled. 'All the time we spent together. Comes to nothing the first time someone flashes a pair of tits at you.'

'He's not worth it,' Lucy said, as she bundled Summer into the wall.

As Jay moaned in pain, Summer wrapped her arms around Lucy's back and started to sob.

'Coco, get one of his brothers to come scrape the loser up,' Lucy ordered.

As Coco dashed off, Lucy nursed Summer back into the bedroom. Michelle's curiosity got the better of her and she closed up on Jay, who flinched, half expecting another kick.

'You're bleeding all over my Hollister shirt!' Adam wailed, as he rushed on to the scene with Theo in tow.

'His nose is mashed,' Michelle observed, as she snapped a picture. Then she scowled at Jay. 'I'm tweeting this,' she told him, as she backed away. 'Loser.'

30. Brand New Pigbag

@MicheleWeiISS Check this pic of @JayThomasJET! Its wot happens when you mess with my girl @SummerSmithISS Retweets 22,943 Likes 314,560

The rain had been lashing all day, but it hadn't stopped a crowd of several hundred – mostly teenaged girls – gathering outside Manchester's Ogel Hotel. The mob turned crazy as a gold open-topped bus turned into the hotel drive, trailed by a Channel Six satellite van.

Up top, steel drums and a lively-but-soggy brass section belted out a festive version of 'Papa's Got a Brand New Pigbag' by Pigbag.

'We're broadcasting live on 6point2,' Lorrie shouted, from the front of the bus, as a tall intern shielded her with a Channel Six golf umbrella. 'The *Rock War* Battle Zone semi-final kicks off in just over two hours and the atmosphere here is electric.'

As the bus braked to a gentle halt, the crowd mobbed the bus and a dozen burly security guards battled to keep the open rear platform clear.

'Are we ready to meet the bands?' Lorrie shouted.

Down below, a girl got as far as the first step to the upper deck, before being grabbed and thrown down by a brute of a female security guard. Cameras flashed as the fan hit the wet pavement, grazing her palms.

'In alphabetical order we give you, Frosty Vader!' Lorrie announced.

Dozens of camera flashes reflected off Noah's wheelchair as he pushed himself down a ramp and wheeled over a section of sodden red carpet towards the back of the bus, followed by three jogging band mates.

'Half Term Haircut!'

The four smartly-suited band members drew a huge cheer as they came out, stopping along the way for kisses and autographs.

'Industrial Scale Slaughter!'

The whole crowd started to chant, Summer, Summer, as the four girls walked out. Summer was devastated by what Jay had done and she walked in the middle with Lucy and Coco's arms around her back.

'You'll do better than him!' someone shouted.

Summer got a huge cheer as she gave the shouter a thumbs-up and a coy smile. Then Lucy squatted down, with one knee on the wet carpet.

'Hop up, bitch!' Lucy said.

The crowd gave its biggest roar yet as Summer jumped on Lucy's back and waved with one hand as she took a slightly wobbly ride down the red carpet towards the bus.

'Jet!' Lorrie announced.

The whole crowd turned as the four boys came down the ramp. Babatunde made an instinctive move to sign a few autographs, but the girls by the barriers were jeering and pulled their autograph pads away. Jay hid behind his big brothers, wearing sunglasses to shield a swollen nose and two black eyes.

The crowd continued to chant Summer's name as Theo flipped the crowd off and called them all wankers.

'Last but definitely not least, the Pandas of Doom.'

As Max and Eve led the Pandas on to the red carpet, a girl broke through the security guards down by the bus. She was holding a Frozen Fanta drink – or rather several Frozen Fanta drinks that had been purchased at the local cinema and tipped into a much larger popcorn bucket.

As a security guard lunged, the girl flipped the giant slushy into the side of Jay's head.

'Now who's orange?' the girl shouted. 'Manchester rules!'

Jay spasmed as the ice filled the back of his hoodie, ran into his ear and down his collar. Besides the cold, his already throbbing nose twinged with pain, as did a couple of torn stomach muscles. Babatunde caught frozen shrapnel as he moved in to stop Jay stumbling.

As the attacker got dragged away by security, soft drink cans, a tennis ball and even an old shoe came flying in, as part of the crowd began chanting, *We hate Jet!*

Theo grabbed the shoe and lobbed it back as he scrambled aboard. Jay shook the ice out of his hoodie as he stood on the bus's open rear platform, and Max skidded in it as he stepped up.

'And now we're off to The Sandpit,' Lorrie told the crowd, and the audience at home.

Dylan was the last to board. The elderly bus threw out a cloud of soot as he found a seat on the lower deck next to Jay.

'Hey, pal,' Dylan said, his voice nasal because his tubes were scabbed from his epic nose bleed the previous night. 'You doing OK?'

Jay didn't answer because he was afraid he'd burst into tears.

*

Lucy, Coco and even Michelle had been super-supportive. They'd kept an eye on Summer all day, brought cups of tea, made sure she ate lunch, gave her lots of cuddles and constant reassurance that everything was Jay's fault and that they'd have done exactly the same if he'd cheated on them.

At times their attentiveness had been cloying, and while flattening Jay had been extremely satisfying, Summer regretted it now. Might was never right, and while she was still too hurt to take Jay back, or even speak to him again, she'd accepted that he was a nice guy who'd done something stupid, now that the initial shock had worn off.

All this was tangling her brain as she settled in a make-up chair, waiting for Kia who always did her hair. Summer didn't mind having a few seconds' peace and stared at herself in the mirror, looking at all the brushes and potions as she wondered what her future held.

'Sorry to keep you waiting, pet,' Kia said, as she charged in. 'Disaster with Lorrie's hair. Open-top bus in the rain does a girl no favours!'

Kia checked a clipboard, to see if there were any special requirements for Summer's look.

'"Austere", it says here,' Kia said, as she sprayed distilled water on to a cotton cloth. 'Gonna clean you off to start. I hear you've had a rough day.'

Summer almost said, *I'd rather not talk about it*, but she was saved the bother by Karolina bursting in, followed by two of her production assistants.

'Have you seen Earl?' Karolina asked. 'Patrick mentioned that you're friendly with him.'

'Earl left,' Kia said, surprised. 'I saw him with Moirin and his luggage, getting into a car. He gave me a kiss goodbye.'

Karolina's eyes went huge. 'Pardon me?'

Kia looked awkwardly towards Summer. Then lowered her voice, which was ridiculous because Summer was less than two metres away and heard anyway.

'People were talking about what his daughter did on social media. Earl said he didn't want her in the limelight and he'd chartered a plane back to Los Angeles.'

'And you didn't tell anyone this?' Karolina hissed.

Kia shrivelled under her boss's glare. 'I just bumped into him. I assumed he'd told people first.'

'*Schweinebacke!*' Karolina shouted, glancing up at the show clock beside the make-up mirror. 'I've got a live show in forty minutes.'

'Could the show work with two judges?' one of the assistants asked thoughtfully.

Karolina shook her head. 'All the timings would be out and it would look like amateur hour.'

'Anthony the music director could sit in, or maybe one of the girls from the Black Swans,' the other assistant suggested.

'Both possibilities,' Karolina agreed. 'But the Swans have been unco-operative since they arrived, and since votes are involved, I'd rather it not be someone employed on the show. So here's what we do: we're less than five miles from Media City. Call the Channel Six studio, and anyone else you know around there. BBC, ITV, Channel Five and a dozen indies have shows running out of there. We want a famous face. Preferably with a music connection, but I'll take a comedian if that's all we can get. Even a newsreader if we get desperate.'

'How much?'

'Twenty grand,' Karolina said. 'Hell, this show is making money. Stretch to fifty if you really need to.'

Kia shook her head and tutted as Karolina and her assistants headed off, starting calls on their phones.

'Fifty grand for two hours on TV,' Kia said. 'That's more than I make in a year.'

31. Pesky Chipboard

The rain was coming through the venue's tented roof and Babatunde splashed through indoor puddles as he raced between plywood partitions backstage.

'Earl's gone,' he blurted, as he charged into Jet's dressing room.

Theo was preening in a mirror, Adam fiddled with his guitar, while Jay lay on a tatty sofa with a clean hoodie and an ice pack over his swollen nose.

'You're shitting us,' Adam said, as Jay sat up.

'On my mum's life,' Babatunde said. 'I was taking a crap and Patrick – sound guy Patrick, not director Patrick – was talking about it with one of the interns. He said Earl flew his daughter back to LA, before the media dug their hooks into her.'

Jay managed to grin, even though the swelling made his face feel like it was tight-wrapped in clingfilm. 'Any idea who they'll get to replace him?'

'Nope,' Babatunde said. 'But it can't be worse than a guy who caught our lead guitarist in bed with his fifteen-year-old daughter last night, can it?'

*

The Sandpit was packed with four thousand fans. Lorrie glanced anxiously at the empty judge's chair as she watched *Rock War*'s opening titles on the stage-side screens.

'Hi, everyone!' Lorrie shouted, as the stage lights came up. 'Wow! It's amazing to be here.'

As Lorrie spoke, Patrick the director sounded in her earpiece. 'We're going straight into the first song. Judge three is still in make-up, but will be ready by the end of Half Term's set.'

Lorrie looked a tad flustered as the crowd noise subsided. 'Semi-final!' she shouted, making the crowd go crazy again. 'Five bands start. The two with the highest scores will be voted through by our panel of judges, and the third finalist will be picked by you, the people at home. But you know what I really love about *Rock War*? For all the hype. The publicity. The craziness, violence and complicated teen romances . . .'

Lorrie paused while the audience made a big WOO sound.

'. . . What *Rock War* is *really* about is the music. All our bands are playing two songs tonight. One is a free choice, one is a song by a famous Manchester band. And to kick things off, it's Half Term Haircut, with The Verve's classic, "Bitter Sweet Symphony".'

The lights cut across to Half Term Haircut, in their skinny jeans and tweedy jackets. Owen cracked a gentle smile and flicked up one cheeky eyebrow as his keyboardist played the lilting opening melody.

It was one of the least 'rock' performances any band had done on the show, but the audience swayed to the melody and burst into cheers when it finally wound down.

'We reckon you'll like this one,' Owen told the audience. 'It's currently number two on iTunes and maybe you'd be kind enough to help make it number one. It's called "Puff".'

The plastic roof practically blew off The Sandpit as 'Puff' began. The crowd stamped their feet and security had to move in as an overexcited fan tried to climb on stage. When 'Puff' ended, the roar lasted a full half minute, while Half Term Haircut moved to the edge of the stage and did their trademark Japanese bows, to the audience and then to each other.

'How the hell is anybody going to stop that!' Lorrie gushed, as the director cut back to her. 'What an amazing start to the show. Now before we hear what our judges think of that song, I have to share a piece of very sad news.

'Earlier today, our legendary *Rock War* judge Earl Haart was taken ill, and I'm sorry to say that he won't be with us tonight. Our producers have been scouring the nation for a replacement and I'm delighted to say they've found one at very short notice. She's generously interrupted a busy schedule to be here tonight. She certainly doesn't need any introduction to fans of talent shows. Ladies and gents, I give you the one, the only . . . Miss Karen Trim!'

*

'Are you *bloody* kidding me,' Theo shouted as he launched a kick at the dressing room's partition wall.

The size twelve smashed clean through chipboard, making the live monitor feed flicker and scaring the hell out of Sadie, who was sitting in Frosty's dressing room the opposite side.

'Watch it, you crazy ass!' Sadie screamed, scrambling up as clocks and pictures fell off both sides of the wall.

Out on stage Karen Trim was doing a royal wave. 'It's so good to be on the second best talent show on Channel Six,' she announced, oozing her own importance.

'Great,' Jay said, as he buried his head. 'They've replaced the one guy on the planet who hates me more than anyone else with a woman who Theo punched on live TV, and who I've spent most of the past two weeks trying to goad into donating half a million quid to charity.'

'It's arguably not gonna be our night,' Adam noted wryly.

The wall shuddered as Theo tried to break free. 'Little help,' Theo urged. 'My boot's stuck.'

'You can't make this shit up,' Babatunde said, laughing and shaking his head, as Sadie grabbed the boot sticking through her side of the wall and gave it a twist and shove.

Theo fell backwards into a table. Then he sprang up, streaming expletives as he launched another kick. This time a huge piece of chipboard caved in, leaving a half-metre hole into the next room.

'Calm down, you idiot,' Adam said.

On the other side, Noah had rolled up to peer through the new hole, while the monitor showed that Half Term Haircut had scored twenty-seven points. Eight from Karen Trim, ten from Jack Pepper and nine out of Beth Winder.

'That basically puts them in the final,' Sadie noted, as she climbed through Theo's hole and sat in a chair. 'Ain't it cosy in here!'

'Are they even rock?' Jay asked bitterly. 'They should rename this show *Harmless Indie Band in Tight Trousers War.*'

32. Dance Like Ian Curtis

Max would never admit he'd crashed and burned two weeks earlier, but the Pandas played it safe, opening with the Muse track 'Psycho', then letting Eve take over vocals as they segued into 'I Wanna Be Adored', by Manchester's Stone Roses.

The band exchanged high fives and sweaty hugs. The crowd's reaction was good, but not the roof-blower that Half Term Haircut received. Karen gave six, and Beth and Jack added eights for a respectable twenty-two points.

'Are you happy with that?' Lorrie asked Max.

'It'll be tough, but that score gives us a real chance,' Max told the audience. 'Eve was really sick two weeks ago, so I want to thank all the people out there who showed faith. And voted for our potential, rather than our performance on the night.'

Dylan was conflicted as they headed off stage. Vote rigging had got them through the last round and two of his three band mates pissed him off. But he'd enjoyed the buzz of a good performance, and it had stirred his basic human desire to win.

On stage, Lorrie introduced the first of two songs by guest act, the Black Swans. Behind stage, Dylan eyed Industrial Scale Slaughter in the waiting area. They were next up and he strode over to wish them luck.

'You were great tonight,' Lucy told him. 'Might even avoid the vote-off.'

'Doubt that,' Dylan said. 'We lack your star power.'

'We'll be using your changes to "Neon Zipper",' Lucy said appreciatively.

Coco nodded. 'It's way better now. You're gonna be a producer or something someday, Dylan. I fiddle for hours and can't work stuff out. You hear it once and instinctively know how to fix it.'

Dylan liked having two hot older girls throwing compliments his way and couldn't stifle his smile. 'So, where's Summer hiding?'

'Throwing up, most likely,' Lucy said.

'Jay usually sits with her when she's nervous,' Dylan noted.

'The little shit did have a knack for that,' Lucy admitted. 'Have you got a cold? Your voice is . . .'

'Bad nosebleed,' Dylan said, as he noticed Will from the *Rock War* website calling him over for an online interview with his band mates. 'It's all scabbed and nasty. Better go answer stupid questions. Good luck up there!'

Summer was jogging back from the toilet as Dylan left.

She smelled of mouthwash, and trembled as he gave her a hug and wished her luck.

'I think I've had more hugs today than in the last five years,' Summer grinned. 'Did we say thanks for your help rearranging "Neon Zipper" for my vocals?'

'Lucy covered it,' Dylan said. 'You go knock 'em dead.'

Summer felt light-headed as she waited with her band mates. She thought she might puke as the Black Swans played a track either side of a commercial break. Her face got touched up and she swallowed a heave as the stage manager urged them on to the stage.

The Black Swans had four platinum albums, had headlined Glastonbury and regularly sold out twenty-thousand-seat arenas on both sides of the Atlantic. But the *Rock War* crowd was teenaged and invested in the competition, so their reaction to the Black Swans' set was muted and the female trio's sour mood got worse as they heard the vast cheer when Summer took to the stage.

Summer's nerves usually improved when the noise enveloped her, but she was jarred by a group of girls close to the stage holding up home-made banners. One had Michelle's Twitter picture of Jay after the beating and a *Don't mess with Summer* slogan; another fan had photoshopped Summer's head on to a picture of a female UFC fighter.

It wasn't how Summer wanted the world to see her. Her eyes glazed with tears, but she didn't dare touch them because there was a camera in her face, and she could imagine the *Summer Sobs* headlines.

'They're performing as a full quartet, for the first time in over two months,' Lorrie gushed. 'Let's hear it for Industrial Scale Slaughter.'

'Neon Zipper' was one of Industrial Scale Slaughter's original songs. It had gone down decently two weeks earlier, with Michelle screeching the vocal. Now Summer was back, and Dylan had helped to rearrange it, with a slower tempo and Summer sharing lead vocals.

With Michelle kicking things off, Summer's nerves had a few seconds to settle. Once the song began, the crowd was invisible and she felt a kind of glow from her band mates.

She'd been the band's accidental star since she'd first opened her mouth at boot camp. The soap-star drama of hospitalisation and absence from the competition had made things awkward, but when it mattered Michelle, Lucy and Coco had supported Summer, and she now felt she belonged in a way she'd never done before.

Industrial Scale Slaughter had formed as a thrash metal band and even the toned-down 'Neon Zipper' was a wall of noise, about as far from Half Term's radio-friendly melodies as it was possible to get.

It was never going to be a mass-market sound and Summer sensed the crowd's frustration as the track wound down.

'This one hails from Manchester,' Summer said. 'The original was by Joy Division and it's called "She's Lost Control".'

Lucy switched from her kit to a drum machine, to recreate the original recording's sparse drumbeat. Joy Division's singer,

Ian Curtis, had been famed for frenzied, robotic dance moves. The crowd was too young to recognise that Summer and Michelle were mimicking Curtis, but they appreciated the manic intensity in Summer's dusky vocal and flailing arms.

As the song died down, Michelle joined Summer at the microphone for the repeat chorus. The crowd roared as the lights came up and Michelle jumped in the air to give Summer a chest bump. Unfortunately, this wasn't choreographed, Summer stepped back at the wrong moment and Michelle went head first into a microphone stand.

The hit wasn't hard, but the heavy stand rocked, then rocked back, whacking Michelle in the nose. Summer wiped some of the sweat pouring down her face. She initially smirked at Michelle's misfortune, but was then horrified as blood started to stream from a gashed forehead.

Lucy stepped out to comfort her sister as the audience gasped. But Michelle wasn't badly hurt, and while most teenagers might have been mortified after making a fool of themselves in front of a crowd, Michelle loved any kind of attention.

Michelle smeared the streaking blood over her sweating cheek and down the front of her dress, then moved to the edge of the stage and took a bow.

Lorrie had seen the funny side and fought laughter as the director cut to a shot of her standing beside the judges' bar.

'That didn't happen in rehearsal,' Lorrie ad-libbed. 'But up to that point it was *intense*. I think Summer might have sweated a whole bucket.'

The director cut to a brief shot of the girls hugging and a stage hand passing Michelle a bar towel. Then it cut to Karen Trim.

'I'm not a rocker,' Karen began. 'At times tonight, I must admit I've wished I had some broccoli sprigs to stick in my ears.'

The girls felt nervous as the crowd hissed their disapproval.

'But, but!' Karen teased. 'Let me fin-*iiiiish*! Thrash metal may not be my bag, but I know talent when I see it.'

Now the crowd boomed approval.

'Summer's got *that* voice, the musicianship was spot on and I felt like I was sucked right into the action. So I'm giving you . . .'

After a pause, Karen held up a nine. The crowd went crazy and the girls jumped up and down. Summer even wound up with Michelle's bloody handprint on the back of her shirt.

'Me likey!' Jack Pepper said, as he stood up and flashed the crowd his pearly whites. 'This band struggled a bit as a trio. But tonight they absolutely kicked ass! Ten out of ten!'

The director cut to Beth Winder. 'There's been so much talk about Summer,' Beth began. 'But that unit behind her was tighter than Jack's leather trousers. Awesome, awesome, awesome!'

The crowd went bananas as Beth held up a number ten. Lorrie dashed across the stage and tried to get Summer to speak.

'Girls, you must feel you've got one foot in the final, with twenty-nine points.'

Summer and Michelle were wrapped in a tearful, bloody hug, forcing Lorrie to point her microphone at Coco.

'Best night ever, best crowd ever!' Coco shouted. 'Bring on the final, bitches!'

33. Frosty Reception

In the true spirit of rock, Theo and Sadie enlarged the hole in the chipboard partition, creating a single joined dressing room. As the night wore on, the space became a hub for bands who'd already played, with all attention focused on a pair of tiny LED monitors, relaying the action from on stage.

The girls from Industrial Scale Slaughter were cheerful, and stayed on Frosty Vader's side of the partition to avoid any awkward encounters with Jay. Half Term Haircut brought in fruit shortcake biscuits and their own chairs. Dylan and Leo had cushions, which left Max and Eve as the only absentees.

Frosty Vader kicked off their set with a note-perfect cover of The Smiths' 'What Difference Does It Make'. Early in the series, Frosty had played their own weird brand of effects-laden rock, and survived two vote-offs. But with the stakes so high, they'd decided on a pair of hits, and had the crowd singing along to Nirvana's 'Smells Like Teen Spirit'.

A great performance was capped by Noah high-wiring off

the stage. The crowd were aware of the circus net strung above their heads, but the director had lit the audience carefully and ensured that the net was never seen in audience close-ups. So for a few tantalising seconds, the crowd at home thought Noah might be plunging to his death.

'Noah's got bottle doing that,' Theo said admiringly. 'Heights really put the wind up me.'

The judges started their business as the two Romanian acrobats helped Noah out of the net and wheeled him back to the stage through a crowd having the night of their lives. Noah took a hundred high fives, as Karen gave Frosty Vader a nine.

'She's marking high for an evil troll,' Dylan noted, as he watched in the dressing room.

Babatunde smirked. 'If Karen Trim marks everyone else high, it hurts more when she gives us zero.'

'One,' Jay corrected grumpily. 'They don't have zero.'

There was a huge roar in the merged dressing room when Jack awarded Frosty Vader a ten. With nineteen points and ten to play for, it meant a ten from Beth would put them level in the lead with Industrial Scale Slaughter. Eight or higher would beat Half Term Haircut and mean that the competition favourites would drop into the vote-off.

Half Term Haircut had a superior air that rubbed some of the other bands the wrong way, but they were balls of angst as the camera cut to Beth Winder.

'Come on, Frosty!' Theo shouted, as he gave Owen from Half Term Haircut's chair a kick that edged the line between friendly and menacing.

'I think the standard tonight has been amazing,' Beth began, as contestants' eyes locked on the little screen. 'The bands have all worked so hard . . .'

'Get on with it, you fat tart!' Owen shouted anxiously.

'. . . But I don't think I saw the real Frosty Vader out there tonight,' Beth continued. 'I *love* their idiosyncrasy and for me, they just played things too safe.'

The crowd hissed as Beth held up a seven. Half Term Haircut were still second and howled with relief. Industrial Scale Slaughter started screaming, because they were now leading, with only Jet left to play. They'd booked their place in the final.

While Sadie and Otis were up on stage, telling the crowd they were disappointed to be in third by just one point, but still hopeful of making the final, one of the runners came to the dressing room to give Jet their stage call.

Jay was full of aches and wanted to be in bed. He popped a couple more Ibuprofen and drew muted *good lucks* and a couple of high fives. As he exited, he glimpsed Summer at the back of Frosty's dressing room, squeezed between her band mates, looking more troubled than you'd expect from someone who'd just made the final.

'Everyone's against us,' Theo roared, as he led his band into the waiting area at the side of the stage. 'But you know what? Everyone's been against me my whole life and I won't stop fighting now.'

The four lads hugged, being gentle on Jay's wounds. He heard a notification on his phone. He expected the message to be from his mum, but it was his cousin Erin. It was the first time he'd heard from her since she'd been voted off with Brontobyte two weeks earlier.

Always my fave cousin! Go play your balls off! XXX

It meant a lot to Jay. After the Summer thing and the Frozen Fanta, it was a relief to know there was one girl in the world who didn't think he was a dickhole. There was no time to text back, because a stage hand was waving them on.

The crowd reaction was mixed. For every Summer fan that had decided to hate Jay, a Theo fan stood ready to shout them down. The lights and noise made Jay's head throb with pain as Babatunde kicked things off, proving why he was easily the best drummer in *Rock War*.

Oasis's 'Live Forever' was made for Theo's in-your-face vocal. Jay's vision was blurring, but his fingers kept strumming. The night had been dominated by bands playing it safe, and Jet kept up the trend, following Oasis with 'Dakota' by the Stereophonics.

As the set ended, Jay saw Babatunde looking his way, mouthing, *You were way off . . .* Jay was short of breath and stumbled as the band stood, awaiting the judges' verdicts. Karen Trim screwed up her nose and made a kind of snorting sound.

'Well, I know what I like,' Karen Trim said, earning some laughs for a catchphrase she'd coined as a judge on *Hit Machine*, 'And that, my friends, was *not* it.'

Karen held up a number three. Divided between the Theo and Summer loyalists, the jeers and cheers were about equal.

But since three bands had already scored high, even tens from Jack and Beth wouldn't get the twenty-seven points Jet needed to tie with Half Term Haircut and avoid the vote-off.

Babatunde reacted by kicking over a cymbal stand, while Jay sat back down, numb to the verdict because his swollen nose throbbed and the stage lights felt like needles in his eyes.

Adam tried to tackle Theo, who grabbed the microphone stand that Michelle had wounded herself on and ripped it off the floor. Theo held the thin end as he charged across stage towards Karen Trim.

'Die, hag, die!' Theo shouted.

Karen Trim squealed and exited on the opposite side of the stage. Jack Pepper stood bravely to stop Theo going after her, but this wasn't the completely crazy Theo of old. He knew bashing Karen Trim's brains out on live TV would probably end badly for him, but after an average performance, he needed to go out with a bang.

Few people are strong enough to throw a heavy-based microphone stand like a javelin, but Theo was one of them. Turning away from the judges' bar and to the back of the stage, he sent the stand spearing into the giant neon *Rock War* logo.

Glowing glass tubes shattered. The stand caught in the plastic framework that held up the neon and its weight was enough to rip the entire logo out of its mountings in the lighting gantry. Lorrie and Theo dived for cover as the entire sign crashed down on to the stage.

'Karen Trim,' Theo raged, as he stuck his face up to a

camera. 'I will haunt you! I will eat your brains!'

As Theo sprinted off and dived head first into the crowd, the entire lighting gantry above the stage creaked precariously. Nobody liked what they were hearing and Lorrie, three quarters of Jet and the two remaining judges charged off stage.

'He's *completely* lost it,' Jay gasped, as he scrambled away.

Fortunately the lighting gantry was designed to withstand the collapse of even the largest pieces that hung from it. The electrical wiring was also designed with safety in mind and fuses popped, shutting down everything from lights, to remote cameras, the sound system and stage-side screens. As emergency lights came up over the audience, the stage stayed black.

Viewers at home briefly saw a colour card. Patrick was directing the show from a production truck parked outside the venue. All his camera feeds were dead, apart from a wide view taken from the back of the audience and a live feed from backstage. It was a two-person team, running a shoulder-mount camcorder. The camera operator was an intern, and with him was teenaged presenter Will, who usually filmed backstage interviews for the *Rock War* Facebook page.

'Ahh,' Will said, as the stage director rushed back and told him he was going live to an audience of fifteen million. 'Clearly, err . . . I guess we have a technical issue here . . .'

34. Down To The Decimal

Semi-Final Result		
Industrial Scale Slaughter	29	FINALIST
Half Term Haircut	27	FINALIST
Frosty Vader	26	VOTE-OFF
Pandas of Doom	22	VOTE-OFF
Jet	16	VOTE-OFF

Dylan stood in a shaft of light, stubbing out a smoke and enjoying the kind of air you get when it finally stops raining. There was a humming generator truck parked in a big puddle, and a hundred cables running out the back of The Sandpit to a mobile production van.

Dylan pulled his phone and glanced furtively before opening up the QStat Terminal App. After confronting Harry and his dad, Dylan had agreed to keep the vote rigging secret, as long as all future rounds were honest. And he'd been given a login for the voting system, so that he could be sure.

The connection to the on-site Wi-Fi wasn't great and Dylan was about to try a different spot when the three-way pie chart finally showed on screen. Frosty Vader were at 42.7% of the votes, Jet at 42.6%, with the Pandas trailing on 14.7%. The Pandas' status was disappointing, but no surprise to anyone who'd seen the real result from two weeks earlier.

QStat updated a couple of times per minute and the next refresh had the leading bands tied on 42.7%. Dylan tapped the chart to get the actual numbers and saw that Jet were ahead by eighty votes, out of over a million cast.

Frosty retook the lead, as a wind howled off The Sandpit's tented roof. Entranced by the updates, Dylan jolted when he heard a foot in a puddle a couple of metres away.

'Hey,' Summer said, as Dylan urgently shoved the phone into his pocket. 'You looking at porn or something?'

'Course not,' Dylan gasped.

Summer smirked. 'The way you shoved that back in your pocket . . .'

'You made me jump is all,' Dylan said defensively. 'Congrats on the final. You deserved it.'

Summer pointed up the alleyway towards a main road. 'There's a car waiting to take us back to the hotel. I just wanted to wish you luck in the vote-off.'

'Appreciated,' Dylan said, smiling. 'You feeling OK? You know, with Jay and shit.'

'Mixed up,' Summer admitted. 'I was so angry at first. But Jay's *not* a bad person.'

'Just a horny teenaged idiot like the rest of us,' Dylan said, smiling.

'And I shouldn't have hit him. Well . . . He deserved a slap, but I got carried away.'

'I certainly won't be getting on the wrong side of you.'

'No jokes!' Summer said, raising her hands. 'It sucks so bad. This time yesterday I had this cute, funny boyfriend. And now . . .'

'You think you might get back together?'

Summer shrugged. 'Even if I was sure I wanted to, we live a hundred and twenty miles apart. Day return London to Birmingham costs fifty squids.'

Dylan felt rich-person guilt, but couldn't resist a dig. 'I didn't think you paid your train fares.'

'Ha-ha,' Summer said, then looked down at her feet. 'Seriously though, I'm not saying you're gonna get knocked out tonight, but whatever happens I really hope we stay in touch. I met so many good people at the manor and you're one of my favourites.'

'You're one of mine,' Dylan said, as he pulled Summer into a hug. 'And I'll be at an all-boys boarding school, where the height of sophistication is butt-tagging someone else's pillow. So you can be *sure* you'll hear from me.'

'Boys are gross,' Summer smirked.

Dylan felt weird as Summer walked away. His attraction to her was one of the reasons he'd ditched Eve, but she'd got with Jay, and then vanished while she recovered from her accident. Now he sensed the possibility of something, right as he was about to get voted off *Rock War*, go back to Scotland and possibly never see Summer again . . .

*

Thanks to Theo, the *Rock War* semi had ended with Lorrie and Will presenting from a damaged stage, with no monitors or timing system, while filmed by camcorder and improvised lights running off a twenty-five-metre extension lead from a regular wall socket.

The stage crew needed every minute of two frantic hours between the main and results shows to clear out the damaged neon, replace the dodgy wiring and get most of the lights and two out of four remote stage cameras working.

This frantic scramble meant the crew hadn't been able to perform their regular task of swapping the performance stage and judges' area for the spartan set with three white circles that had been used in previous result shows.

After he'd created so much extra work for the technicians, several burly fellows had sworn in Theo's face, and there was much black humour around the possibility of a sixty-kilogram stage light 'accidentally' dropping on his head during the results show.

So Theo expected more abuse when he came out of the toilet and got approached by the big Yank who'd been trailing Karolina for much of the past week.

'Rick Cosgrove,' he said, as he held out a huge hand. 'Vice President of Commissioning, ANT. That's American Network Television.'

Theo usually swaggered, but Jet being in the vote-off and

the focused hatred of a thirty-strong technical crew had knocked him off stride.

'I guess you know who I am,' Theo said warily.

'I do indeed,' Cosgrove said, as he flicked a business card. 'I'd like you to take this. I'd also very much like to take your agent's details.'

'I don't have an agent,' Theo said. 'Closest thing is my stepdad Len, who kinda manages the band.'

Rick seemed to have twice as many teeth as anyone else Theo had ever met. They glowed as he slipped a Samsung Note out of an ostrich-leather case and gave Theo the plastic stylus. 'Would you mind scrawling your contact details on there?'

'Right,' Theo said. 'Can I ask why?'

'I find you interesting,' Rick said, as he slapped Theo's shoulder. 'I'll have someone touch base with you shortly.'

Theo resumed his walk back to the dressing room, but only made a couple of strides before he encountered his band mates coming the other way, led by a runner.

'It's showtime,' Babatunde said. 'All bands on stage.'

'That American guy just asked for my details,' Theo said, as he let his band mates go by before turning to follow them. 'What do you reckon that's about?'

Jay was usually the brains of the operation, but he was zoned out with his headache. Win or lose, he just wanted to go to bed.

'ANT are supposedly close to a deal to bring *Rock War* to the US,' the runner said. 'At least that's what I heard.'

'Maybe they want Jet on *Rock War* in the USA?' Babatunde suggested.

'That would just be weird,' Theo said. 'Can you imagine Mum's face?'

Adam smirked. 'Maybe he's gay and wants to lure your hot ass back to his hotel room.'

'That's *got* to be it,' Babatunde grinned.

They'd reached the edge of the stage. The timing and scheduling screens were still down, but there was a monitor tuned to Channel Six. The weather forecast was on, which meant the results show would begin at any second.

Jet were the first band to arrive alongside the stage, but Noah wheeled up a few moments later, followed by the rest of Frosty Vader. The *On Air* light flashed as three quarters of the Pandas arrived. The contestants didn't know what to say to one another, as Lorrie got a cheer from the crowd and started her intro to the results show.

'Welcome back to this eventful evening. Lines are still open for another few minutes and voting instructions are on screen now. And just in case you still haven't decided who to vote for, here's a recap of what happened earlier this evening.'

Dylan was the last contestant to hit the waiting area. He'd faked the need to pee and stayed back in his dressing room for a final glimpse at QStat. The Pandas had dropped below 14%. Jet and Frosty Vader had each drawn more than two million votes. Frosty had been six hundred ahead when Dylan last looked, but votes continued to pour in and the lead kept switching.

'Amazing,' Lorrie told the audience, when the highlights package ended. 'Now I'm hearing that some of you at home are struggling to get through to register your votes. I'm incredibly sorry if you missed out. We're going to do everything we can to beef up our systems so that everyone gets their chance to vote in the final. But we do have to close the lines in just a few seconds.'

A pair of tens appeared on the stage-side screens and the audience began a countdown. 'Ten, nine, eight . . .'

As the audience counted, the members of Jet, Frosty Vader and the Pandas filed on stage. Since the results stage hadn't been erected, each band had been told to stand around one of three yellow Xs taped to the stage floor. Jay's vision blurred as lights dimmed and the countdown hit zero.

'That's it!' Lorrie announced. 'The votes are in and in a few seconds we'll be ready to announce the first band to be eliminated.'

There was a drumroll as the lights flashed between the three anxious quartets.

Lorrie spoke in her most doom-laden voice. 'The first band to be eliminated from the *Rock War* semi-final is . . .'

The wait felt like a million years.

'The Pandas of Doom.'

Dylan looked down at his feet as Leo put an arm around his back. Max looked slightly psychotic and a tear streaked down Eve's face. Jay didn't absorb the words as Eve and then Dylan did the whole *thank you, we came so far but we're devastated* type stuff. He saw one of the crew moving high up in the gantry and imagined a light coming down on Theo's head.

'And we'll find out who our third finalist is, right after this break!'

Dylan and his band mates hugged everyone before filing off. Rather than stand separate like the director wanted, Frosty Vader and Jet merged. Theo stood behind Noah. Sadie put her arm around Jay and Adam's backs, while Babatunde did the same with Cal and Otis.

The crowd went completely silent as the drums rolled and the stage lights flashed between the two spots where the bands were supposed to be standing.

'The third and last band to reach the final of *Rock War* 2016 . . . which will be held at the Emirates Stadium on Saturday December 24th . . . will be . . . announced . . .'

Noah clutched the arms of his chair. Adam felt Sadie's nails digging into his back. Babatunde was sweating so much that he pushed down his hoodie, revealing a bald head and a birthmark shaped like Norway.

'The third *Rock War* finalist will be Frosty Vaaaaaaaader!'

35. That's That

The Sunday Post, *Arts & TV section*, December 11 2016

TRASHING THE SET CAN'T SAVE JET

Former favourites fail to make final

. . . *While other shows fight to gain publicity, Rock War has struggled to stay out of the headlines.*

On any other show, a sex scandal involving an underage contestant might hold the limelight for weeks. But it barely raised an eyebrow in a show that has outraged its key sponsor, dabbled with bankruptcy, fired its host, driven its creator into rehab and seen one of its contestants fight with a Hollywood superstar, while another almost died in a traffic accident.

It almost seemed routine when last night's semi-final

ended with a complete power failure after a contestant threatened to kill a judge, before demolishing a huge portion of the set with a microphone stand.

An estimated sixteen and a half million tuned in to watch the chaos and the final on Christmas Eve is widely expected to top that.

There's even another scandal brewing over Channel Six's last-minute decision to sell 48,000 tickets to the final for £70, instead of the originally advertised price of £10.

This estimated £3 million windfall will come on top of the profits from Half Term Haircut's song 'Puff', which is being widely tipped for the coveted Christmas number one slot.

A performance of contestants Summer Smith and Theo Richardson singing The Pogues' Christmas classic 'Fairytale of New York', which was broadcast early in the series, will also be released in time for Christmas.

The night's biggest losers were Jet. As little as two weeks ago, they were joint favourites to win, led by the snarling on-stage presence and off-stage antics of Theo Richardson, and backed by competent guitar work from Theo's younger brothers and the outstanding drums of Babatunde Okuma.

The run-up to their performance was a car crash, as Jet lurched from one public relations disaster to another. They hurled insults at their host city, while the band's youngest member allegedly slept with show judge Earl Haart's daughter and was then assaulted by his girlfriend, rival contestant Summer Smith.

In the end though, it was most likely an average performance on the night that cost Jet a place in the final.

The teen quartet plodded through tracks by Oasis and the Stereophonics, before what turned out to be Theo Richardson's final act in Rock War: smashing up neon signage and reducing the last ten minutes of the show to the production values of a YouTube video.

But this rampage seemed like it had been calculated to distract attention from a poor performance. In its own way, it was every bit as manipulative and tacky as the slick Karen Trim productions from which Rock War seeks to distance itself.

While Jet were undeniably the night's big losers, the winner of last night's show was music itself. Instead of Jet, the audience chose to save Frosty Vader, whose erratic but often innovative sounds have shown the potential to mature into something of real quality.

And while Rock War has thrived on controversy, it is ironic that the favourites to win are now Half Term Haircut. A talented and well-groomed quartet, they hail from Surrey's affluent stockbroker belt, rarely speak out of turn and end each performance with an eccentrically polite round of Japanese bows.

Monday

The yell came from the bottom of the stairs. 'Jayden, breakfast!'

He got called Jayden when he broke the Xbox, forgot to collect younger siblings from play centre, or hid the letter from school after he lobbed his mate Salman's bag out of a second-floor window in science class.

Jay's face had almost stopped hurting, but everything else sucked as he snuggled up to the wall with his duvet shielding him from the universe. He hated the fact that after all of Theo's craziness, it was the chain of events he'd set in motion that wound up getting Jet kicked out.

To add insult, Half Term Haircut were storming the charts with 'Puff', which was based on an idea Jay had given them. And then there was Summer. Jay's brain ached as he rolled on to his back and thought about how hot she was. One time when they'd kissed, she had blades of grass stuck to her legs and her mouth had tasted like everything he'd ever wanted . . .

'Don't make me come up there, Jay! I will *not* be happy.'

Jay closed his eyes and braced as he heard his mum's slippers on the stairs. She crashed in and slapped the foot poking out the end of the duvet.

'You're not deaf,' she yelled. 'Adam's already in his uniform.'

Jay reckoned he'd have been dressed too, if he'd had the second hottest girl in Year Ten for a girlfriend and enough muscle to stop anyone talking shit.

'My eyes are all puffy,' Jay whined. 'What's the point going when I can't even read?'

'Eyeballs seemed all right playing Xbox with Patsy and June yesterday afternoon. And when you showed me them trainers you're after on your phone . . .'

Jay sat up, his hair a tangle, two slightly black eyes and the most miserable expression he could muster.

'I hate my life,' he moaned. 'Everyone at school's gonna rip the piss out of me.'

Jay knew his mum loved him, but with eight kids and a chip shop to run her maternal style was mean and lean.

'You're going to school and that's that,' she said, as she whipped the duvet off and flung it across to Adam's side of the room. 'Up you get!'

'It's practically Christmas,' Jay moaned. 'It's not like anyone's gonna be doing any real work this week.'

'When I agreed to let you do *Rock War*, what did I make you promise?'

Jay cast his eyes down. 'That I'd work really hard to catch up when I got back . . .'

'And now I can't even get your ass out of bed.'

'I . . .' Jay mumbled, as he felt a tear welling in his eye.

'I know it's crap right now,' Jay's mum said, as she opened his side of the wardrobe and pulled out a school shirt and trousers off hangers. 'But you're gonna be like this *whenever* you go back to school. Probably worse if you have until New Year's to sit around angsting over it.'

Jay nodded reluctantly as his mum gave him a quick hug and a kiss on the forehead. 'I bet all your mates will want to hear your stories.'

'What mates?' Jay said warily, as his mum reverted to form and charged out.

'You got five minutes or Len gets your bacon,' she warned, as she ran back downstairs and started yelling at Jay's little sisters June and Patsy. They were by the door, bickering over who a pink umbrella belonged to.

The black school trousers felt like handcuffs as Jay stepped into them. He cut across the hall to the bathroom, just as his younger brother Kai swaggered out and barged him into the wall.

'Stinks in there, mate,' Kai grinned. 'Laid a nice floater for you.'

36. The Deal

BizBuzz.com, Monday December 12th

$94 Million Deal Brings Rock War to US Screens

\# American Network Television secures 5-year deal for hit UK talent show

\# Four major US networks entered bids

\# Show set to replace ailing *Hit Machine USA* in Saturday primetime

Shares in American Network Television (ANT) rose 2.7% upon the announcement that smash UK show Rock War *will premiere on US screens this fall.*

The five-year deal will see the show anchoring ANT's Saturday night schedule beginning summer 2017. Bonus payments and profit shares could see payments to the show's creators Venus TV exceed $150 million over the life of the contract.

*Shares in Channel Six UK (ChSix), which owns a 25%
stake in Venus TV, were also up 1.4% on the news.*

*Karen Trim was unavailable for comment, but is said
to be considering legal action over the axing of her longest-
running US show.*

Cocaine was playing havoc with Dylan's pipes and he
woke with dried blood spattered on his sleeve. After burying
the shirt in his laundry basket, he cheered up when he sat
on the toilet and saw a message from Summer.

> How's living in the real world?
>> Miss the Rock War gang. Told my dad Yellowcote has
>> broken up for Christmas and he believed me!!!!!
> Hahahaha. Con artist ☺

The cooks and cleaners rarely disturbed the peace inside the
huge manor house, so Dylan was surprised by a racket as
he strolled barefoot towards some breakfast. The main door
was open and a bunch of roadies were carrying equipment
through to the ballroom. He found his dad having breakfast
with Uncle Harry.

'Here's our little moral crusader,' Harry teased cheerfully, as
Dylan stepped up to a fifteen-seat dining table.

'You both look happy,' he noted.

'We have our reasons,' Dylan's dad, Jake, said. 'Ninety-four
million of them!'

'Fifty per cent of ninety-four million,' Harry corrected, as

Dylan looked baffled. 'The deal got inked with ANT. *Rock War* is crossing the Atlantic.'

'So, we can afford shoes now?' Dylan joked.

As soon as he sat down, one of the kitchen staff stood behind, gave a polite nod and asked what he wanted.

'Kippers,' Dylan said. 'Potato waffles. And a smoothie, like mango, mint and strawberry. You know how chef makes it for me?'

'I'll go prepare it, Mr Wilton,' the kitchen hand said, before shuffling off.

'So what's the mayhem in the ballroom?' Dylan asked.

'Band needs to rehearse,' Jake explained. 'And if you want to keep things under wraps, this is about the best place there is.'

'Terraplane?' Dylan said.

His dad smiled and nodded, as Harry beamed. 'I've got the tour fixed. A hundred and two gigs over sixteen months. One point two billion dollars in ticket guarantees from the promoters. We'll release a couple of new tracks. Plus a live album, merchandise, concert film and a three-part documentary about the band.'

Terraplane had broken up before Dylan was even born. Two of his dad's former band mates were his godparents, but while he'd met all the band members at parties and weddings, he'd never seen them play.

'There's gonna be a film crew coming by too,' Harry said, as he formed a TV screen with his hands. 'It'll be the opening scene for the documentary. You know, voice-over, moody shots of dust being blown off guitar cases. Five band mates getting together and amping up for the first time in twenty years.'

'Historic shit!' Jake said, making all the glassware rattle as he pounded the table. 'Is my boy too cool to hang with us old geezers?'

Harry smirked. 'Can't stay in your room jerking off *all* day, Dylan.'

Dylan quickly flipped his Uncle Harry off before cracking a smile. 'Just to be clear, I'm in a manor house, with a band and a TV crew?'

Jake saw what his son was getting at and slapped him on the back. 'Exactly son, you'll be right at home.'

*

You get used to smells, but Jay had been away from Carleton Road long enough to catch the whole set: floor polish, body spray, playground funk, bad lunch and farts. The noise was more intense than he remembered, and there was drizzle in the air, which made the hallway floor a mass of wet shoeprints.

Jay wasn't being paranoid. Every eye *was* on him as he found his form room. A tiny Year Seven got shoved into his path with squeals of, 'She fancies you!'

A mountainous Year Ten barged him, and his pal's raised hand made Jay flinch.

'Theo's his brother, dickhead,' one of the Year Ten posse whispered. 'Leave him alone.'

Jay hated having to rely on Theo and Adam, though plenty without muscular backup envied it. He felt better when

Babatunde came by and high-fived him, but the drummer was back with his Year Ten pals and that reminded Jay that *Rock War* was over. And while nobody had discussed it, maybe Jet was over too . . .

He was a couple of minutes late to form room. He hadn't seen most of his class in six months, so there had been growth spurts, hairstyle changes, serious acne eruptions and a new girl who he put in the hot-geek category.

'Ahh, the last of the pop stars has returned,' Jay's form tutor, Mr Oxlade, said, raising a couple of laughs.

'What's it like being beat up by a girl?' a little brat called Reubens taunted, getting a much bigger reaction.

Reubens was all mouth, so Jay mouthed back as Mr Oxlade pulled a copy of the class timetable out of the register.

'Grab this, find a seat.'

There were a few empty chairs at all-girls' tables, but Jay knew they'd be pissed off if he joined them. There was a space up back, where Aidan and David sat. They were hard cases. Weight training, football, and part of a big crew you hoped never to meet on the street.

That left Jay's old spot as his only real choice. Tristan and Salman were the other *pop stars* Mr Oxlade had been talking about. They'd been Jay's mates from the start of primary school, up to the fight before Easter that led to Jay getting kicked out of Brontobyte.

Jay hadn't spoken to Tristan in months, but he'd never fallen out with Salman, and Tristan was too scared of Theo to try anything physical, so it was his least bad option.

Salman was on the end, with an empty chair between him and Tristan. Jay's only choice was to sandwich between his two former besties. It was a squeeze with the row of desks behind and when Tristan pulled the empty chair back, Jay's first thought was that he was pulling it away. But Tristan was letting him in.

'Hey,' Jay mumbled, eyeing Tristan warily as he dropped his backpack and sat down.

'When'd you get home?' Salman asked.

'Yesterday afternoon,' Jay said, as he took in the classroom, and the familiar view over bike racks out of the window. 'Feels so weird being back here, after everything. What was last week like?'

'Shit,' Tristan said, which was the first non-insult he'd spoken to Jay in six months.

'Everyone wants to have a pop at the TV stars,' Salman said sourly. 'And teachers are moody as, because we're behind with our work.'

'Aidan nabbed me cutting through the park on Friday,' Tristan said. 'One week you're on TV. The next you're flat on your back, with ball ache and dog shit on your blazer . . .'

'The novelty will wear off,' Salman said.

Jay was surprised that Tristan was talking to him. They'd been rivals in *Rock War*, but apparently being back at school with everyone against them had changed the dynamic. He wondered whether to say *So we're OK now?* or something, but they'd known each other forever, so it mostly felt like a return to normal.

'Bloody PE,' Jay said, as he saw what the timetable had in store for third period. 'I haven't got my kit.'

'I'm sure Mr Fox will find something nice and ripe in the spare kit box,' Salman teased.

Jay rested his head on the desk top. 'Kill me now.'

'Look on the bright side,' Salman said, as he patted Jay on the back. 'None of us won *Rock War*, but at least *you* got a shag out of it.'

37. Brand Theo

Theo got out of his stepdad's van, a battered Transit with *Big Len* painted on the side and a counterfeit disabled badge in the front window.

'Shoreditch,' Len grunted, looking into a shop that sold handmade leather belts and a coffee place called Has Beans. 'Trendy wankers.'

They passed a line of ethnic food carts, where one of the vendors offered him a taste of paella.

Len was strictly a meat and potatoes man. 'Be on the bog for a week with all this foreign muck,' he told Theo warily.

The ground-floor lobby of Motion Talent Agency had a glass-topped reception desk and a hipster receptionist wearing a headset mic. He saw Len's scruffy jeans and looked down his nose.

'There's a separate entrance for deliveries around the back, in Greek Avenue. Red doors . . .'

'I have an appointment to see John Motion,' Len said, as

Theo ate a jelly baby out of a bowl on the counter.

The guy still looked suspicious as he made a call, but before he'd finished speaking a dude in a tailored three-piece suit came down spiral stairs and spread his arms wide.

'Welcome, Theo,' he said, shaking hands, then with Len. 'You were signed to my father, back in the eighties?'

Len nodded as they headed towards the stairs. 'I was a session musician. Had my own group for a while. Your father, Jackie Motion, thought we might be the next Def Leppard or Terraplane. But our album peaked at thirty-two on the heavy metal chart and that was that.'

'Can't all hit the big time,' John Motion said, smiling. 'But I'm glad you remembered the name and looked us up.'

'Does your father still work?' Len asked.

John shook his head. 'He retired around ten years ago. Had a stroke recently.'

'Sorry to hear that,' Len said.

The stairs topped out into a hallway. There was a meeting going on in a conference room and glass-fronted offices branched in either direction. The floor was trendy polished concrete and the artwork looked pricey.

'I hope I'm not wasting your time,' Len said. 'This Cosgrove guy spoke to Theo. Then his assistant called twice last night and again this morning. So whatever they're after, they're keen, and I don't want the lad signing things until a professional looks at it.'

'Wise words,' John said, as they reached the end of the hallway and stepped into a large office. There was a concrete desk, with nothing but a phone on it, and a Salvador Dali melting clock painting on the wall.

John turned to Theo. 'So when do you turn eighteen?'

'April fifth,' Theo said.

'Sit down, guys. Can I get you anything to drink?'

John buzzed his assistant to bring in a pot of coffee, before taking a notebook and fountain pen out of a desk drawer. Theo sunk into a retro leather chair as he noticed a signed picture of John Motion with Lionel Messi on the glass shelf behind.

'So, Cosgrove is worth getting excited about,' John began. 'ANT has been getting its ass kicked by Netflix and the other US networks. Cosgrove just came from CBS as new head of programming, and shelling megabucks for *Rock War* is his first big move.

'I Skyped Cosgrove's assistant right after your father . . .'

'*Step*father,' Len corrected.

'. . . After your stepfather spoke to me this morning. He *really* wants you, Theo.'

Theo squinted. 'You mean Jet?'

John laughed. 'I'm sure America has no shortage of talented teen rock bands. He wants you to be the co-host on the American version of *Rock War*.'

Theo practically fell out of his chair. 'Me?'

'Your profile went stateside when you de-toothed DeAngelo Hunt. The rebellious angle is key to the success of *Rock War*, and your brand says young and rebellious like nothing else out there.'

'Are you sure he's not yanking us off?' Theo asked.

'We've not even signed a contract for me to be your agent yet,' John said dismissively. 'But we *do* need to move fast. Cosgrove's assistant said they're looking to make a big splash by announcing the team to present *Rock War USA* and get bands setting up online profiles ASAP. They're looking at the rapper Q Bott to work with you, which will also bring in a more diverse audience.'

'Bott is smoking hot!' Theo said.

'I wouldn't kick her out of bed either,' John grinned, as he pointed to Theo's watch. 'Did you buy that?'

'Got given to me at the *Chequered Flag* premiere,' Theo explained.

'What are you, six foot two?'

'Six one.'

John smiled. 'Perfect. You're in great shape, good jawline, V-shaped torso. Motion Talent Agency has an in-house modelling agency. You might need some time on a sunbed, but I can see you modelling all kinds of shit. And that's good bread and butter money – two, three grand for a photo shoot, fifty plus for a brand endorsement. Family brands won't touch you. But I think you'd be an easy sell for lad fashion. Your Fred Perry or Ben Sherman type brands.'

Len knew enough about showbiz agents to see that John was trying to get Theo all hyped up, so that he'd sign a contract that would give the Motion Agency a healthy cut of any future income.

'Before we get carried away,' Len said firmly, 'did ANT

make any kind of firm offer for my stepson's services, or is this all blowing in the wind?'

'He's good for you, Theo,' John said, pointing at Len. 'Doesn't fall for my horseshit. As a matter of fact, I did manage to squeeze some numbers out of ANT. Their initial offer is thirty-five thousand dollars, two-year contract, option for a third and fourth season. It would probably be hard to push for more cash on the first season, but I'm sure I can negotiate bonus payments for season two, subject to the show hitting certain viewing targets.'

Theo counted with his fingers. 'Thirty-five thousand per year, that's twenty-something thousand pounds, isn't it?'

John burst out laughing. 'Thirty-five thousand per *episode*. The show will run twenty-two episodes, starting this September. Seven hundred and seventy thousand dollars per season, which at today's exchange rate is a little over half a million pounds.'

Len and Theo grinned at one another.

'Get me a pen, where do I sign?' Theo blurted.

'But like I said, if *Rock War USA* is a hit there's *huge* upside potential. Ryan Seacrest gets fifteen million for hosting *American Idol*. Regis Philbin was on twenty plus for *Who Wants to Be a Millionaire*.'

'Wow,' Theo said.

'Wow indeed,' John smiled. 'Why do you think I came running down the stairs when you arrived? You're seventeen years old and my twenty per cent cut of your future could be *massive*.'

'Twenty?' Len gasped. 'The ANT contract's already on the table. You're worth twelve and a half, tops.'

John ignored the attempt to negotiate commission as he stepped around the desk and crouched beside Theo. 'There's one *really* important thing here, young man.'

Theo glared sideways, not liking the sudden change to a patronising tone. 'What?'

'If *Rock War* hits big in the US, salary and endorsements could earn you a hundred million bucks over the next few years.

'But you are *not* a US citizen, which means they don't have to give you a work visa. United States Department of Immigration don't play games. I know you've had some scrapes with the law . . .'

Theo looked anxious. 'I did six weeks in young offenders' when I was fourteen.'

'You were a minor, so it doesn't count,' John said. 'But juvenile convictions within the last two years are taken more seriously, and you have to be even more careful once you turn eighteen. Get caught with a joint, criminal conviction – no US work permit. Someone winds you up in a nightclub, you throw a punch and get done for assault, criminal conviction – no US work permit. Same goes for stealing cars, bonking underage girls, drunk and disorderly, burglary, trespass, arson . . . Do you understand?'

'Sure,' Theo said.

'So can you stay out of trouble and let John Motion make you rich?'

Theo's brain was full of dollar signs and he cracked one of his cockiest smiles. 'Course I can, bruv,' he said. 'Don't sweat it.'

38. Like Old Times

Mr Fox showed mercy and let Jay off PE. The afternoon was double tech in the woodwork room. There was only a week and a half until Christmas break and everyone else was finishing off spice racks that had taken all term, so Ms Heron told Jay he could work quietly on his homework.

While all kinds of crashing and general mayhem went on around the woodwork benches, Jay sat at a regular desk along the side wall. The new girl – Bailey – had been given the same deal. She had a chunky build and stockings laddered just above the ankle. She stared at her science book, biting a well-chewed black thumbnail.

'Do you get this refracted light thing?' Jay asked, as he tilted his chair towards her.

Her almost-new exercise book was filled with neat girly writing and she'd stuck all her worksheets in with Pritt Stick.

Bailey looked around to see if the teacher was nearby before asking, 'What bit don't you understand?'

'This bit,' Jay admitted, as his pointing finger circled the entire page.

Aidan was walking past in his woodwork apron, and two floating chair legs proved irresistible. There was a grinding sound, then a yelp, as Jay landed with his face next to Bailey's black pump.

The whole class laughed as Jay stumbled up, with Ms Heron closing in her steel-toe-capped boots. 'What have I told you lot about tipping chairs?' she growled.

'Don't tip chairs,' half a dozen kids droned back.

Once Ms Heron had made sure Jay was OK, he settled back down, flushed with embarrassment. Bailey was laughing too, but she offered Jay a tissue to wipe sawdust off his hands.

'Aidan's a knobhead,' she said. 'My last school was all girls.'

'Was that better?' Jay asked.

'Different,' Bailey said. 'Boys seemed like these weird mystical creatures. Now they're just a bunch of annoying dickheads in my class.'

'I'm Jay, by the way.'

Bailey's face lit up. 'Everyone knows who you are. My last school was obsessed with *Rock War*. I told my Facebook that Tristan and Salman were in my new class, and everyone was like, *screw you, you're full of crap*.'

'You should get a selfie with them.'

Bailey shrugged. 'It's weird asking. And I don't wanna get my phone confiscated.'

'Meet us by the gate, after school. We'll sort you out.

Especially if you tell me what the hell an *angle of incidence* is supposed to be . . .'

*

While *Rock War* was banged out for TV, the crew that rocked up at Dylan's house to start on the Terraplane documentary fancied themselves as artistes. They had lights, baffles, snoots and ultra-HD cameras that ran on tracks. They spent thirty minutes just lighting a couple of moody close-ups of Terraplane's drum kit.

While the crew prepared to film the historic moment when the rock gods jammed together for the first time in twenty years, the rock gods themselves spent two hours in the adjoining library, smoking joints and working their way through crates of Mexican beer and aged whiskies from Jake Blade's cellar.

To begin with Dylan felt like a kid intruding on the grown-ups, but once the booze started flowing and his dad let him have a few puffs on a joint, everyone wanted to regale him with stories about crazy stuff his dad did.

'Remember that joint in Austin?' Terraplane's bassist 'Mad' Max McTavish asked Dylan. 'Was that the eighty-five or eighty-eight tour?'

'I was born in two thousand,' Dylan pointed out.

'You missed a good bloody night,' Max explained. 'Stolen fire engine backed into a swimming pool. The cocaine got delivered in a suitcase. We were getting it on with a bunch of little cookies and then this cowboy turns up with a shotgun. Naked but for his hat, hallucinating on LSD. Jumps off the roof and impales himself on a flagpole.'

'You guys knew how to party,' Dylan said dubiously.

'Texas cops don't mess,' Max continued. 'Whole band spent a night in jail and Harry had to tip a hundred grand in the local sheriff's hat to bust us out.'

The director came in and announced that she was ready to film. Dylan's dad took several attempts to dig his way out of an armchair, then took two steps forwards and fell flat on his face.

'I am so high!' he announced, as he convulsed with giggles.

It took ages to get the five band members in place. Max left a little packet of cocaine behind. Dylan swiped it, before taking it into a side room and snorting it off the top of his wrist. He wound up high in the back of the ballroom, behind the cameras with a bunch of girlfriends, wives and other hangers-on. His Uncle Harry was teetotal and gravely warned Dylan to be careful.

'I just had a few beers,' Dylan said defensively.

Harry's stare said he didn't believe Dylan, but he said no more.

When the cameras started rolling, Dylan expected a disaster. But even after a twenty-year break and an afternoon getting wasted, Terraplane could play. There was nothing great about it, but there was a real sense of history amongst the crew and hangers-on and a good round of applause when they called it quits after three tracks.

'Real rehearsals start tomorrow,' Harry announced. 'Just the band, not this bloody circus.'

The craziness kept going through a dinner made up of a Brazilian all-meat barbecue. It was past nine when Dylan found himself by the pool, making out with a twenty-something in a striped top. He thought he was on to something good, until she hopped up, vomited in a Jacuzzi, then started sobbing something about how she was in love with a guy named Sam.

Stuffed with booze and meat and with marijuana and cocaine in his blood, Dylan was the most wasted he'd ever been. He had lipstick smears on his face and a big wet piss stain on his chinos. He'd lost a shoe and he'd dropped his iPhone in one of the swimming pools. He'd decided to retreat to bed when a blurry version of his dad grabbed him by the shoulders and shook him hard.

'I love you, son!' he shouted. 'Bloody love you.'

'Love you too, Dad.'

'We're racing the Group Bs.'

Some men collect stamps or war medals. Jake Blade collected Ferraris, vintage helicopters, and Group B rally cars. Group B rallying involved cars with four-wheel drive and more power than a modern Formula One car. They were stupidly fast and the whole thing got banned in 1987, after three drivers died in a matter of weeks.

'Dad, no,' Dylan said firmly. 'You can barely walk.'

Jake wouldn't let Dylan go. After some more shaking and a boozy hug, Dylan found himself at the rear of a posse ambling towards the manor's underground garage.

Besides the servants, the band's manager, Harry, was the only sober person in the house. After some fruitless verbal attempts to urge everyone to go to bed, the fearsome manager vanished for several minutes, then charged into the garage with a double-barrelled shotgun, which he fired into the grille of a 1971 Mini Cooper.

'I'll be making too much money from this tour to let you assholes go killing yourselves,' Harry roared, as he reloaded. 'Now get some bastard sleep before I lose my temper.'

39. Fairytale

'Hey it's me!' Summer told her camera. 'I'm at the BBC!'

She sat in a little dressing room, with a bowl of tangerines and a plate of custard cream biscuits on a table in front of her.

'I'm sorry that this is my first vlog since before the semifinal. But it's been a manic week and I didn't feel like talking after the whole thing with Jay. And I know a lot of people were laughing and photoshopping my photo on to MMA fighters, but I'm a peaceful person and I'm not proud of what I did.

'I actually Skyped Jay last night. He's been at school all week, which seems weird. We both apologised for what we did to one another and we've agreed to stay friends.

'Apart from that, it's been a good week, but really hectic. I had to go up to the Midlands to see my doctor, who says everything's fine, and she says the muscle in my bad leg is almost back to a hundred per cent. We've also been doing loads of rehearsing, obviously.

'Each band has to play three songs in the final and the theme is supergroups. So we play one original song that nobody has heard before, one song by one of the biggest bands of all time and our third song is a free choice, but it must have a Christmas theme.

'It's dead quiet at the manor with only three bands left. And they're already packing up a lot of stuff, like one of the classrooms, and the offices on the top floor. And we had eight kitchen staff back in the summer and now there's only three.

'So, I don't know if you can see,' Summer said, rolling her chair back so that the camera got a wider angle. 'I'm all done up in this fancy dress, which I had to come up to London and have fitted yesterday. And I swear, the woman fitting it must have stuck a pin in my thigh a dozen times. And now I'm here for Jon Sanders' talk show.

'The main guest tonight is that Aussie guy Jason wotsit, who plays Keyhole in that movie where the trucks crash off the cliff in the trailer. I'm sorry, but I'm useless at movie names . . . So we passed in the hallway and the publicist introduced me. And Jason shook my hand. And he was just *soooo* fine, with muscles out to here and the bluest eyes I have ever seen. I just got totally tongue-tied and blurted, "Wow, you look like a movie star." And he looked a bit confused and said, "I am a movie star," before walking off.

'So that was a *total* embarrassment . . . And I'm recording this vlog, because we're on last so I've got half an hour to kill and I'll just get really nervous if I sit still. I'm supposed to be on with Theo, but he disappeared to get coffee half an hour ago.

'We'll be singing "Fairytale of New York", which we recorded together way back in the summer. With so many songs and so much *Rock War* stuff going on, I'd almost forgotten about it, but now it's been released on iTunes and the publicists are hyping it up as this big battle between us and Half Term Haircut for Christmas number one.

'And I spoke to my nan earlier, and they've sorted it so that she'll be at the stadium for the final in eight days' time. I actually got the afternoon off to go shopping for her Christmas present yesterday, but the shops were rammed and people kept recognising me and asking for autographs. I got her present in the end, but it was exhausting . . .

'Not that I should really be complaining, because last Christmas it was just me and my nan sitting home, with a Bernard Matthews turkey roll and crackers from Poundland. And now, I . . . Basically all this stuff that's happening is insane. So yeah, that's me doing a big update on everything I can think of right now. Thanks for watching, everyone!'

Theo came in as Summer leaned forward and switched off her camera. His cheeks were stuffed and he held a silver tray stacked with sliced roast beef, a whole crabmeat-stuffed lobster and an unopened bottle of Prosecco.

'Just borrowed this from the catering trolley outside Jon Sanders' dressing room,' Theo explained, as he placed it next to the custard creams. 'I'm sure he won't mind.'

*

Jay wouldn't have admitted it, but his mum had been right about not wallowing at home. By Wednesday he'd started getting back into routine and his presence in school hallways no longer drew stares. There were still bullies, boredom, bad food and teachers with IQs lower than the wattage of an energy saving bulb, but having some mates made it tolerable.

The resurrected relationship with Tristan got cemented after school on Tuesday, when Jay got invited round to play Xbox at his house. Salman, Erin and Alfie were there as well, along with all of Brontobyte's drums and equipment. But nobody had any appetite to jam, or even talk about bands and music. After five months at the manor, everyone wanted a break.

But the best thing about Jay's first week back was Bailey, the new girl. Jay had a couple of chats, then made a bold move on Thursday morning. When he saw there was no empty desk close to Salman and Tristan in religious studies, he sat next to her. In the afternoon, Jay invited her to join himself, Salman and Tristan around a table in maths and after that they sat together in almost every class.

'So Theo's on Jon Sanders tonight,' Jay told Bailey, Friday lunchtime. 'It's not a big deal, but they're gathering round to watch in my aunt's pub. Do you fancy coming?'

'Erin's mum?' Bailey asked, and Jay nodded.

Jay gasped when Bailey arrived at the pub with her dad. It was the first time he'd seen her out of uniform and she was all gothed up, in black tights, shoulderless black dress and purple eye make-up. He wanted to tell her she looked great, but her dad came into the pub behind her, making the whole thing awkward.

'It's dark out and she doesn't know the area,' Bailey's dad explained, as his daughter went red.

While Jay's aunt Rachel poured Bailey's dad a free pint, Jay led his new pal upstairs to the living room. She nodded to Tristan and Salman, before Jay introduced her to a bunch of girls from Erin's class, plus various cousins and siblings. It was strictly a Coke and crisps affair, but everyone was lively and since there wasn't much space Jay found himself sat on a floor cushion with Bailey squeezed up, close enough that their knees touched.

All attention turned to the screen as Theo and Summer walked on stage. Jon Sanders gave her a kiss.

'Real pleasure to meet you both,' Jon said. 'Now before you sing for us, there's a couple of things to clear up. Theo, we've heard the rumours of a multi-million-dollar deal to host the US version of *Rock War*. Can you tell us any more about that?'

'I've always admired you, Jon,' Theo said, grinning. 'And I'm honoured to be following in your footsteps, by being a dummy who earns a packet for standing in front of a microphone asking daft questions.'

The line was scripted, and Jon roared with fake laughter. Back in the pub, Tristan spluttered, 'Theo's gotta be the luckiest bastard on legs.'

Jay had an instinct to defend his brother, but more or less agreed. On screen, Jon moved on to his next question.

'And Theo,' Jon said, as the chubby host dropped into a

boxing stance and threw a couple of fake jabs. 'You're a bit of a boxer?'

'Sure,' Theo said, as he slapped his stomach. 'Won a few amateur belts, but I've been out of training while I was at the manor. So I'm a bit flabby at the moment, but I'll be hitting the gym big time in the new year.'

Jon grinned. 'But I understand Summer packs quite a punch too. Would you be brave enough to step into the ring with her?'

Summer dipped her head with embarrassment as Theo answered. 'Jon, I'd never hit a lady. That's why I'm still angry she floored Jay's skinny ass.'

Jay gawped as the audience on screen cracked up laughing. Back in the pub, Tristan leaped into the air, flicking his wrist. 'Burn!' he roared to Jay. 'Oh my god!'

'You'll *never* live Summer's beats down,' Salman added.

Erin hated the tension between her boyfriend and cousin and gave Tristan a whack on the back of his jeans. Jay hurt on the inside, but fought off the urge to storm off in a huff.

'So good luck in the big final,' Jon told Summer, on screen. 'And good luck to both of you with your shot at number one.'

The camera panned out to the show's band, as Theo and Summer stepped across to a pair of waiting mic stands. Jay was all tense and irritable, but Bailey put a hand on his wrist and gave him a sweet smile.

'Don't worry about it,' she said, resting her head on Jay's shoulder as Theo began singing on screen.

40. Barcelona Thrashed

ROCKWAR.com HEADLINES

1. *Who will be the 3rd judge in Rock War Final?*
   Show's producers remain tight-lipped as Karen Trim rules herself out of 2nd appearance.

2. *Xmas No.1 Announcement Looms.*
   'Puff' from Half Term Haircut and Theo and Summer's version of 'Fairytale of New York' are both in the running. The chart will be announced at midnight on Thursday.

3. *Theo Inks $2.5m Deal to Host Rock War USA.*
   American Network Television has announced a 3-year deal for our former contestant to host American version of show. Venus TV has also announced deals that will see local versions of Rock War screened in Mexico and Australia in 2017.

4. *Stage Crew Arrives at the Arsenal Stadium.*
   Following Arsenal's 6–1 Champions League thrashing

of Barcelona yesterday, Rock War *crew descend on stadium to begin setting up for the final.*

5. **Cobb Arrives at Rock War Manor.**
    Celebrity chef Joe Cobb has arrived at Rock War Manor *to cook a Last Supper for the contestants. The three bands will have a final chance to rehearse on Friday morning, before a limousine convoy takes them to London for Saturday's final.*
    rockwar.com
    21 December

Terraplane had been rehearsing for ten days and sounded sharp as Dylan pottered away from the breakfast buffet table with a bowl of fruit and some coffee. He wore the T-shirt and boxers he'd slept in as he shuffled back towards his room.

Uncle Harry was too busy talking on the phone to say good morning, but Dylan had less luck being ignored by Dimitri. Dressed in Adidas three-stripe trackie bottoms and a neon yellow vest, his father's buff personal trainer peered approvingly into the bowl.

'Fruit is a good choice, but beware of the high sugar content,' he said, acting as if it was perfectly normal to begin a conversation with nutritional information.

'So glad you approve,' Dylan said grudgingly, as he tried to keep walking.

But a wall of muscle and neon Lycra blocked his path. 'I've been working with the band, getting them in shape for touring.

But I'm free while they're rehearsing and your father suggested that you could use some exercise.'

'I'm good,' Dylan said forcefully. 'I have to do sport at school, and these are my holidays so . . .'

'What sports do you like?' Dimitri asked. 'I can devise a workout that incorporates elements from . . .'

'I hate all sports,' Dylan said firmly. 'Sweaty doofuses getting excited cos they kicked a ball through a hoop.'

'You're too young for this flabby belly and slouched posture,' Dimitri said, still beaming. 'What's a lady going to think when you take off your shirt and she sees *that*?'

Dylan finally lost his patience. 'Can't you just go drink a protein shake, or something?'

Dimitri scowled as Dylan marched off towards his bedroom. Dylan drank some of his coffee, before stepping into a bathroom that was almost as grand as his dad's. A shower would help him feel less groggy, but so would the sprinkling of cocaine he had left in his bedside drawer. And he could easily pop across the hall for more, seeing as his dad was rehearsing.

But it was only nine thirty and Dylan didn't like the idea of being high all day. Plus he kept getting nosebleeds and the cocaine was wrecking his sleep. But on the other hand, if he snorted the gear he wouldn't care about any of that stuff . . .

The buzz from cocaine was incredible, but it didn't last long. If he snorted the stuff by the bed, he'd soon be crossing the hall to his dad's room to steal seconds and then he'd spend all day trying to keep a buzz going. And Dylan was scared, because his dad was a light user and it was only a matter of time before he worked out who was snorting his gear.

Dylan reckoned he could try blaming one of the staff. But then they'd lose their job, and his dad would move his supply somewhere more secure. Like the safe where he kept his fancy watches. And then Dylan would be stuck in this house all over Christmas, with no mates, no drugs and nothing to do.

He strolled back to his bed, feeling awful. He'd got used to Rock War Manor, where there was always something going on and the day felt like it was going to last a hundred hours. He thought about stealing and hiding his dad's entire stash. Then he'd be fine for a week or two.

I'm going to get addicted.

But as Dylan sat on his bed, he realised that he was spending all of his time either thinking about cocaine, getting high on cocaine, or feeling crappy and guilty about having done cocaine. He wasn't getting addicted, he was addicted *already*.

Dylan grabbed the iPhone that replaced the one he'd dropped in the pool and navigated to a number he'd saved the night before. According to their website, the *Addiction Buster* helpline offered confidential help and advice to anyone with a drug problem.

But he was sure the first thing that they'd say was that you had to tell an adult, and he couldn't stand the idea of going to his dad and telling him he'd been snorting his cocaine. Especially not with Uncle Harry, and the band, and a personal trainer in the house.

Dylan thought about how shit he'd suddenly made everything and how he only had himself to blame. The phrase

I'm a drug addict clanked around his brain like a coin in a washing machine.

What would all his *Rock War* pals say? What if the press found out? What about school? *So I'll just stop. I'll be strong. I'll never snort that evil crap again.*

But he also hated the thought of being in this giant house until school went back. With no mates and nothing to do but read, or watch TV, or fiddle around in the recording studio. He'd be so bored without that beautiful cocaine high . . .

Dylan buried his face in a pillow and hated himself. Then he jumped up, tears streaking his face as he crossed the hall, and delved into the secret drawer in his father's bathroom.

41. Turning Green

Thursday December 22nd

Back in July, Summer had arrived at Rock War Manor with two Tesco bags for life. The clothes inside were mostly hand-me-downs from the Wei sisters. Five months on, the room she shared with Michelle overflowed with everything from cards made by fans, to designer clothes and jewellery sent by publicists keen to see Summer dressed in their brand.

'Eighteen pairs of shoes,' Summer noted, as she looked at the boxes stacked on her bed. 'They won't fit in my little bedroom, and even if they did I can't walk in the stupid heels half of 'em have got.'

'There are kids in the Third World with no shoes at all,' Michelle said, as she picked up a pair of neon yellow strappy shoes. 'Though arguably these wouldn't be ideal in darkest Congo.'

'I was thinking eBay,' Summer said. 'Should easily make enough to cover gas and electric for the winter.'

Michelle laughed. 'Only you could talk about paying some dreary gas bill two nights before the big final.'

'It's not a cash prize even if we win,' Summer noted. 'We get to record an album, but there's no advance and no guarantee our record will sell.'

The door was open. Noah gave a gentle knock and rolled in, looking stressed.

'Got a spare bed for Christmas?' he asked.

Michelle put on a stupid posh accent. 'Always for you, Noah dah-ling.'

'What's the problem?' Summer asked.

Noah smiled. 'The competition finishes on Christmas Eve. So win or lose, me and Sadie were supposed to fly home to our families in Belfast on Christmas morning. My dad said he'd organise it, but he faffed about trying to save a few quid on the fare and they all got booked up.'

'Bummer,' Summer said.

'We'll probably just do Christmas in a hotel in London,' Noah explained. 'But I was looking forward to seeing my nanna and doing all the regular boring turkey and tinsel stuff.'

Noah saw the time on Summer's bedside clock. 'You sitting up to see the Christmas chart going online at midnight?'

'I'm already tired,' Summer said, yawning at the thought. 'And we've got this whole Christmas meal with Joe Cobb to get through.'

'They're inviting friendly journalists,' Noah said. 'So we've got to dress up, and behave.'

Summer made a soft groan. 'I wish they'd just let us spend

our last night hanging out together.'

'Is there such a thing as a friendly journalist?' Michelle asked. 'I *really* miss Theo at times like this.'

Noah smiled at the thought. 'He'd certainly know how to liven up a posh dinner.'

*

It was five to midnight when Jay stepped out of his bedroom and hopped across the hallway to take a pee. His little siblings had blobbed toothpaste everywhere, the floor around the toilet was splashed with pee, the laundry basket overflowed and the air stank of Kai and Adam's boxing gear.

The chip shop closed at eleven on weeknights, but Jay's mum was still up, making Friday's packed lunches in the kitchen. She'd moan if she caught Jay out of bed on a school night, but there was also noise coming out of the living room. He crept downstairs and found Theo with his feet on the sofa, and a Doritos bag on his lap.

The TV was showing the crappy Mark Wahlberg *Italian Job* remake, but Theo was focused on his phone.

'Chatting to Noah,' Theo told him. 'He says hello.'

Jay considered Theo's confusing nature as he flopped into an armchair and got one of Hank's Skylander figures wedged in his back. Theo definitely had a nasty streak, but at other times he'd spend hours playing Lego video games with Hank and he'd always looked out for Noah at Rock War Manor.

'Tell Noah I said hi back. Did he say what's going on down there?'

'He's at some dinner, bored off his head,' Theo said. 'Says

he's trapped between Owen and a journalist and they're both talking about their coloured vinyl collections.'

'Half Term Haircut are so boring!' Jay gasped. 'It's like those dudes were born aged thirty-five.'

'So you still sniffing around that Bailey chick?' Theo asked, but before Jay got a chance to confirm that he was, Theo realised it was only a few seconds to midnight and flipped to a music website on his phone.

Jay had only got up to pee, so his phone was on charge by his bed. Too lazy to fetch it, he squatted on the arm of the sofa looking at Theo's. Theo found the chart page. He refreshed it a couple of seconds after midnight, but it stayed on the previous week's chart.

'Come on,' Theo moaned.

It was a couple of minutes past when the Christmas Top 100 chart finally downloaded. Theo swore, because the screen only showed the bottom half.

'Click there,' Jay said, pointing impatiently at a link titled *050-001.*

'All right, Bony Boy,' Theo said, using a nickname he knew Jay hated.

A pair of messages popped up on screen. Clearly lots of people were trying to find out what was Christmas number one, because the top fifty download was stalled.

Theo's first message was from Summer and just said, *Not too shabby, mate!*

'What does that mean?' Jay gasped, as his mum stepped into the room, drying her hands on a tea towel.

'You've got school and college in the morning,' she growled.

Theo liked to present a *couldn't give a damn* image, but he was gripping his phone tight and torn between asking Summer to clarify and leaving the screen clear for the chart to download.

Then nine-year-old Patsy screamed from the top of the stairs. 'You're number one, you're number one, you're number one!'

She came bolting downstairs in striped pyjama legs holding her Kindle Fire, followed by her younger siblings, Hank and June.

'Is anyone in this house asleep?' Jay's mum groaned, as the chart finally appeared on Theo's screen.

There was no denying it now. 'Fairytale of New York', by Theo & Summer, had shot straight into the singles chart at number one. There was a charity record at number two and 'Puff' by Half Term Haircut was only at number three.

'I am a golden god!' Theo shouted, as he stood up, thumping his chest.

His mum finally seemed to snap out of grumpy-tired-mum mode and gave Theo a huge hug. Kai was coming downstairs in his boxers, moaning about the noise, and apparently Erin knew too, because she was clambering in through a balcony window from next door, followed by her two older sisters and her mother.

'Champagne,' Auntie Rachel shouted, as she ran into the living room brandishing two dusty bottles from her pub cellar.

Jay got kissed and hugged by his cousins, as Patsy jumped on the sofa chanting, 'Number one,' over and over, while

Hank and June fought over who got to sit on Theo's shoulders. The only family members absent were Adam, who was at his girlfriend's, and Len, who was driving back from hosting a Christmas sing-along night.

'He's number one in the charts and the Yanks are making him a millionaire,' Jay's mum said proudly, as a champagne cork popped. 'And I'd have bet me left tit he was gonna end up in jail.'

'He probably still will,' Kai noted sourly.

Auntie Rachel had champagne dribbling everywhere, and Jay felt his mum tap him on the back. 'You run and get some glasses. And a bottle of Pepsi for the little ones.'

Erin ran to the kitchen after Jay. She grabbed an assortment of unmatched glassware as Jay passed it down from a cupboard.

'Best Christmas present ever!' Jay's mum shouted.

Patsy had found Theo and Summer's recording on her Kindle and Hank cheekily shouted, 'Turn that racket off,' after she hit *play*.

Theo and everyone else started singing along, and the scene in the living room was so chaotic that Jay couldn't get back in the door with the bottle of Pepsi. Even Kai was having a ball, hugging his big brother and suggesting that Theo might want to buy him a new bike.

Jay knew he was witnessing a family moment that people would remember until they shrivelled up and keeled over. But his smile was fake. Forming Jet and entering *Rock War* had been Jay's idea. But while Theo had the number one single and the multi-million TV contract, all Jay had to look forward to was the last day of school and the Year Nine Christmas disco.

He wanted to enjoy the moment, but all he could muster was jealousy.

42. Mighty Convoy

One of the unpaid runners helped Summer tape up the last of her boxes and Shorty the cameraman filmed as she closed the door of her empty room and headed downstairs for the last time. Vans and trucks had descended to collect gear. Anyone late for breakfast found the tables stacked up and the serving cabinets being jet-washed on the back patio.

While Joe Cobb had done his gourmet thing for the contestants and journalists the previous night, the remaining crew and runners held their own last-night party in the ballroom. There were many sore heads as Summer joined in a round of tearful hugs.

Lorrie, the presenter who'd joined the show as an unpaid intern, and some of the senior staff like the stage manager and head of design, had already signed on for *Rock War* season two. Patrick the director was taking a couple of months off, before taking on the job of setting up *Rock War Australia*. Plenty of other staff would be heading abroad, as *Rock War* transitioned from a UK start-up to a global television brand.

Karolina had been a tough boss since she'd taken over from Zig Allen, but everyone agreed that she'd been decent about helping the dozens of unpaid runners. They'd spent months working for free, hoping to get a foothold in the competitive TV industry, and she'd helped find paying jobs for many, and given all but the most useless ones a two-grand bonus from *Rock War*'s profits.

Summer hugged an editor with a contract in Mumbai, a seven-months-pregnant sound engineer, and an intern in the web team, who'd landed a lucrative job running the online team for *Rock War USA*.

There were a lot of emotions as the twelve surviving contestants waited just inside the main door. Sadness at leaving the manor for the last time, fear of winning, fear of going back to normality. Anxiety about an extended two-and-a-half-hour final show in front of an audience of close to fifty thousand people.

As the final approached, channel 6point2 had dropped all its regular programming for 24/7 coverage of *Rock War*. There were interviews, repeats, highlight shows and reruns. They were live on air as the manor doors swung open and the contestants ran, or rolled, towards three waiting limousines.

They were long-wheelbase Rolls Royce Phantoms, but each one had been covered in garish neon shrink-wrap, complete with the *Rock War* logo and posterised photos of band members. Lucy led the way into the buffalo leather and foot-gobbling carpet of Industrial Scale Slaughter's bright pink model.

They had two motorcycles leading the convoy. These were followed by the three band limos, then a satellite truck and a tail of various media and crew vehicles. The journey took three and a bit hours, with horns blasting and phones snapping on every kerb. They got mobbed when they stopped at a service station and there were even phones being poked under the toilet door when Summer sat down to pee.

After the chaos at the hotel in Manchester, the bands' digs for the night before the final were a closely guarded secret. There's rarely much news in the run-up to Christmas, so the live convoy of neon Rolls Royces had spread beyond 6point2 and got shown live on several news channels.

A crowd of over two thousand had gathered in front of the Emirates Stadium. The weather had turned bitter, but the gloved and hooded crowd didn't seem to mind as the convoy stopped by the gate to the stadium's underground car park. There were quite a few cops out to police the unplanned mob and they didn't seem happy when the bands wound down their windows.

Bodies hit the side of the cars and *Rock War*'s twelve remaining contestants found hands probing inside the windows, either with autograph books or just seeking a high five or handshake from their favourite contestant.

It was a popularity contest. Half Term Haircut got surrounded. Industrial Scale Slaughter had a crowd that was just as big, but it was all around one side trying to get Summer's attention. In the third limo, Frosty Vader dealt with a small-but-fanatical gathering, that seemed to confirm their status as the final's underdogs.

Noah got handed a teddy whose T-shirt bore the Frosty Vader logo, while Sadie picked up a Northern Ireland flag, which she trailed out of the window as they rode the last couple of hundred metres into the stadium's underground parking.

It was a gloomy space, with *Rock War*'s equipment and production trucks parked beneath the underside of the stadium seats. With the crowd safely locked outside, the twelve contestants stepped out and followed thick bunches of cabling down fifty metres of corridor. The light grew as they reached the mouth of the players' tunnel.

'Jesus,' Summer gasped, as she stepped out, taking in a football pitch covered in a protective blue matting, tens of thousands of red seats and a huge stage, sandwiched by loudspeakers stacked five storeys high.

A live crew from 6point2 had followed the band mates down the tunnel and a director urged them to start walking towards the stage. There were eighteen steps from the pitch to the stage and Lorrie was waiting as Summer reached the top.

'So,' Lorrie asked, sticking a microphone in Summer's face. 'Do you think you can win here tomorrow night?'

*

Jay really liked Bailey, but he still had feelings for Summer and after the whole Moirin mess he was wary of getting into anything else too quickly. School ended at one and the disco sounded lame, so they went to see a film. It was terrible, but they had fun giggling and pointing out holes in the plot. Bailey laughed so much that a lady sitting two rows behind shushed them, and then moved seats.

'Need a pee,' Jay said, as they headed out.

He checked his phone after he'd dried his hands and saw a text from one of the *Rock War* stage crew.

'Good news,' Jay said, when Bailey came out of the ladies. 'You know how all former *Rock War* bands and their parents are invited to the final tomorrow night? And I just got this text back, saying that seeing as me Adam and Theo share parents, there's enough space to bring a plus one.'

Bailey's jaw dropped. Jay grinned.

'So, can you think of anyone who might like to go to the final? And watch it all live, and probably meet the winners at the after-show party. And maybe take some photos and make certain Facebook friends from their old school a tiny bit jealous . . .'

'EEEEEEEEEEEEEEEEEEEEEEEEE!' Bailey squealed, so loud that about ten people looked around.

'So that's a yes then?' Jay asked wryly.

43. On A Sunbed

With an audience expected to exceed the 16.4 million who watched the semi-final, Channel Six are charging £400,000 for a 30-second ad slot during the Rock War *grand final.*

AdvertisingUK.com, December 23rd

'It's Christmas Eve, babes!' Lorrie told a crazy forty-eight-thousand-strong crowd, some of whom had paid up to £800 for a pair of scalped tickets. 'We thought we'd got rid of him, but Theo's back to kick off our final, with Summer Smith, singing *Rock War*'s very own Christmas number one!'

Dressed all in black, Theo came on from the left of the huge stage. Summer came on at the other side, barefoot in white. Fake snow wafted down as she blew the audience a kiss, while Theo sang the opening verse of the duet.

Jay was a hundred metres away in one of the plastic seats, directly outside the stadium's directors' box. Bailey was next to him, but his mind was with Summer on stage. He looked around at Adam, who sat in the next seat with one arm around his girlfriend, Meg.

'Remember how nervous she was at Rock the Lock?' Jay asked. 'She's a totally different person.'

'You're quite a fan, considering she gave you two black eyes,' Bailey noted waspishly.

'Can I join you?' someone asked from behind. The voice was so croaky that nobody recognised it until they looked around.

'Dylan, me darling!' Adam said, before introducing the girls.

The temperature was just above freezing and Dylan shivered as he breathed steam off his cup of tea.

'You don't look too good,' Adam noted.

'Touch of this flu that's going around,' Dylan lied. 'But don't worry, I think I'm past the contagious phase.'

Theo and Summer got a warm reception and ended their performance with a hug.

'You vote for this girl!' Theo told the crowd. 'Not those boring squares!'

The crowd in the stands was roaring as Lorrie came back on stage yelling, 'I think this is gonna be quite a night!'

Since it was the middle of the football season, the crowd weren't allowed on the pitch. This left an expanse of empty blue matting in front of the stage. The lighting changed, so that there was a single spot over the unoccupied judge's chair.

'It's all about the threes tonight,' Lorrie explained. 'Three bands performing three songs. We've also got three performances lined up by some of the biggest bands in rock, including our judges, Beth Winder and Jack Pepper.

'The format of tonight's final is slightly different to the previous rounds. The judges will each give their scores out of ten, and at the end of the show, the band with the lowest score will be eliminated. It will then be down to you at home to cast your votes for the winner.'

Lorrie gave a couple of seconds for the crowd to cheer.

'But the question everyone's been asking this week is, who is that third judge going to be?'

A pair of spotlights fired up from the far end of the stadium, lighting up a big yellow H in the centre of the pitch. While the audience in the stands heard chopper blades closing in, the screens beside the stage cut to a live shot from inside the helicopter.

There was a middle-aged man in the back seat of the chopper, dressed in ripped jeans and a trendy jacket with lots of zips. He wore a black knitted balaclava, like he was about to rob a bank, and the only clue to his identity were some tentacles of greying hair poking from the bottom of the mask.

'Who is he?' Lorrie asked.

Usually *Rock War* was timed out to the second and carefully planned in rehearsal. But with media attention so intense, this was a genuine secret. Lorrie was one of half a dozen people inside the stadium who knew, and she'd only been told because it would look massively stupid if she had no clue when the secret broke.

The chopper landed noisily and the hooded figure jogged across the covered pitch and up a temporary ramp in front of the stage. He went down on one knee, facing the crowd, as Lorrie stepped up behind. Since he hadn't played a gig or released a record since before most of the crowd were born, the reaction was muted as Lorrie peeled off the balaclava.

'I give you the lead man from one of the biggest bands of all time. Mr Jake Blade of Terraplane!'

His face wasn't recognisable after so long out of the spotlight, but every rock fan knew his band.

'Welcome to *Rock War*,' Lorrie said, as Jake found his feet.

'Good to be here,' Jake said, his rich Scottish accent ricocheting through the stadium's PA.

Up in the directors' box, Dylan cringed with embarrassment as a cameraman lined a shoulder cam up to his face.

'But you've actually been involved in *Rock War* for some time,' Lorrie said. 'As some *Rock War* trivia buffs may recall, your son, Dylan, is a member of the Pandas of Doom.'

The camera on Dylan went live, showing his tired face to the viewers at home and on the giant stage-side screens.

'Love you, son!' Jake shouted, as the audience cheered.

Dylan gave an awkward thumbs-up, as Jay reached behind his head to make finger horns.

Lorrie smiled, before continuing. 'But a little bird tells me you had another even more important role in *Rock War*. A financial one?'

'Ahh well,' Jake said, staring down modestly. 'You see, my boy was made up being in a TV show. I was proud as any parent would be. But then Rage Cola pulled their sponsorship, and the show was about to close down, so I chipped in with Channel Six and my pal Nick Cobb to keep things running.'

Lorrie took a step back and gave a little bow. 'Ladies and gentlemen, you are not *only* looking at one of the biggest rock stars of all time, you are literally looking at the man who saved *Rock War*. We are not worthy!'

Jake acted embarrassed. 'It's not been a bad wee investment,' he admitted. 'But to start with, I just put the money in for my son.'

'So you must have made a few quid out of this?' Lorrie asked cheekily.

'That I have,' Jake admitted. 'But I'm pleased to announce that I'll be donating my share of the money we made selling *Rock War* to the Americans to a bunch of kiddies' charities.'

'And I'm told that share is around twenty-two million pounds?'

'Something thereabouts,' Jake said modestly, as the audience roared. 'I also persuaded those tight wads at Channel Six to donate all the ticket money from tonight's final!'

This got the biggest cheer of the night so far.

'And our other judges, Beth and Jack, are going to perform tonight. So do you fancy giving us a song?'

Jake smiled. 'My band hasn't performed on stage together in twenty-two years, so we might be a bit rusty. But do you mind if Terraplane play a couple of tracks?'

The audience at home saw several cutaway shots of shocked faces, including those of the other two judges.

'You know, Jake,' Lorrie beamed as she wagged a finger. 'I think we might just be able to squeeze you in . . .'

Jake gave Lorrie a kiss, then started a brief walk towards the judges' bar.

'Now *that's* what I call an exclusive,' Lorrie said. 'But now it's time to get down to business, with the first song from our three finalists. I give you Cal, Sadie, Otis and Noah. It's Frosty Vay-derrrrrrrrrrr.'

44. Gorilla Fart Video

Trending on Twitter:
#Terraplane
#RockWarFinal
#GorillaFartVideo

Frosty delivered a kick-ass version of Black Sabbath's 'Paranoid', and after Beth told them they'd played it too safe in the semi, their new composition was full of static bursts, whale song and a lyric about a kid getting lost in a supermarket and being chased by giant crabs. The judges were positive, though their marks wouldn't come until after the bands returned to play their Christmas song.

Half Term Haircut were next. With Jet failing to reach the final, most felt that Jet fans were more likely to defect to Industrial Scale Slaughter's brand of high-speed thrash metal than Haircut's indie sound. To try and counteract this, they'd ditched suits for jeans and shoes for boots or scruffy All Stars.

The requirement to play a song by a rock supergroup, a new song written by the contestants and a Christmas song meant that Half Term Haircut couldn't play their hit 'Puff' for the third show running. Their set kicked off with an adequate cover of the Beatles' 'Revolution', but they'd never possessed great songwriting skills, and with Jay or Dylan no longer around to help, the Haircuts performed a track called 'Unknown Place' which went flat with the audience.

'Not your best effort,' Beth commented.

'Guys, I hate to be a downer,' Jake Blade added. 'But "Unknown Place" is a track that belongs in a screwed-up paper ball on your rehearsal room floor.'

There was a commercial break, then Beth Winder performed her only hit before Industrial Scale Slaughter took the stage. Michelle got the biggest laugh of the night so far, coming on stage with a half-metre flashing LED Christmas tree strapped to her head.

Unlike the other bands, the girls had the sense to kick off with their original song. It was a decent effort called 'Horny Skater Put That Away', then they really got the audience going with Summer and Michelle doing a duet of Metallica's 'Ride the Lightning'.

Terraplane were next on stage. They did two of their biggest tracks, but while their historic return was huge news, the reception inside the stadium was flat. Everyone was confident that they'd sell out their billion-dollar tour, but the tickets would be bought by middle-aged rock fans, not a teenaged *Rock War* audience who just wanted to hear the final songs.

Channel Six were determined to sell as many £400,000 ad slots as possible. With fewer contestants but an extended running time, the show started to drag as Lorrie stepped off stage and did a segment where she asked the audience how they thought it was going. Then one of the 6point2 presenters stood in the directors' box, asking former contestants who they hoped would win.

Finally, Frosty Vader took the stage for their Christmas song. Otis started off crooning a version of Bing Crosby's 'White Christmas', which quickly turned punk, with several off-colour adaptations to the lyrics.

'Seven points,' Jake Blade said.

Beth had criticised Frosty Vader for playing it too safe in the semi-final, but their original composition was anything but and she rewarded them with a nine. Finally, Jack Pepper gave them another seven, before sliding across the bar and taking his turn at singing his biggest hit.

'Twenty-four is a tough score to beat,' Lorrie said. 'Can Half Term Haircut do it?'

Making the three rock bands play a Christmas song was either the idea of a genius, who wanted to set an unusually complex challenge, or a total idiot, who didn't understand the awkward juxtaposition between hard-core rock and sappy Christmas songs.

While Half Term Haircut had stumbled with their original composition, they nailed the festive season. John Lennon's

'Happy Christmas (War is Over)' suited Owen's voice and the band's indie sound, and they made no attempt to alter a great song, even if it wasn't rock.

Jake gave them an eight, and given the average reaction to their original song Beth shocked everyone by handing out a nine. The camera cut to a shot of Frosty Vader looking nervous, as Jack gave his verdict. Since two out of three bands were going to the viewer vote-off, an eight or higher would give Half Term Haircut a spot.

'Sometimes I don't like it when a band simply makes an exact copy of an original song,' Jack began. 'But it can also be a beautiful thing to see a great song treated with respect. And I think that's *exactly* what you boys did.'

Jack held up a number nine and Half Term Haircut started yelling and hugging.

'And will it be Industrial Scale Slaughter or Frosty Vader who joins Half Term Haircut in the final audience vote?' Lorrie asked dramatically. 'You'll find out after this short break.'

*

Summer reckoned they'd done better than anyone else with their first pair of songs. But Industrial Scale Slaughter's sound meant they'd risk the judges' wrath if the band stepped back and let Summer sing another Christmas classic. But rocking out risked alienating the audience.

The girls' unconventional solution was to have Summer belting out the classic gospel hymn, 'Amazing Grace'. Some heavy rearrangement, with help from *Rock War*'s music director

Anthony, meant that the Industrial Scale Slaughter version came with a mass of crashing guitar and wild drumming.

Noah knew Frosty Vader were screwed the instant Summer opened her mouth, and he looked around to see Sadie shaking her head.

The crowd erupted as Industrial Scale Slaughter wound up their most explosive performance of the series, and the director cut super-close as Summer ended the song with tears streaming down her face.

'Win or lose,' Summer told the crowd emotionally, when she finally finished, 'this has been the most amazing five months of my life and I love you all.'

'If you want to come on tour and be Terraplane's backing singer, you've got the job,' Jake Blade told the screaming crowd from behind the judges' desk. 'But I wouldn't do that if I were you Summer, because your band mates are incredible too. There's only one score I can give. Ten out of ten.'

Beth drew wild cheers with a second ten, before the director cut to Jack.

'Half Term Haircut got the first ever perfect score earlier in the series,' Jack told the audience. 'And tonight, you girls banged your own perfect score home with a nine-inch-nail. Ten outta ten!'

The director flashed between shots of the three bands. Summer and the girls going crazy. A close-up of Noah looking upset as his band mates group hugged. But it wasn't just the eliminated band that looked shocked. Half Term Haircut had won more Battle Zone rounds than anyone else, but only one of their three songs had completely hit the mark tonight and the four clean-cut teens looked like they'd just had a tray of ice cubes dropped down their backs.

45. FTW

'Beth Winder ticked me right off tonight. Giving Half Term Haircut a nine was the biggest stitch-up I've seen all series. We've wound up with the final pair everyone expected, but those boys totally rode their luck . . .'

Irate caller on London Live Radio

***ROCK WAR* – ODDS TO WIN FINAL**

Industrial Scale Slaughter	7–5 Favourite
Half Term Haircut	3–2
Betforce.com	

After all the Saturday nights backstage, Jay found it odd spending the ninety-minute gap between the main and results shows as a spectator way up in the directors' box.

While the stands were packed with fans, none of the other boxes on the stadium's corporate level were out of use. Jay had enjoyed catching up with contestants he'd not seen in months, but the box was hectic inside, the outdoor seating area was freezing and it was hard to relax with 6point2's camera teams ready to pounce for live interviews. Bailey was happy being a fangirl and getting her photo taken with former contestants, so Jay snuck out for some quiet time.

The corporate boxes formed a complete ring around the middle tier of the stadium. Jay walked down the gently curved hallway that ran behind them. He kept wondering if he'd reach a locked door, or get sent back to the directors' box by stadium security, but the corridor was an unbroken circle and he was almost back where he'd started when he saw Dylan staring out of a window at a clear night view of the city.

'Where'd you spring from?' Dylan asked.

Jay shrugged. 'Stretching my legs.'

'Can you see St Paul's or anything from here?'

'Central London is south of here, and you're looking north,' Jay explained, before pointing. 'That's Hampstead, where Tristan and Alfie live. I'm from the scummy bit over there, where you see all those council blocks.'

'You been back to school?'

Jay nodded. 'Sucks.'

'I lied to my dad,' Dylan said. 'Spent the week at home, bored off my head.'

'Living at the manor is gonna be hard to top,' Jay said. 'You kept it close to your chest, about your dad being the secret investor.'

'I only found out a few weeks ago myself,' Dylan said.

'Seems like a cool guy,' Jay said. 'Wish my family was rich.'

'Money only does so much,' Dylan sighed. 'At least your mum gives a shit.'

Jay made sure nobody was close by before asking a question. 'Are you really OK? You don't look like yourself.'

'It's this cold,' Dylan said.

'Did you take that cocaine I sold you?'

Dylan felt a little shot of adrenaline. *Is it that obvious?*

'I was curious is all . . . I did try a couple of snorts, but I binned most of it.'

'Good to know,' Jay said. 'I'd feel terrible if I was responsible for something . . .'

'Like I said, the cold. Plus Terraplane have been rehearsing at our house, so it's been pretty noisy at night . . .'

Dylan's body language was off, making Jay suspect he was hiding something.

'If you ever need any help . . .' Jay said.

Dylan was irritated. 'Jay, I may puff the odd joint, but I'm not into hard drugs, OK?'

'I didn't say that you were,' Jay said, surprised by the strength of Dylan's indignation. 'I was just surprised by how rough you looked. Adam said exactly the same thing.'

Dylan had been lonely all week. He didn't want Jay to go away, but he didn't like being quizzed about his wellbeing, so he changed the subject to something that was certain to hold Jay's attention.

'Can I tell you something in confidence?'

'Always,' Jay said.

'My dad's not the great guy he made himself out to be on

stage,' Dylan explained. 'He didn't invest in *Rock War* because of me. He invested because his manager, Harry Napier, told him *Rock War* had to be a money-spinner if Karen Trim was sniffing around. As an afterthought, he also tried to rig the show so that I won.'

Jay gawped. 'You what?'

'That's why we survived four weeks ago when Eve was sick and Max played that godawful Africa song. Brontobyte got way more votes, but the Pandas stayed in. I went nuts when I found out. Told my dad to stop it, or else I'd splurge the whole story to the press.'

'Bombshell!' Jay gasped, as Dylan pulled his phone out and glanced around before opening up the QStat app.

'I made them put this on my phone, so that I could see that all future voting was a straight deal,' Dylan explained, as he keyed a login. 'I checked the voting about ten minutes ago. It's been a consistent ten to twelve per cent lead, right since the voting lines opened.'

Jay was shocked as he looked at the pie chart on Dylan's phone. 'Forty-four, to fifty-six,' he said.

Dylan smirked. 'If you're quick, you've got ten minutes to put a bet on.'

*

With a straight choice between winner and loser, *Rock War*'s producers struggled to drag out the show with highlights, interviews and even a charity appeal.

Finally there were eight teens, plus Lorrie, on the stage. The screens at the side of the stage flashed with *Results Counted*.

'I understand that it's been really close,' Lorrie told a crowd as silent as forty-eight thousand people are capable of being. 'I'm told that I'm being watched by twenty million people, which is making me a little nervous . . .'

At home, the viewers saw cutaway shots of the four girls stood in line, holding hands, while the Half Term Haircut bandmates formed a circular hug. Fireworks and streamers were set in the stage floor around both bands, but only one set was destined to go off.

'It's time,' Lorrie said, as a stage hand passed a gold envelope. 'The winner of *Rock War* two thousand and sixteen, is . . . coming up right after this commercial . . .

'I'm kidding, I'm kidding,' Lorrie continued. 'The winner is . . .'

'... Half Term Haircut!'

46. Uncle Harry

It was fingers-in-the-ears time as fireworks ripped across the stage. The lights switched to the performance area left of the stage and Half Term Haircut brought the house down as the victors finally got a chance to play 'Puff' over *Rock War*'s closing credits.

The last thing the viewers at home saw was a title card:

Have you got what it takes to win Rock War 2017?
Upload your band profiles from January 1st
rockwar.com

While the audience flooded into the streets, eager to get home before public transport shut down at midnight, crew, contestants, family and a couple of hundred VIPs kicked off a wrap party in the stadium's banqueting suite.

'How does it feel, coming so close?' a journalist asked Summer.

She'd prepared her answer well in advance. 'JLS and Olly Murs were runners-up in X *Factor*. Day's End were runners up on *Hit Machine*. Those guys prove that not winning isn't the end of the world.'

Lucy and Michelle were close by and crashed the interview screaming, 'The future's bright!'

'We'll be selling out stadiums when Half Term Haircut are playing holiday camps,' Coco added, before taking a swig of her Bacardi Breezer.

The girls laughed together as the interviewer went off to ask Frosty Vader the same questions. Karen Trim was being photographed fake-strangling Theo, as Summer tried to escape.

'Summer,' a photographer yelled. 'Come and join in.'

'Sorry, but I'm gonna piss myself!' Summer said, as she jogged out of the room.

She got collared again when she came out of the toilet. This time it was Karolina, introducing a man Summer had seen a couple of times at the manor.

'Harry Napier,' he said brightly. 'I run Wilton Music. I know you're tired, but I'm based up in Edinburgh, so I'd like to take you aside for a few moments while I have a chance.'

The hallway outside the banqueting suite had some leather benches, and Harry invited Summer to sit down.

'You were astonishing tonight,' Harry purred. 'There's not many fifteen-year-olds who can carry "Amazing Grace" like a three-hundred-pound gospel singer.'

'Thank you,' Summer said.

'You've got that once-in-a-generation voice. Like Janis

Joplin, or Amy Winehouse.'

'Didn't Amy Winehouse die of a drug overdose?' Summer asked.

'So did Janis Joplin . . .' Harry said thoughtfully. 'So maybe ignore that example . . . But my point is, as part of Jake Blade's deal to buy Venus TV, our company Wilton Music owns the recording rights for all the bands who entered *Rock War*. But I'd really like to launch you as a *solo* artist.'

Summer shook her head firmly. 'Coco, Lucy and Michelle are my best friends. I never asked to be the star . . .'

'Maybe you didn't ask, but you *are* a star,' Harry said forcefully. 'You don't belong in a thrash metal band, sweetheart. It's the musical equivalent of buying a Van Gogh painting and hanging it in a cupboard under the stairs.'

Summer pointed towards the banqueting room. 'Those girls did *everything* for me,' she said. 'They invited me to their houses. Gave me their clothes. Mr Wei's been paying two thousand pounds a *week*, to keep my nan in a nursing home while I was at the manor.'

'Mr Wei owns a very successful architectural practice,' Harry pointed out, as he slipped a folded sheet of paper out of his jacket and handed it across. 'Two grand a week is *nothing* to him.'

Summer opened the paper and saw that it was a set of particulars for a newly built bungalow a few miles from where Summer had grown up. It was priced at £265,000.

'It's part of a warden-assisted community,' Harry explained. 'So you'd be able to live with your nanna, but she can call on the warden if there's ever a problem, leaving you with the freedom to do gigs and be a normal teenager without worrying all the time. I'll also get Buick Partners on your team if social services start sticking their noses in.'

'I don't understand,' Summer admitted.

Harry smiled. 'I'm offering you a half-million-pound advance as a solo artist. Normally, only a third of a recording artist's advance is paid on signature of the contract. But I'm prepared to front-load it, so that you have enough to buy and furnish the house.'

Summer felt a lump in her throat. It was everything she'd ever wanted, wrapped in a poisonous shell.

'We'll start off with a couple of singles,' Harry explained. 'Then we'll release an album around Easter time and get you on the road, probably as the opening act for someone's arena tour.'

'I really appreciate the thought you've put into this, Mr Napier,' Summer said. 'But I can't abandon my friends.'

Harry grunted. 'Sweetheart, it's called the music *business* for a reason. I did market research on all twelve bands as soon as we invested in Venus TV. Three things came out of that research.

'The first was that Half Term Haircut had a more loyal fan base than any other band, so I'll have them working hard on their first album in the new year and I'm expecting them to make me a lot of money. The other two standouts were Theo, who's unfortunately been snapped up by the Yanks, and you.'

'I don't know . . .' Summer said.

'In our research, seventy-three per cent of *Rock War* fans said that they'd be *likely* or *highly likely* to buy a record released by Summer Smith. When we asked the same question about Industrial Scale Slaughter, that number drops to nine per cent.'

Summer pushed hair off her sweat-glazed face and sighed. 'Can I think it over? At the very least, I have to talk this over with my nan.'

'I'd be happy to arrange for someone to show you both the house,' Harry said. 'It's newly built, three bed, two bath. Nice fitted kitchen, microwave, double oven, American-style fridge-freezer, Bosch washer and dryer. I even checked on your route to school. The 53 bus stops a few hundred yards away, though a taxi may be more becoming for a young lady of your status . . .'

'Can we see it?' Summer asked guiltily.

Harry had put deep thought into the best way of separating Summer from her band mates, and he felt like he was winning the battle as a noisy cheer erupted from inside the banqueting room. He glanced at his gold Rolex and cracked a big smile.

'One minute past midnight,' Harry said warmly, as he stood up and patted Summer's shoulder. 'Happy Christmas, sweetheart. Go have fun with your friends and I'll sort out that house viewing for the twenty-seventh.'

Seven Months Later

47. Community Service

'Thank you, thank you. I'm Theo Richardson and this is Rock War, with you every Saturday between now and Thanksgiving. In a moment, my co-presenter Q Bott will be taking you live to the Rock War Penthouses in Las Vegas, to introduce the first of our sixteen bands and tell you what Rock War is all about. But to kick this show off with a bang, giving their first performance on US television in more than twenty years, I give you, the one, the only . . . Terraplane!'

American Network Television, July 2017

It was just past eight on a fine July Saturday as Summer Smith crossed the threshold of a swing park a couple of miles from her new home. Her hair was tied back and she wore grubby slip-on Vans, old jeans and a washed-out green hoodie. She got a scowl from Ted the supervisor as she handed over a little log book and a photo ID, issued by

Restorative Justice.

'You know the rules,' the moustached supervisor said. 'If you're more than ten minutes late, I have the right to send you home and make you come back another day.'

'I've *never* been late before,' Summer pleaded. 'My nan's not feeling too good. It took a while to get her sorted.'

The supervisor looked unhappy, but Summer was no trouble compared to the surly young men who copped the vast majority of community sentences.

'Just this once,' Ted said, as he took Summer's log book, 'I'll mark you down as arriving on time. *But* since you're last to arrive, you can do the worst job.'

'I don't mind,' Summer said brightly. 'Thank you.'

'Should be through with this lark in a couple of weeks,' Ted said, as he inspected Summer's log book. 'Only ten hours left to serve.'

Summer's lawyer had hoped she'd get off with a warning. But her profile as one of the stars of *Rock War* meant the magistrate decided to make an example, giving all four members of Industrial Scale Slaughter forty hours' community service for fare evasion, and sixty more for her role in the assault on Tina the train guard.

The little park was on a steep hill, bordering a covered reservoir. After donning knee pads and thick gardening gloves, Summer said hello to a couple of lads who were around most Saturdays, then dragged a set of gardening tools up a steep embankment.

The embankment was topped by a low brick wall that

separated the park from the reservoir. There were shrubs at the base of the wall and Summer's next five hours were to be spent picking litter, clipping back overgrown shrubs and weeding.

Some of the guys doing community service were lazy on principle and only worked if the supervisor stood right over them, but Summer found the hours passed quicker if she kept busy. Even with padding it was tough on the knees, but the worst part was that half the dogs in Dudley seemed to have used the wall as a toilet.

It took less than fifteen minutes to sweat through her hoodie. But she couldn't take it off, because she only had a T-shirt underneath and there was broken glass and spiked branches everywhere. Every few minutes, she had to take off one filthy glove and mop the sweat streaming into her eyes.

The only compensations were the fact that she only had today and one more Saturday, and Tim. The baby-faced seventeen-year-old iPhone-snatcher came by with a wheelbarrow every half-hour, taking the litter and plant cuttings away. His bum filled his jeans out very nicely, and he'd unbuttoned his plaid shirt to show off a six-pack that distracted Summer from shoulder ache and the fresh bug bite on her neck.

She was crawling backwards out of a bush when a shadow moved behind. But there was no squeak from Tim's wheelbarrow and she squinted over her shoulder at a small figure in mirrored sunglasses and gardening gloves.

'Wassup, traitor,' Michelle said sourly.

While Summer had returned to her old school after *Rock*

War, Mr and Mrs Wei had been concerned about the amount of education their girls had missed during the competition. They'd set up their daughters with four months of intense one-on-one private tutoring, before enrolling them into a posh private school in central Birmingham.

As a result, the closest Summer had come to Lucy and Michelle since *Rock War* ended was an exchange of scowls on the day of their court appearance.

'Hey,' Summer said warily. 'Since when do you work on this site?'

'Since I lobbed a brick at my dickhead supervisor at the canal last weekend,' Michelle explained. 'So how's the pop star lifestyle? That last single kinda vanished without trace. And wasn't your big-shot manager dude supposed to be setting you up with gigs?'

Summer cringed as she stumbled tiredly to her feet and held her arms out wide. 'My album got slated, my singles didn't chart,' she admitted. 'I've lost my three best friends, and Wilton Music doesn't even bother returning my calls any more. So, I guess I got *exactly* what I deserved for ditching the band.'

'Poor old you,' Michelle scoffed. 'Still managed to get yourself signed up by John Motion though. Heard he got your solo advance bumped to three quarters of a mil.'

'I emailed your dad,' Summer said. 'I offered to pay back every penny he spent looking after my nan.'

'My family wouldn't wipe their asses with *your* money,' Michelle sneered. 'For some people, it's not all about money.'

Summer felt a lump in her throat. She'd felt ashamed ditching her band mates in return for a fat cheque, but she knew she had to when she'd seen how perfect the bungalow was for her nan.

'It's a lot easier to be all snooty about money when you've got plenty of it,' Summer snapped.

'You're such a sly bitch,' Michelle shouted, before launching herself at Summer with a two-handed push.

Summer was heavier than her ex-band mate, but while the push only knocked her half a step back, the combination of stiff knees and stepping awkwardly on the handle of her shovel left Summer completely off balance.

Michelle maxed this by hooking her boot around Summer's ankle and giving her a second shove down the embankment.

Summer yelped as she felt herself falling. She landed hard on her shoulder and rolled several times down the embankment, sending a dozen sparrows into the air, before coming to a painful stop against the blackened remains of a bin melted by arsonists.

'I'll splatter you, dipshit,' Michelle screamed, as she grabbed Summer's shovel and charged downhill with it raised above her head.

Summer found her feet, stumbling into the arms of Tim, who'd abandoned his wheelbarrow and rushed over when he heard her scream. Ted the supervisor had also heard and got in Michelle's way. He was a big fellow, and while Michelle swung with all her might, he had no problem parrying the blow with a thick arm and then ripping the shovel out of her hand.

'I saw what you did to Summer,' Ted yelled. 'I'm sending you home and reporting you to your support officer.'

'Like I give a toss, ya hairy oaf,' Michelle shouted, before giving Summer the finger and storming out of the park in a hail of foul language.

48. The 2017 Jet

Half Term Haircut have just released their third straight UK number one single. A UK arena tour scheduled for the end of the year has already sold out, and now there are rumours that the band will be opening for Terraplane on the European leg of their tour.
ChannelSixNews.com, July 3rd 2017

Dressed in school uniform, Jay walked up the driveway of a sizeable semi-detached house, followed by his girlfriend Bailey, cousin Erin, plus his mates Tristan, Salman, and Tristan's little brother Alfie.

'Voilà,' Jay said, as he pushed the button on an electronic plipper attached to his door keys.

A metal garage door started to rumble, revealing a space big enough to fit two cars. The walls adjoining the house were lined with black sound-insulating foam. There was a rack with guitars, some amplifiers, basic recording equipment and

Babatunde waiting up back behind Big Len's shabby drum kit.

'You found the place OK?' Jay asked, as Babatunde gave him a high five.

'Twenty minutes on the tube,' Babatunde nodded. 'It's a nice area.'

'All those years of being povs,' Tristan said, catching a whiff of fresh paint as he admired the neat rehearsal space.

Erin and Tristan had been together for more than a year, and she gave his ear a friendly flick. 'Don't diss my family, bitch,' she told him.

Alfie was now in Year Eight. In the seven months since *Rock War* ended, his voice had broken, he'd spurted ten centimetres and he even had a zit just below his right ear.

'So selling that little chip shop paid for all this?' Alfie asked.

Erin explained. 'The pub and chippy belonged to me and Jay's grandparents and were in our family for over fifty years. But that area's getting all gentrified and a pizza chain offered stupid money to buy us out.'

'This is bigger than *your* new place though,' Tristan told Erin.

'Theo helped out,' Jay explained. 'He got some money for "Fairytale of New York", plus his *Rock War USA* deal and a bunch of modelling work.'

'Theo's ridiculously loaded,' Erin said, shaking her head. 'I still can't believe he got paid eighteen grand to model underwear . . .'

'All credit to the guy though,' Jay said. 'My mum didn't want to take any of his money, but he was like *first thing I want is my family to have somewhere nice to live.'*

'Theo's a decent guy if you stay on the right side of him,' Babatunde noted.

Erin nodded, then teased Tristan. 'You love him too, don't you sweetie-kins?'

'In my book, you don't stop being a dick just because you made a few quid,' Tristan grumbled.

Salman smirked. 'Just because he stuck your head down the toilet . . .'

'All right,' Jay said, trying not to laugh at the memory. 'Let's crack on.'

Jay had no appetite for playing music in the first three months after *Rock War*, and it wasn't just his housing situation that had changed when he returned. Theo was off to America, while Adam was all loved up with Meg and quit the band. Brontobyte had a similar situation when Tristan joined a rowing club and did the world a favour by giving up drums.

With both bands short-handed and the remaining members back on friendly terms, a merger seemed the obvious solution. Nobody liked the name Brontobyte, so the 2017 version of Jet was a five-piece. Babatunde on drums, Jay on lead guitar, Salman on bass and occasional vocals, and Erin on lead vocals. That left Alfie as a talented all-rounder, who could play keyboards, extra guitar, percussion and even occasionally make use of his newly broken voice as a backup singer.

While the band mates stripped off school blazers and plugged in, Tristan located the kitchen and got Cokes for everyone, while Bailey found some cushions the pair could sit on while they spectated. Jay's siblings Hank and Patsy wandered in to check on the big kids, but left when Jay told them they could only stay if they sat quietly and didn't keep running in and out.

'What we starting with?' Babatunde asked.

'"Fox on the Run",' Alfie said, as he tapped some buttons on a Yamaha keyboard. 'I think I've got the intro right.'

A high-tempo *wah-wah* sound came from a speaker.

'Nice one, Alfie,' Jay said. 'Everyone ready?'

'I don't think this mic is working,' Erin said.

Jay spent a couple of minutes checking some plugs and hunting through a plastic box for a spare microphone lead.

Babatunde tapped his sticks and counted the band in. Alfie began with his newly programmed intro and the guitars cut in perfectly. Salman and Erin combined on the vocal, and while the smallish space meant the drums were too dominant, it was clear that the tutors during *Rock War* boot camp had done their stuff. This was way more than a bunch of average teens jamming after school.

It was a very different Jet to the one that entered *Rock War*. While still underpinned by Babatunde's drums and Jay's lead guitar, Erin's vocal was silk to Theo's sandpaper. The addition of keyboards gave a more sophisticated sound, though whether that was an improvement depended upon your musical taste.

They'd been rehearsing for an hour and a bit when Jay's mum came in with a tray of nuggets, sausage rolls and oven chips.

'God you lot pong,' she complained, as sweating teens dived in. Then she turned to Jay. 'I just spoke to Len. He's moaning that you've ignored a text.'

'Pretty noisy in here,' Jay said, reaching into his pocket, then realising his phone was still zipped inside his school pack.

'Lovely new house,' Alfie told Jay's mum.

Jay finally found his phone trapped between the pages of a fat history textbook.

'Len, you beauty!' he shouted.

Erin peered over his shoulder as Jay read the message out loud. 'Gig confirmed. This Saturday. At The Cocoon in E8. Twenty-five pounds each plus up to fifteen pounds food and drinks.'

49. Slashed and Dirty

Summer hated the decision she'd had to make, but if you wound back time she'd do it again. The bungalow had loads more room than the flat and the neighbours were friendly old-timers who fussed over Summer.

With more money and no stairs to deal with, her nan – Eileen – had regained some independence, using an app on her new smartphone to order taxis and make her own way to doctors' appointments. She had enough money to get her hair done every Tuesday morning and attended a Wednesday afternoon social at a nearby church.

'How was club today?' Summer asked, as she took a dish of Tesco Finest lasagne out of the oven.

Eileen went into great detail about a lonely guy called Fred whose son had been rushed to hospital and major scandal involving two women who'd been eating all the jam ring biscuits without making their forty pence contribution to biscuit club.

It wasn't exciting stuff, but Summer loved it, because for years Eileen had frequently gone days without talking to anyone but her.

'And how was school?'

'School's school,' Summer shrugged.

It had been hard work catching up after *Rock War*, but she'd had a good report, predicting A and B grades in next summer's GCSE exams. Socially, she got even more attention from boys now that she could get her hair done professionally and had a uniform that didn't comprise wrecked Primark pumps, laddered socks and a blouse with two missing buttons and reminders of a leaky biro.

But she'd not found close friends to replace her band mates, and when it came to talking about serious stuff, Facebook calls and WhatsApp convos with *Rock War* pals like Sadie, Dylan and Babatunde were more meaningful than anyone she saw face to face.

Homework and looking after Eileen took up a lot of Summer's evenings, but she didn't have band stuff any more and she'd partly filled that gap by taking up running. She'd bought proper running gear and had a fantasy where she ran a 10K for charity and raised heaps of money from all of her non-existent friends. For now though, it was just something she did for an hour, between stacking the dishwasher and starting on homework.

It was a beautiful sunny evening and Summer nodded to a couple of regular runners as she did a big circuit of the local park. Her favourite part was taking a couple of mouthfuls from a drinking fountain at the park's highest point and then belting downhill as fast as she dared. If the wind was in her face it was even better.

For the first week she'd started off part running, part walking. As Summer's fitness improved she was able to run three, then five kilometres, and she was reaching the point where she was thinking of extending her current six-and-a-bit-kilometre circuit.

'I've got you a jar of my jam,' Paula, who lived just inside the sheltered housing's barred gate, said.

Summer apologised for dripping sweat as she popped inside and saw Paula's kitchen table covered in dozens of jars of home-made jam.

'Would you like some iced water?'

Summer felt guilty, because Paula always seemed lonely. 'I've got an English essay,' Summer said. 'Maybe you can come round for dinner on Sunday, if your daughter's not visiting?'

Summer ran her last two hundred metres holding a pot of still-warm jam. She was reaching for the front door when a voice came from behind a little hedge.

'Hey, Summer.'

She flew backwards, dropping her key on the front path. 'Dylan?' she gasped.

'I rang the bell,' he explained, as he stood up. 'I can hear the telly inside.'

'My nan nods off after dinner. And you're a long way from home.'

Dylan tried not to look at Summer's sweaty cleavage. He'd grown a couple of centimetres since she last saw him, but his face was thinner. His hoodie seemed to hang off and was all stained around the neck.

'Is that blood?' she gasped. 'And you've got a black eye.'

'I've had a bit of bother,' Dylan said nervously, as Summer picked up her key. 'My dad's away on tour. I didn't know where else to go.'

'Don't you have a bag or anything?'

'If this is weird I'll go away,' Dylan blurted, as he turned his back.

'You're not going *anywhere*,' Summer said firmly. 'You've come all the way from Scotland . . . I'm not turning you away, but I'm just back from a run. So I'm all sweaty and . . . I mean, why didn't you call first?'

'Are you OK, Summer?' Eileen asked, raising her voice over the TV and keeping one hand on the necklace with the button she could use to call the warden.

'It's fine, Nan. It's Dylan Wilton.'

Dylan kicked off filthy trainers and Summer realised he hadn't showered in a while as she closed the front door.

'I wondered where you'd got to,' Summer said. 'I was going to send a message asking how you were.'

'I've switched off my phone,' Dylan said. 'I don't want people knowing where I am. Don't tell anyone I'm here.'

'What people?' Summer asked, as she caught another look at the neck injury. It had scabbed over and the dry blood made it hard to tell how serious it was, but the long straight cut was clearly a knife wound. 'You've been slashed. Who slashed you?'

'Summer, what happened to Dylan?' Eileen shouted from the living room. 'Do I need to call the police?'

'No, please,' Dylan said. 'If you don't want me here I'll go, but don't call the cops.'

Summer put a hand on Dylan's shoulder. 'Nobody is saying they don't want you here. You're one of my best friends and I want to help you. Come and sit in the living room. Try to calm down and tell me what happened.'

Dylan was a scared, grubby little boy as he sat on the sofa in the living room. One hand trembled slightly.

'I was getting bullied at Yellowcote,' Dylan explained. 'I've always hated it there, and it's been ten times worse since *Rock War* ended. So my dad's on tour and doesn't even answer messages. In the end I got so sick of it and ran away. I got a night bus to Edinburgh and these guys – I think maybe they recognised me. I was in the station waiting for the first train and they pulled a knife. I tried to run, but he cut me. Then they gave me a kicking and took my bag and everything.'

Dylan pulled up his hoodie, showing big bruises on his ribs.

'I couldn't go to the cops,' Dylan explained. 'They'd have just sent me back to Yellowcote.'

'You poor love,' Eileen said warmly. 'I think the first step is to get yourself cleaned up. Then get those filthy clothes washed and dried.'

Summer smiled, putting on her practical hat now that the shock had worn off.

'You can be the first guest in our spare bedroom,' she told Dylan. 'Though we haven't got any clothes that'll fit you, so you might have to wrap yourself in a bedsheet until yours come out of the dryer. Have you eaten?'

'I had a Snickers on the train, but got no appetite. I'm actually kinda queasy.'

'I got a new duvet and some covers for the spare room at Debenhams. I can dig out a spare toothbrush and deodorant,' Summer said, grabbing Dylan's hand as she saw his bottom lip trembling. 'God knows how we're going to fix this, but you'll feel better once you're clean and rested.'

A tear streaked down Dylan's face as he squeezed Summer's hand. 'I'm sorry to barge in like this,' he sobbed. 'I just couldn't think of anywhere else I could go.'

50. Nappy Night

Once a month The Cocoon club put on an alcohol-free nappy night. It was supposedly for thirteen- to seventeen-year-olds, though nobody older than fifteen would be seen dead there.

The atmosphere was lively, but the parents were dropping off kids who'd yet to master dressing grown up. Girls had trowelled on the make-up and struggled with heels, while a no jeans, no sportswear rule meant a lot of lads wore the bottom half of their school uniform, or something bought for a family wedding that didn't quite fit any more.

There was a DJ until nine, a chubby nineteen-year-old who called himself ZeroP and who'd got the gig by virtue of his dad owning the club. There were two hundred teens in a room that could take twice that many. A few had coupled up, but mostly groups of boys stood around the edge holding plastic Coke cups, while girls danced in the middle, or queued for the toilets.

'Where's Theo?' a lad heckled, as Jet took to a cramped

corner stage that all but left Jay and Erin's toes hanging off the front.

'Theo's round at your house, shagging your mum,' Erin shouted back.

The boy got teased by all his mates as Jet kicked off playing the always dependable White Stripes track 'Seven Nation Army'. The last time Jet played, it had been to eighteen thousand, with fifteen million watching on TV and a shot at stardom at stake. Now they were playing to two hundred, for twenty-five quid each.

To start, the girls who'd been dancing for the DJ backed off, so everyone was around the edges. By the third track a couple of groups of rowdy boys had started jumping around in front of the stage. One lad went flying and rival groups faced off for long enough to raise the attention of fierce-looking security staff.

But rather than put kids off, a lot of other boys in the room seemed to take this as a battle call and there were soon about fifty boys forming a rowdy mosh pit in front of the stage. There was plenty of space, so girls joined in further back.

The *Rock War* format meant that neither Jet nor Brontobyte had ever performed more than three songs live. The Cocoon had scheduled them to play for an hour and they were sweat-soaked in half that time.

As the set wore on, a virtuous cycle developed between band and audience. As more kids danced, Jet played better. As Jet played better, more people danced and the audience of self-conscious young teens started to relax. When you were hot and breathless after dancing like an idiot for twenty minutes, it felt like less of a massive deal to smile at the girl beside you at the bar and say *hey* . . .

There were shouts for an encore when Jet's hour was up and ZeroP looked annoyed as Jet played an extra fifteen minutes. When the encore ended, Babatunde, Alfie and Salman jumped off the front of the little stage and had no problem finding girls keen to talk to them.

Since Jay and Erin had partners, they stayed back and helped Len start clearing their gear.

'Bloody great set,' Len shouted over a deafening rumble of EDM. 'The way you got 'em going, you're probably gonna be responsible for a wave of teen pregnancies.'

It was quieter out by the van as the club's owner, Muhammed, shook Jay's hand. 'You're welcome back next month,' he said, as Len wheeled out a trolley loaded with Babatunde's drums.

Muhammed counted five twenties out of a Gucci wallet.

'You said twenty-five each,' Len said sternly.

'But the band only had four members on TV,' Muhammed said. 'So it's a hundred, however you choose to split it.'

Len towered over the club owner. 'I told you it was five on the phone,' he said firmly. 'And the way they had your crowd jumping up and down, you must have sold an extra five hundred quid's worth of drinks.'

The tension subsided as Muhammed pulled out an extra thirty, and Len gave him a fiver in change.

'There's your first lesson in *real* rock music,' Len told Jay, as

Muhammed headed off. '*Every* owner and promoter will try and dick you over.'

Erin came out smiling as Jay and Len headed back inside. 'You should see Alfie,' she grinned. 'He's got a girl on each arm, like some gangsta pimp!'

*

Summer lent Dylan a hundred quid and he went into town while she was at school to pick up a few clothes. Both Summer and Eileen urged him to go to hospital and get the cut on his neck checked out, but he insisted it was fine.

Summer had her last five hours' community service on Sunday morning. She bought a celebratory cream cake in Tesco on the way home and was surprised to find the smell of a roast when she came through the front door.

'Who knew a rich boy like you could cook?' Summer said, as she found Dylan in the kitchen. He'd combed and gelled his hair. He was still too thin, but completely different to the mess that rocked up on the doorstep two days earlier.

'It's only lamb chops from the freezer,' Dylan said, sounding relaxed. 'Your nan helped with the timings and peeled the veg.'

'I'm gross,' Summer said, pointing to grass-stained trackie bottoms as she put the cake in the fridge. 'I need a shower.'

Paula from down the street joined them for dinner. They all played Scrabble after scoffing the cream cake and Eileen won by six points.

'I wish I could hang here forever,' Dylan told Summer, a couple of hours later.

He stood in the open doorway of her bedroom as she rested on her bed. 'I'm not distracting you from homework or something, am I?'

Summer was flat out and smiled. 'Back and knees are killing me, is all.'

'There's nobody who loves me the way you and your nan love each other,' Dylan said thoughtfully.

'I'm sure your dad loves you,' Summer said. 'Nobody ever bought a TV talent show for me.'

Dylan laughed. 'But all I ever wanted was a bit of attention. And maybe not to be shipped off to boarding school . . .'

'You never talk about your mum,' Summer noted.

Keen to change the subject, Dylan took a half step into the room and pointed at an acoustic guitar tucked between Summer's desk and the far wall.

'Are you learning?' he asked. 'You kept that quiet.'

'I shouldn't have wasted money on it,' Summer said, sighing. 'I did two lessons with this horrible Dutch woman and gave up . . .'

'Can I?' Dylan asked, as he reached to grab the guitar.

Summer nodded and he effortlessly strummed a piece of classical guitar.

'You're so good I *hate* you,' Summer said, burying her face. 'Was that Spanish?'

'It's a piece by Mozart, adapted for guitar,' Dylan said. 'I'm not a horrible Dutch woman, so I can give you lessons if you want.'

'Is there any instrument you can't play?' Summer asked.

'Bagpipes are tricky,' Dylan smiled, as he sat on the chair at Summer's desk. 'But anyone can learn an instrument with practice. Your voice is a gift.'

Summer was flattered, as she sat up and crossed her legs. She was barefoot and Dylan thought her toes were stupidly sexy.

'I'm done with music,' she said. 'Stupid competitions and an album everyone takes the mickey out of.'

'You're not dumb, you're brilliant.'

'Have you *heard* my album? Q and NME both gave it one star.'

'It's an abomination,' Dylan admitted. 'But that's because my idiot godfather, Harry, totally ignored your strengths. He tried to turn you into some tacky Britney Spears wannabe and make a quick buck. If you went into a studio with me, I'd give you a totally different sound. Like, a proper soul singer. Maybe a jazz band, and some simpler tracks where it's just your voice accompanied by a guitar.'

'I know you're talented,' Summer said. 'Jay and Owen both said you were better at producing and arranging than the professionals working on *Rock War*. But I'm not joking about being done with music. I got what I wanted: a good place to live with my nan and some financial security. But I don't miss all the headaches that came with it.'

'Financial security,' Dylan scoffed. 'Where's your *passion*?'

Summer riled up, reminded of her row with Michelle a week earlier. 'People with money always say that,' she snapped. 'Maybe when I'm older, or something. Right now, I'm very happy being Summer the schoolgirl. Keeping out of the limelight, trying to get good grades . . .'

'Waste of an amazing voice,' Dylan said. 'But I totally get where you're coming from. And who am I to go dishing out advice when you seem sorted and my life is a shambles?'

51. Cheque Mate

Jay panicked as his mum knocked on the door of his attic bedroom. 'Yeah,' he said, as he straightened his covers and kicked shoes and junk off the floor. 'Come in.'

It had turned even hotter, so the roof windows were wide open. 'You get a nice breeze up here,' Heather said, as she stepped in, eyeing the mess on the floor. 'You got a letter.'

'Really?' Jay said. He never got mail and he was paranoid that it was something from his school as he grabbed it. But surely they'd address that to his mum?

'It's messy over there,' Jay blurted, as his mum stepped deeper into the room. 'Mind your head.'

Heather looked down at the floor and smirked as she kicked a foot. 'Good afternoon, Bailey,' she said cheerfully.

'Ahh,' Bailey said awkwardly, as she rolled over, dressed only in her bra and some shorts. 'Hi, Mrs Richardson.'

'We were doing homework,' Jay said. 'It's just that it's hot.'

'You've got lipstick on your cheek,' Heather lied.

'I'm not wearing lipstick,' Bailey said, but by the time she'd pointed this out, Jay had incriminated himself by wiping his face.

With three boys older than Jay, Heather was a realist when it came to her prospects of stopping teenaged kids having sex. But she didn't like the fact that Bailey had sneaked into the house behind her back.

'Grounded, one week,' Heather said.

Jay knew he'd cop worse if he made a fuss. 'We were just snogging.'

'*Please* don't tell my dad,' Bailey begged.

Heather smiled. 'There's condoms in the boys' bathroom any time you need 'em.'

'Mum,' Jay gasped, flushing red with embarrassment.

'We're not having sex,' Bailey said truthfully.

But Heather liked how the two teenagers were squirming. 'I've got a sex manual Bailey can borrow so you know you're doing all the different positions properly. Len keeps a few Viagra by the bed if there's any problems in that department . . .'

Jay was horrified, until he saw his mum's wicked smile and realised she was just trying to freak them out.

'I want a normal mum,' he joked.

'You're not a bad kid, all things considered,' Heather said. Then she looked at Bailey. 'Put your gear on. You can hang out downstairs or in the garden, but not up here.'

'Sorry,' Jay said, as his mum left and Bailey started looking for her blouse. 'She's crazy.'

'She's pretty cool, actually,' Bailey said. 'If my dad caught us like that I'd be grounded till I left for uni.'

'So you wanna watch a movie or something downstairs?'

'Better go,' Bailey said. 'Got my geography project to write up for Monday.'

After a goodbye grope, Jay found himself sitting on his bed in shorts and a T-shirt, feeling pretty lucky to have a girl like Bailey and only slightly pissed off that he was grounded. Then he remembered why his mum had come up in the first place.

The letter wasn't from school, because the franking mark said *Edinburgh*. Inside were about six sheets of folded A4 paper. The first sheet was a letter. It was on *Wilton Music* headed notepaper with a tear-off cheque at the bottom of the page.

Dear Mr Thomas
Please find your royalty statement and attached cheque for the period January to July 2017. If you have any queries regarding this matter, please call the Wilton Music Edinburgh office between 9am and 5pm Monday through Thursday.
Yours,
Morag McGovern
Head of Royalties

Jay's eyes practically came out on stalks when he saw the amount. *Pay Jay Ellington Thomas, the sum of, Thirty-one thousand, eight hundred and sixty-three pounds, only.*

'Only,' Jay gasped to himself, as his heart raced. It surely had to be some kind of mistake.

*

Summer got home an hour late, because two girls started fighting in history class. Then the class kicked off while their teacher was out of the room dealing with the fighters and the head of year came in, read the riot act and gave detention to the whole class.

So Summer wasn't in the best mood as she came up the driveway. She vented to Dylan about the injustice of getting detention when she'd just been sitting quietly at the back, after which he cheered her up with a hug and a reminder that it was less than two weeks until summer holidays. Then he surprised her by giving back the hundred quid she'd lent him to buy clothes and he gave her a little gift, in a small plastic bag from a shop called MK Music.

'Milton Keynes?' Summer noted, as she saw the address on the bag.

'I had a cash card inside my jacket that those assholes didn't get when they ripped my wallet and phone. But if my dad has the cops looking for me, they'll trace where I use my card, so I took the train to Milton Keynes and drew cash there.'

'You really are a proper little fugitive, aren't you?' Summer teased, as she looked into the bag at her gift.

'I know you said you want nothing to do with music for a while,' Dylan said warily, as Summer pulled out a rectangular box. 'It's a high-quality digital recorder, with a pair of microphones. It plugs into a phone or tablet, and there's an app that turns it into a mini recording studio. It's not studio quality, obviously, but if you know how to set up the microphones you can record a damned-fine demo.'

'Maybe you should take it back,' Summer said. 'Was it expensive?'

Dylan looked sad. 'Not for the guy whose dad is set to earn over three hundred million for a tour this year. I know you've had a crappy day and bad experiences with music. But there are things I can show you. I can make a demo with your voice and that acoustic guitar. It won't be anything like that horror show pop album Harry made you release . . .'

Summer looked worn-out. 'Guess I've got no community service this Saturday.'

'I've got a couple of song ideas we can kick around,' Dylan said excitedly. 'And it's just a demo with an acoustic guitar. It'll take two hours, three tops. If I don't persuade you after that, I swear I'll *never* pester you about music again. Deal?'

Summer cracked a slight smile. 'Deal.'

52. Supercop

'I can't go to yours, I'm grounded,' Jay told Salman, as he came out of the school gates after last lesson.

'Is it true you gave Bailey crabs?' Tristan teased.

'Your mama,' Jay said, grinning.

'This sucks,' Salman said. 'Bailey and Erin are on a field trip. We could have just hung out as guys, like old times.'

'You *seriously* need a girlfriend,' Jay noted. 'What happened to that chick you snogged at The Cocoon?'

'Seeing *Chequered Flag Five* with her on Saturday,' Salman said proudly. 'And don't try to wuss out by changing the subject.'

Jay shook his head. 'I'm grounded and my mum's like a supercop these days. She's got way too much time on her hands now she's not running the chippy.'

'She'll probably get pregnant again,' Tristan teased.

'Is that even possible?' Salman asked. 'Your ma must be like, fifty or something.'

'Forty-seven,' Jay said flatly, not rising to Tristan's bait.

They'd reached the end of the street. Tristan was going left with Salman. Jay had to go right to catch the Tube up to his new digs in Barnet.

Jay probably could have gotten away with going to Salman's if he'd only stayed a couple of hours and told his mum they were doing homework, but the truth was his mind had been focused on the thirty grand. He'd not bragged to anyone in case it was a mistake, and he jogged all the way from Totteridge station to his house.

Jay had to duck Hank and some playmates having a water fight as he came up the driveway. Len was in the living room, with his feet on the coffee table, listening to music on a set of headphones. Jay's stapled royalty statement was spread out on the arm.

'Did you call the record company?' Jay asked.

Len took the cans off and cracked a big smile. 'The good news is it's really your money,' he said.

'Awesome,' Jay said. 'What's the bad news?'

Len laughed. 'There isn't any, I was just being dramatic.'

'Did they explain the gobbledegook on the statement?'

'Do you remember your song "Strip"?'

Jet had only played 'Strip' once, during the *Rock War* quarter-final. The track had come out of the same jam session where he'd given Half Term Haircut the idea for their hit 'Puff'. Both songs were based on a riff that Jay had created, and since Haircut's songwriting skills were modest at best, Jay still occasionally tormented himself, wondering whether the outcome of *Rock War* would have been different if he hadn't given the eventual winners the basis of their first big hit.

'How is "Strip" making money?' Jay asked. 'It wasn't even released as a download.'

Len smiled. 'Apparently one of the American TV bigwigs who was bidding to buy *Rock War* heard you playing "Strip" on the quarter-final. She thought it would be a good fit as the theme song for a new comedy drama called *Tenured*.'

'And they're paying us money?' Jay said, grinning as he Googled *Tenured* on his phone. This came up with hundreds of results led by *Judd Marsh shines as Lebowski-esque college professor in new HMC bittersweet stoner comedy* . . .

'I don't think it's been on yet,' Len explained. 'Morag said the show premieres in a few weeks. The money you've been paid is for acquiring exclusive rights to the song you wrote, plus adaptation rights for an acoustic version that will play over the end titles. Adam, Theo and Babatunde will also be getting money for playing on the record, though not as much as the songwriter. And you'll all get royalties every time the show runs.'

'How much?'

'Morag said it's a thousand and something dollars for every episode made, then there's a royalty every time it's shown. She said she'd email the *Tenured* contract over, but she was having trouble locating the paperwork.'

'So are they going to release it as a download?' Jay asked, as he tapped the *video* button on his Chrome browser.

The first video was a trailer for *Tenured* on HMC's YouTube channel. Jay hit *play* and turned up the volume, hearing Babatunde's unmistakeable drums and a voice-over about a stoner professor, who'd blackmailed his way to a tenured professorship, and who was simultaneously growing marijuana while hopelessly in love with a twenty-year-old student.

'Bloody hell,' Len said, smiling as Jay moved around so he could see.

Jay was buzzing. 'Even if I never see another penny, thirty grand will pay my uni fees. And if the show's a hit . . . I mean, shows like *Modern Family*, they wind up making *hundreds* of episodes.'

Heather came in from the kitchen, smiling. 'There's a rumour going around that I've got another wealthy son,' she grinned, before putting her arms around Jay and giving him a kiss.

'But how come nobody from Wilton Music told us this was happening?' Jay asked. 'Shouldn't they be releasing the single? Maybe even getting us interviews about the show . . .'

'There are a lot of bullshitters in the music biz,' Len said. 'But Morag was refreshingly honest. She told me that a year ago Wilton Music handled Terraplane back catalogue and a couple of other dinosaur bands with a staff of three. Now they've got Terraplane on a billion-dollar tour, Half Term Haircut exploding, twelve more bands to promote for *Rock War* season two and the whole shambles with Summer Smith. They're short-staffed, and the careers of Jet and the other losing bands from *Rock War* season one are way down their priority list.'

'But it could be Jet's big break in the States, couldn't it?' Jay asked. 'If one of our songs is the theme to a hit new show, and our former lead singer is hosting their version of *Rock War* . . .'

'You know what I think?' Len said. He was liked by all his stepkids, but his tone was unusually firm. 'If you have a hit, you have a hit. But your head is shooting up in the clouds, fixating on instant success and some Yank TV show that might flop and get cancelled.

'Look at what happened with Summer. She takes the big bucks, gets partnered with an absolute dickhead producer, puts out a poor album and now she's a fifteen-year-old has-been. You *need* to get in that garage and rehearse three times per week. You need to write great songs. If you play as well as you did at The Cocoon last Saturday, you'll build a following and I'll be able to get you better gigs and start building a *real* fan base.

'I know the last thing someone your age wants is some boring adult telling you to buckle down, work hard and be patient. But this new incarnation of Jet is genuinely excellent. And if you want real success, rather than some one-hit TV bullshit, you gotta stay humble and grind it out, one gig at a time.'

Len was surprised to see that Jay was smiling at him.

'How can Jet fail with a great manager like you?' Jay said cheerfully. Then he turned cheekily to his mum. 'Now I'm rich, can I buy my way out of being grounded?'

53. The Whole Truth

It was a sunny Friday evening as Dylan and Summer sat on a blanket on the back lawn with a guitar, the digital recorder linked to Summer's phone and a jug of iced tea.

Dylan strummed The Vaselines' 'Jesus Doesn't Want me for a Sunbeam'. Summer's voice was perfect, as always, but she kept mixing up the lyric and getting the giggles. Eileen sat on the patio in her wheelchair. She'd had a bad day with her asthma, but her head bobbed behind her oxygen mask and she had a huge smile when Summer finally sang a complete take.

'That voice . . .' Eileen purred, as she lifted off her mask.

'Do you think she should give up singing, Mrs Smith?' Dylan asked.

'I think she's a clever girl who can do whatever she wants,' Eileen said. 'I'm going inside for *EastEnders*.'

'You want a push?' Dylan asked politely.

'I'll manage,' Eileen said.

Summer lay back on the blanket as Dylan put the guitar

down. She put a hand on his leg.

'I really like having you around,' she said.

Dylan expected some sting. Like, *but you have to go back and face the music*, but she just tailed off and he lay down beside her, looking at a low sun as the *EastEnders* theme wafted out of the living room.

Dylan thought about kissing Summer, but he didn't have the guts and instead it was Summer who slid across the blanket, so she was resting against his chest with her toes touching his ankle.

'I've still got my *Rock War* social media,' Summer said. 'Maybe I could upload one of the demos?'

'Wait a while,' Dylan suggested. 'Give it a few months for memories of the album-of-doom to fade. But my dad's company owns your recording rights. So maybe I can twist Uncle Harry's arm and let him give you another shot. There's a great studio at my house in Scotland . . .'

Dylan tailed off and Summer sensed that he was choking something back. 'What's wrong?'

'It's kinda perfect here with you,' he said. 'But this isn't my real life.'

'Everyone has problems,' Summer said, as she propped herself on one elbow, and gently ran her finger across the long scab on his neck. 'I'll be around, even if you have to go back to living in Scotland.'

And then she kissed him.

*

It was three a.m. when the doorbell rang. They were banging

on the door, as Summer sprinted out of her room, pulling on a bathrobe.

'Who is it?' she yelled.

'Police,' a woman shouted. 'Open the door, now.'

'What happened?' Summer asked, catching a glimpse of a police car and van parked out front as she jogged along the hallway. 'I'll be there in two seconds.'

'What's going on?' Eileen asked from her bed.

'Nan, stay where you are,' Summer yelled, undoing the bolt on the front door as the cops pounded on the door again.

'Step back, hands in the air!' the woman shouted, as two male cops charged into the hallway. They were all done up with riot helmets and protective vests and Summer yelped as a size-thirteen boot mashed her toes.

'Is Dylan Wilton here?' the female cop asked.

'He's in the spare room, at the end.'

Eileen opened her bedroom door and saw the two burly cops running past.

'Nan, I told you . . .' Summer said anxiously.

The two cops burst into Dylan's room. 'Police!'

'Window's open, he must be out the back,' the other one shouted.

Since Dylan wasn't athletic, he hadn't been able to scale the garden fence and came scrambling around the side of the bungalow in his boxer shorts. The female cop closed up and barged him. He bounced into the wooden fence and stumbled face first into a tangle of shrubs.

'Got him,' the officer yelled, as she dragged Dylan out of

the bushes and on to the front drive.

The officer was all bulked up with her protective gear, while Dylan looked skinny and pathetic. His boxers got snagged and he stumbled before the officer slammed him face first into the driveway.

'Hands behind your back,' the officer shouted, as she pulled cuffs off her belt.

Summer rushed out. 'He just ran away from school,' she shouted, as one of the other officers dragged her back. 'This is ridiculous.'

'If that's what he told you, he's a big liar,' the officer said as he jerked Summer back. Then he shouted to his colleagues. 'Search the house.'

'No,' Dylan shouted as his captor yanked him to his feet, handcuffed. 'Don't trash their house, they're nothing to do with this. The drugs are in the kitchen, taped to the underside of the sink.'

'Check under the kitchen sink,' the female officer yelled.

'What drugs?' Summer shouted, stepping up to Dylan as the officer let her go.

His arm was bleeding where it had scraped along the fence and tears were streaking down his face.

'I didn't get mugged,' Dylan confessed tearfully. 'I was doing a lot of coke. I tried to buy drugs off this guy and he slashed my neck. But he tripped, and I stabbed him and stole his gear.'

'Cocaine?' Summer gasped, as she froze to the spot. 'I . . .'

'I'm sorry I lied to you,' Dylan sobbed. 'I shouldn't have dragged you into this, but I didn't know where else to go.'

'Found the drugs,' an officer shouted from inside the house. 'Looks like half a kilo, at least.'

Dylan looked so pathetic. Part of Summer wanted to hug him, part of her wanted to slap his face. But she could do neither, because the cops were dragging him round to the back of their van.

Is Dylan heading for jail?

What will Jake Blade spend 94 million dollars on?

Will Theo make it big in the US of A?

Is Jay really happy with Bailey?

Can Half Term Haircut get any more smug?

Can Jet fight their way back to the top?

Find out in **Rock War: Crash Landing** – *coming soon!*

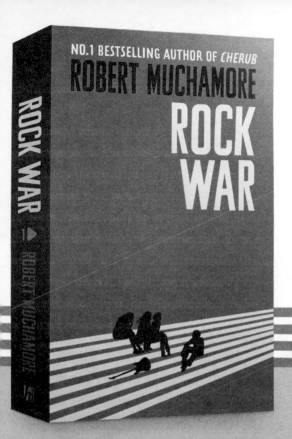

MEET JAY. SUMMER. AND DYLAN.

JAY plays guitar, writes songs for his band and dreams of being a rock star. But seven siblings and a rubbish drummer are standing in his way.

SUMMER has a one-in-a-million voice, but caring for her nan and struggling for money make singing the last thing on her mind.

DYLAN'S got talent, but effort's not his thing ...

These kids are about to enter the biggest battle of their lives. And they've got everything to play for.

ROCKWAR.COM

JAY, SUMMER, DYLAN and their bands are headed for boot camp at Rock War manor. It's going to be six weeks of mates, music and non-stop partying as they prepare for stardom.

But the rock-star life of music festivals and glitzy premieres isn't all it's cracked up to be. Can the bands hold it together long enough to make it through the last stage of the competition, or will there be meltdown?

THEY'VE GOT EVERYTHING TO PLAY FOR.

Hodder
Children's
Books

Also available
as an ebook

ROCKWAR.COM

THE ESCAPE
Robert Muchamore

Hitler's army is advancing towards Paris, and amidst the chaos, two British children are being hunted by German agents. British spy Charles Henderson tries to reach them first, but he can only do it with the help of a twelve-year-old French orphan.

The British secret service is about to discover that kids working undercover will help to win the war.

Book 1 – OUT NOW

CHERUB

THE RECRUIT
Robert Muchamore

A terrorist doesn't let strangers in her flat because they might be undercover police or intelligence agents, but her children bring their mates home and they run all over the place. The terrorist doesn't know that one of these kids has bugged every room in her house, made copies of all her computer files and stolen her address book. The kid works for CHERUB.

CHERUB agents are aged between ten and seventeen. They live in the real world, slipping under adult radar and getting information that sends criminals and terrorists to jail.